UNDERSPIN

A Novel

E. Y. ZHAO

Astra House   New York

Copyright © 2025 by E. Y. Zhao
All rights reserved. Copying or digitizing this book for storage, display, or distribution in any other medium is strictly prohibited.

For information about permission to reproduce selections from this book, please contact permissions@astrahouse.com.

This is a work of fiction. Names, characters, places, and incidents are products of the author's imagination or are used fictitiously. Any resemblance to actual events, locales, or persons, living or dead, is entirely coincidental.

Astra House
A Division of Astra Publishing House
astrahouse.com
Printed in the United States of America

Library of Congress Cataloging-in-Publication Data

Names: Zhao, E. Y. author
Title: Underspin : a novel / E.Y. Zhao.
Description: First edition. | New York : Astra House, 2025. | Summary: "An intimate, bruising debut novel about the short and tumultuous life of a charismatic and enigmatic table tennis prodigy, as seen through the eyes of those pulled into his orbit"—Provided by publisher.
Identifiers: LCCN 2025011656 | ISBN 9781662603266 hardcover | ISBN 9781662603273 epub
Subjects: LCGFT: Sports fiction | Bildungsromans | Novels
Classification: LCC PS3626.H376 U53 2025 | DDC 813/.6—dc23/eng/20250402
LC record available at https://lccn.loc.gov/2025011656

ISBN: 978-1-6626-0326-6

First edition
10 9 8 7 6 5 4 3 2 1

Design by Alissa Theodor
The text is set in Sabon MT Std Regular.
The titles are set in Abadi MT Condensed Extra Bold.

For my families, blood and chosen

You wanted greater still, but love forces
All of us to the ground; suffering bends powerfully,
    Still our arc does not for nothing
        Bring us back to the starting point.

—FRIEDRICH HÖLDERLIN

CONTENTS

Prologue — xi

Game

Kevin — 3
Kagin — 20
Ellen — 35
Rahul — 55
Anabel — 78
Herr Doktor Eckert — 94
Susanne — 118
The Yaos — 141
Dennis and Dennis — 151
Marcy — 177

Deuce

Kristian — 195
Joan — 216
Hannah — 236
Epilogue — 248

ACKNOWLEDGMENTS — 253
ABOUT THE AUTHOR — 255

UNDERSPIN

PROLOGUE

THE LOS

They would start the service when Coach Kristian arrived. Not once in all the times he picked up and dropped off Ryan from home, his school, the airport, Sacramento, LA, Houston, thousands of times across fifteen years of practice and tournaments, had Kristian been late; and as the clock above the door ticked seven past the hour, the Los had to believe he would appear on their son's behalf one last time.

They stood before the packed Chinese Community Center auditorium, aisle lights blaring despite the efforts of two pimply technicians. Behind them, photographs of Ryan spanned a black-draped table, rising from piled white flowers like headstones from a rich sea foam. In Justin Lo's family, the tradition was one formal portrait of poster proportion, too severe to burden with real anguish, but Annie Lo insisted on framed photos from their house: Ryan at three, sprinting down Victoria Peak in a backwards cap, striped tank top, and trilobite sandals that fit in the palm of Justin's hand. Ryan at four, arms crossed above the tide of Half Moon Bay. Ryan at five on his school steps, squinting against a wedge of morning sun that trisected his face. Ryan at eight, back to the camera, hitting a table tennis ball for the first time, arm and paddle one pendular blur. After that, the photos crispened around the harsh geometries of his sport, end lines and corners, taut crosshatched nets, Ryan's teeth bared and fist pumped in celebration.

"Let me know when you're ready," said the chaplain, who, along with Ryan's friend Alvin, had helped the Los post the obituary. They had been so proud of him, and of themselves for entrusting him to the world, but now neither pride nor the world could tell them who their son had really been. The child who, at the only tournament Annie Lo spectated, entered his own parallel reality, swaggering among coaches and players, regarding with courtly gravitas the bulletin board flayed by tack marks and tables streaked with finger grease, so brutally separate from her that Annie felt no desire nor right to spectate again? The teenager, training twenty-five hours a week, who resented intrusions on that reality? The young man who came home six months ago, after he quit the Bundesliga and coaching, whom Annie twice found prone across the back of the couch, snoring, reeking of beer and something metallic? The one they had last seen two weeks ago fastening gold cuff links for Alvin's wedding, which took place in this very room, and to their proposal for a long-overdue trip to Hong Kong replied, *Don't plan around me*? Who had been talking of going back to school, whom ambition had separated from extended family for twenty years, to be reunited only in death, his relatives now filling the front row and wondering whether time and loss had reduced them as severely as their kin, Justin Lo bald and stricken and the skin of Annie's throat crinkled like a bleached riverbed, wondering how this was the driven young couple who had struck out so fearlessly thirty years ago?

Or the very same eight-year-old Annie had first driven to Coach Kristian's club, drawn by a neighbor's talk of a world-class coach nearby? A coach who promised glory—American titles, US Men's National Team, a professional league in Germany—and delivered on it while Annie went back to school, recertified, did her residency, joined an otolaryngology practice. The boy who nightly approached the threshold of his parents' bedroom and inclined his head in genteel good night, and sometimes, for Annie's amusement, pantomimed kung fu moves across the enormous dining room windows, floating in all the greens and purples of the Bay hills?

No—Kristian knew their boy best, even if they had grown apart, and the farther the minute hand tilted past the hour, the hazier the shape of the man in whom all their uncertainty and grief coalesced, until Justin said, "We should have called him. Why hasn't he called? We shouldn't have—" "He'll be here," Annie said. She had vouched for Kristian from the start, and hadn't it worked out until now? If she had never taken Ryan to that club—but who was regret for anyway, she thought, throat beginning to ache, the strongest sensation her body had produced since hearing the news. Soon she would have to speak. She glanced at the clock again. Thirteen minutes past, enough time for one hard-fought set of table tennis. Taking it for a signal, someone at the back began to pull the doors shut. Before Ryan died, Justin would have shaken his head or sliced a flattened hand across his neck, *No*. Now he only watched the rectangle of light narrow, face suspended in childish puzzlement, both disbelieving and reveling in his helplessness. He had looked that way, too, watching their first game of professional table tennis in the Hong Kong airport after a delayed boarding—transfixed, bleary eyes aglow with the sparks of the 1991 World Championship as Jörgen Persson served to the middle, Jan-Ove Waldner flicked down the line, Persson levitated sideways to hook it wide, and Waldner arced his whole body toward the ball, paddle's contact a lightning strike, no premonition of what was to come. *No way*, Annie thought, then and now, as the door swung shut on the last points of a long struggle, as the ball fell dribbling to the scuffed purple floor, *no way this is happening, no, how, no.*

GAME

2002–2005

KEVIN

For a time fizzy, and golden in retrospect, we trained with Coach's favorite boy on Coach's favorite table. Just like Ryan, we served, pushed, blocked, and looped. We served pendulums forward and reverse, and a hooked Tomahawk that became the club's specialty. We ran to the haunted yellow house and back. We were the Court One boys.

Every night at Coach's club was the same. We arrived in the vehicles of parents or grandparents, or in Rahul's case in the bus that trundled hourly up the hill, past the truck depot and the seafood warehouse. If we arrived before the blackout curtains came down, we stared out toward the cobalt mirror of the South Bay. We unpacked in the bleachers and fooled around until our two-mile run to the yellow house and back. We sat in a circle, crisscross applesauce, and counted up and down by increments to focus our minds: one-four-seven-ten . . . thirty-one, twenty-eight, twenty-five . . . one. Then it was grapevines and ladders and jump rope on the red polyester floor, freshest on our court; multiball, a hundred balls in a row served from a caddy behind our net, the sturdiest, attached to the brightest blue table, where we then rallied, served, and scrimmaged. We were the only ones whose strokes Coach deigned to correct himself, hand cold as he repositioned arm, wrist, elbow. Everyone else made do with the assistants who, having traveled far from their homes in Korea or China or, in one case, Nigeria, lacked Coach's seamless authority and pulled you around too hard or not at all.

Ryan was never the tallest or strongest of us, only the fastest and most precise. His face was a lean triangle of focus. In excitement his left eyelid fluttered; that was how you knew you were dead. We didn't remember meeting him, or any of each other. We had always been there, Ryan running three seconds ahead, Alvin leading the rest of us—Rahul, Nicklas, Kevin.

Coach filled our life with punishment. The slowest runner did fifty push-ups; the fastest, Ryan, wore three-pound ankle weights. The slowest drill runner did fifty sit-ups; the fastest, Ryan, did three burpees for every two of ours. The least consistent in multiball and rallying did fifty push-ups and fifty sit-ups; the most consistent, usually Ryan but sometimes Alvin, had to help instruct the rest of us. Anyone who took the elevator, down into the basement or up to the third-floor weight room, ran to the yellow house and back. Anyone caught drinking Gatorade out of the ancient vending machine ran to the yellow house and back. Coach never shouted, just informed us, calm as a judge, in an irrefutable and almost pleasurable way, how our lives would worsen. Alvin said Coach was like a Chinese Face Changer: hidden by a mask beneath which could flash, at any moment, a demon's hooked teeth, the rippling hell-red skin of a horror movie villain. Or like Orochimaru, the snake ninja in *Naruto*, whose split head, right when you thought you'd killed him, regenerated a stolen body.

We accepted everything with equanimity—partly in imitation of Ryan, who never complained, as Coach corrected his every stroke and loomed over him to count sit-ups and pulled him aside at the fountain or into his office to remind him how much better he must be, that he had it worst, though we knew his stoicism was a result of his talent, not the other way around; partly because punishment was the way of our world, in practice and out.

Relegation was the only punishment we feared. Every Thursday, the club's busiest night, Coach relegated one of us—usually whoever lost the most scrimmages that week, or messed up the counting game most often—to Court Two, with Assistant Coach Haesun. In descending order, the best table tennis countries were China, Sweden, Japan, Germany, Korea; what a downgrade from German Kristian to Korean Haesun, from training alongside Ryan to writhing in the morass of lesser boys! The relegated slunk up to us during water breaks, begging for the merciful illusion of having been included in the night's jokes. If we felt benevolently powerful, we granted it. If we felt malevolently powerful, we teased: *What's it like down there? How does losing smell?* If we felt disenfranchised, we ignored him altogether, perhaps the cruelest outcome.

Did this ultimate humiliation sometimes bring out the desire, normally tamped by modest success, to usurp Ryan and claim Coach's affection? Did it make us think we understood what powered Ryan's arm as he hit multiballs onto the white lines that circumscribed our lives outside school, that *we could have done that, too*? Did we suspect that Coach relegated us not for purely economical reasons, but to drum up this very feeling, without any real intention to pick one of us instead? Yes.

But for now, that diverged not at all from what we felt we deserved.

Outside the club, the world turned onward.

The war started.

The lights blacked out on the East Coast.

The president was reelected.

Ryan was relegated three times.

The first time was simple. Running back from the yellow house, halfway up the final hill, Alvin grabbed the back of Ryan's shirt. Coach, who stood watching at the top, must have seen it; saw Ryan stumble, catch his footing, let Alvin pass him across the last sidewalk crack, and then, before Alvin had fully stopped, sprint past and shove him back across.

When Coach announced that Ryan would play on Court Two, Alvin said, "I'll go with him."

"There's not space," Coach said.

"I'll—"

"You're making it worse," Ryan said, and that, despite all the scathing words we'd heard from Coach and Haesun, for whom we never played well enough, was when we really understood contempt.

Alvin and Ryan were always together, at private school and at training. For weeks at a time their scrimmages were evenly matched, and they couldn't stand each other after. Until they made up, the rest of us had to fill in with good humor. Packing up in the bleachers, we asked: Had they watched the match with Joo Sae-hyuk?

Did Nicklas suck at short pips, which Coach forced him to play on his forehand? (We kicked at the red birthmarks dribbling down Nicklas's left calf.)

Did they prefer Persson or Waldner?

Would Rahul get his dad to show us his new BlackBerry? If his dad had a BlackBerry, why'd he still have to ride the bus? (We pinched at Rahul's paunch and stomach hair.)

Was Wang Liqin the greatest of all time?

"I'm Bam Margera, and I feel like kicking my dad's ass all day today," Rahul liked to say, no context. (Of course Rahul's parents, who wouldn't drive him to practice, let him watch *Jackass*.)

"Hi," another of us would echo, "I'm Johnny Knoxville, and this is *Jackass*!"

"If your asshole can't see the camera, then the camera can't see your asshole!"

"I feel like my eyes have gonorrhea!"

We whispered *ass* and *gonorrhea*. If Coach or the assistant coaches heard, we'd have to run to the yellow house and back.

"Secret Jutsu," we shouted, joining index and middle fingers like Naruto to jab each other's buttholes, "One Thousand Years of Death!"

Between Ryan and Alvin, whoever laughed first made things up to the other. Alvin was way funnier about it: "If your asshole can't see the camera"—he'd sidle up behind Ryan—"then the camera"—and jab his lower back!, so hard Ryan flailed and sent his water bottle flying into Rahul's crotch. Ryan would grab Alvin's shoulders and pretend to shake him till his neck snapped; Alvin stuck out his tongue and crossed his eyes, and we all released silent sighs and farts of relief.

Whispers about family crept into the club sometimes. Nicklas had a stepmom he talked about like a slug he'd love to squash. Rahul's parents, in addition to enforcing the bus thing, ran an "internet store" stretching across southern India and the United States. (They were the only parents considered fair game: when Rahul whiffed a ball, or bent to stretch his hamstrings, butt parked defensively against the wall, we'd screech, "Stretching across southern India and the United States!") Ryan's dad was a famous surgeon and Alvin's mom worked at their school as an art teacher. Kevin lived with his grandparents in Chinatown, and only his grandma could drive, which was why he came to practice the least. We boys didn't think of ourselves as "a family," though. We were accustomed to spending our days around other kids, and if what we felt around each other was sharper and more heightened than at school or home, that seemed a natural result of Coach's intensifying presence, the proximity of his club to the open water and the haunted yellow house, the enchanted hours they occupied between the end of school and bedtime.

The second relegation was related to something at school. Alvin had persuaded Ryan to participate in a heist. A third grader's desk had been carried behind their school and dumped in a field.

The rest of us were always tipping vending machines and sticking gum beneath teachers' chairs, but their fancy school called Alvin's and Ryan's parents. Coach sent them both to Court Two.

The third time Ryan was relegated, the week before our first tournament, he'd lost to Alvin every night. Coach dressed him down for losing focus and let Alvin take the first turn in multiball. At the fountain after scrimmages, Ryan and Alvin did not make up. Things between them were coming to a head.

The next night, we went into the haunted yellow house.

The house wasn't particularly scary: according to two wooden signs on the yellower lawn, the first driven into the dirt and the second hanging from an orange scaffold, it had been occupied by a wealthy Hollywood producer then some dentists. The windows still gleamed with unbroken glass, through whose dust you could see the emptied interiors, hardwood and strewn with planks. The tiles on the broad veranda were persimmon red. Rahul hypothesized that there was a dentist's chair somewhere, but there was no way to scale the flaking siding to peer through the second-floor windows.

It was the Thursday before our first-ever tournament. Coach had relieved us of the timed two-mile run. "Go have a jog," he told us, "two laps," which meant four miles instead of two. Of course there was a catch. It didn't dampen us, though, because we expected no breaks. We ran faster than practical down to the house. The slowest of us, Nicklas that day, had barely caught his breath on the scorched lawn before we realized we were having the same idea. Kevin might have tried to stop it, but only remembered hoisting himself up to ride the orange scaffold like a horse, the wood splintering against his palms and the insides of his thighs.

Alvin said, "If you kick doors at the right spot, they explode."

"What about the tournament?" Rahul said.

How moving, to remember when it was our *only* tournament, standing alone in the flume of time, like the house on its drought-scorched hill.

"What *about* it?"

"It's just, if we do this right before . . . I don't know . . ." Ryan rolled his eyes. "It'll be dope," he said sagely.

Alvin rolled his eyes in turn. Since the shirt-pulling incident, he had started wearing a wristband to practice, copying Ryan's headband, and he snapped it impatiently against his arm. "Let's each kick the door once," he said. "If it doesn't open, we'll go back."

We lined up on the steps, Alvin at the top, Ryan beneath, then Rahul, Nicklas, Kevin. Alvin looked back at us and hopped down to Ryan's step.

"You first," he said.

"Why?" Ryan asked. We knew what he was doing: he didn't want to go inside, but he also didn't want to be called a teacher's pet. He had to make Alvin admit he was scared, or make him so uncomfortable *not* admitting that he'd invent another excuse to retreat. While Alvin spun his wheels, the rest of us tried to imagine whether we would be too scared.

"Because you're the best player," Alvin finally said.

"If you say so," Ryan said. We giggled. Ryan shoved Alvin, lightly, the resulting stumble mistakable for Alvin's own clumsiness, and stood wide-stanced on the landing. A few boards stood up jagged, mostly to the side, but sharp enough they made us nervous. Ryan swung his feet up to touch his hands, puffing out breaths. In practice he had the best breathing of us all, rhythmic and explosive just ahead of his stroke, blasting the ball past us like a Wind-style Jutsu.

"Let's go, Ryan," Nicklas said.

"Yes, let's go," Rahul echoed.

Ryan exhaled once more and launched himself at the door; bounced off, tumbled to the ground, and began to scream. Clutching his shin, just below the knee, he writhed and moaned: "Haaah . . . ! A-haaa-ha-haaaaaa. . . . ahhh . . ."

Rahul knelt first. "Let me see," he said. Ryan's face had gone red, and he was crying so hard the noise stuck in his throat. Rahul slapped at the backs of Ryan's hands, "Let me *see*, Ryan!"

He sat up. The leg was fine. The blood we'd expected was nowhere. Rahul fell onto his butt and hung his head between his knees.

"Wow," he said, "wow."

Ryan walked up to the door, turned its rusted knob, and pushed it in.

"Get up," Alvin told Rahul. "Why are you such a pussy?"

"You shouldn't say that," Nicklas said.

"*You shouldn't say that*," Alvin imitated in Arnold Schwarzenegger's voice.

We followed Ryan. Inside, it smelled like the bathroom after a hot shower. Wood poles sectioned the floor into rectangles, one alongside the next from wall to wall. Its layout reminded us of the club.

Ryan led us up the stairs.

We had never seen the second floor of the club. Coach said it would be converted into another practice hall soon. Alvin claimed to have snuck up one Friday while Coach was sick, and though we had thought nothing of his claim at the time, it returned to us now that it had supposedly been piled with folding chairs, someone's old tracksuit draped on top. And here they were somehow, in the yellow house, the abandoned chairs, and at their peak, like an old slick of movie blood, a faded red hoodie, its hems brown with gunk.

Surely there was an explanation: we had misremembered Alvin's description; or Alvin had broken into the house alone before and, for his entirely private amusement, described it to us instead of Coach's secret second floor; or, improbable but not impossible to us, since we thought him capable of anything, Ryan had snuck in and rearranged the furniture to scare Alvin.

We looked to Alvin, pressed against the wall, toes clenched so tightly you could count the knuckles through the tops of his sneakers. There was nothing inherently creepy about the room, which the wind through the cracked window seemed to have scoured of dust. It should have been cheerful how the bright afternoon sky cast our shadows on walls honey yellow with sun, but we felt we could not leave, that something had to be changed or exorcised.

"Look," Ryan said, "we can get onto the roof."

He strode across the floor. Alvin could only follow, the rest of us trailing gratefully. Ryan patted the sill of the window overlooking the road. "Alvin," he said, "take a look."

Any of the rest of us would have asked *why*, by which we meant *h-e-double hockey sticks no*, but if Alvin did so, it was as good as admitting he had been in the wrong for the desk fiasco and could not take what he dealt. He might as well have dropped to all fours and licked Ryan's sneakers.

As it was, he had to crawl out onto the veranda. His butt blocked the sky, rose and fell as he hoisted his calves and feet over the sill. For a moment he just crouched, looking—out, maybe, at the views, but probably down, scared. A nervous fart echoed back.

"All right?" Ryan asked.

"Yeah," came the quiet reply.

Ryan reached up, slammed the window, and flipped the latch shut. He was down the stairs before we realized what had happened, before Alvin turned and banged on the window and screamed. It was the worst thing we'd ever seen, his palm and finger pads against the dusty glass, raw pink like the inside of a mouth. *Thud thud thud*, went the window, still as solid as in our very own homes, where our families cooked us meals and waited, lovingly, for the lights to go out beneath our bedroom doors.

Then Alvin stopped. He might have been banging and screaming for thirty seconds or ten minutes. Rahul had peed himself; we pretended not to notice. Alvin slowly, slowly turned so we saw his butt and back once again.

Nicklas led us back outside. Ryan stood on the desolate lawn, shouting up to Alvin. Above him swayed a gray wood ladder. The patch of grass where it had lain, bordering the lawn and the slope of spiky trees beyond, glistened a rotted, damp brown.

"PUT IT HERE!" Alvin was screaming, and risked lifting a hand to slap the roof. "HERE!"

"He knows where you are," Nicklas muttered.

Ryan lowered the top of the ladder. Tendons tented the soft skin of his elbows. Again, Alvin lifted a hand, pawing at the air. Ryan tilted the ladder away.

"Guys, please," Rahul said. "Can we just get him down?"

"GUYS!" Alvin shouted. He was losing volume. "GUYS. I'm SCARED of HEIGHTS!"

"I want your wristband," Ryan said.

"*What?*"

"Your wristband!!" Rahul screamed. The justice of the exchange seemed self-evident, the scales themselves forged by the types of people Coach (and other adults), by their treatment of us, prophesied us to be. Ryan could make demands, on the table and off; we could only fit ourselves to their logic.

Alvin's left shoulder shuddered as he raised his right hand, centimeter by centimeter. It shook harder as he closed his teeth around the elastic fuzz and tugged his hand free. The white band dropped like a shot bird.

Ryan called, "I'm going to put it down—"

"OKAY! OKAY! PUT IT DOWN!"

"—over—here."

He hefted the ladder off the grass and carried it to prop against the veranda's back corner. Alvin would have to inch twenty feet or so along the tiles.

We wouldn't have dared offer help. This was between them.

"Are you kidding?" Alvin said hoarsely.

"I've climbed it before," Ryan said, clapping the dust from his hands. "Just come down backwards and take it slow!"

"I can't do it."

"Don't look down."

"How do I put my feet?"

"If your asshole can't see the camera," Ryan said, "then the camera—"

"RYAN."

Ryan checked the black Casio watch his surgeon dad had bought him, which only that day, the lax pre-tournament day, would Coach have permitted him to wear in practice. He turned back toward the club and jogged away.

Looking between Alvin on the roof and Ryan disappearing down the road, we decided we would be safer with the golden boy. We followed. At first it seemed the right choice. He breathed in a cheerful way. He even let Kevin run up next to him, where he felt it first as Ryan began to speed up. Faster and faster he ran, until we had to stop and catch our breaths. Nicklas sat against the chain link fence that ran along the sidewalk. Rahul wheezed that he needed to get up, we needed to tell Coach.

"We're allowed to take as long as we want," Nicklas replied. "Today is our free day."

Now that animosity had been openly expressed, we could not stave off all we found deplorable about each other and ourselves. Rahul was a suck-up, even though every adult turned on him. Nicklas was lazy. Kevin was invisible and no one bet on him. We quarreled against the chain link until Rahul said, "What if he catches up?" It would have shattered the excuse that we left Alvin behind to get help and, more frighteningly (we felt, with a shudder), would have been like being caught by a ghost.

At the top of the hill, Coach and Ryan stood, twin pillars of Rome. "You left him on the roof?" Coach demanded. "He's still up there, you left him?"

"I told them to wait," Ryan said. "I said I was coming to get help. I told you guys not to dare him up there!" It turned out that beneath his sympathetic winner's mask there was another, peeled off for the first time, revealing total indifference toward us.

Coach was winding down his sentencing (we would do burpees until they got back safe and mop all the floors after practice), Ryan serene behind the line of fire, when Alvin sprawled across the last sidewalk crack. "Made it," he panted. It was surely the fastest mile he'd ever run. Our ankles ached in sympathy. His face was nearly purple. His palms and knees were browner than a brown crayon. "Sorry, Coach!"

Coach knelt, his trademark for making us feel (sometimes with a false sense of security) taken seriously. "You're not hurt?"

"Hurt? Why?"

We tried to signal with our eyes, Rahul with his slowly dropping jaw.

"Your teammates said you were on a roof," Coach said.

"I was? That's weird. Don't know anything about a roof."

Coach stood back up and looked us in the face, one by one. One by one he tapped our shoulders. "You're staying home tomorrow," he said. "Home. Home."

"Me too?" Alvin said.

"Especially you."

Coach did not tap Ryan's shoulder. Ryan stared out toward the house, where, on the same hot dry wind that lifted our sweaty hair from our sweatier foreheads, the sign on the scaffold was probably swinging, a ladder tossed down beside it.

"Woo-hoo," Alvin said. "No tournament, woo-hoo!"

"Inside," Coach said.

All through practice, Ryan's face stuck in the expression he'd worn outside. He had lied and backstabbed to protect something dear to him, his primacy in Coach's eyes, and we understood because we, too, had lied to protect something precious: our loyalty to Ryan, our awe of his boldness, our bond. We, too, had perhaps wished Alvin taken down a notch.

No one seemed to understand our motives better than Alvin.

"Hi, guys!" he shouted from Court Two. "Bet you don't miss me!" We pretended not to watch him, but could not unhear the crazed smack of balls off his paddle.

"You guys like that?" he called. "There's more where it came from, you can't keep me down!"

Coach started him at the bottom of King of the Court, and we could not stop him from ripping through us to Court One, where Ryan presided.

Alvin won in an all-time sweep, 11–9, 11–7, 14–16, 11–5.

"Too bad I'm not playing tomorrow," was the last thing he said to us, "*not*."

His mom waved at us through her car window. She was pretty and seemed nice. We imagined waking up to a breakfast she had cooked, the day's horizon tournament-free, and sighed longingly. Alvin ran around to the passenger seat and drove away in style.

On Monday, Ryan's father came into the club for the first and last time. How could we have been so unsupervised? he demanded of Coach.

"No one was hurt," Coach said.

"But they could have been! How could it even get that far?"

"Who do you think competes better," Coach said, "free boys or stunted babies?"

"That's not the point."

"How safe were you as a boy, Doctor?"

The focused triangle of Dr. Lo's face, thicker-boned than Ryan's, two stern divots in his brow like fossilized thumbprints, tightened toward Coach, then wavered. "It was a different time," he said.

"Did you not cherish your freedom?"

"Yes, but—"

"Would you be who you are today without it?"

We held our breaths. Coach spoke again: "Mischief is sign of a strong will. We harness that. The boys have been punished for this trouble, which I agree went beyond the pale. Believe me: I know I must take more care than even parents. Your son is safe, Dr. Lo."

It cowed us, how seamlessly Coach rewrote such a momentous day, how easily he defeated a man we had all assumed to be great.

"Stop staring, boys," Coach said, "it's rude."

We ran ten suicide sprints in penance.

•

Ryan represented us alone at the tournament.

I, Kevin, stuck around for one more year, but for me and Alvin, missing the step of that first tournament set us behind Ryan once and for all on the spiral staircase of progress, which spun tighter and tighter the higher you went, so that by two months later Ryan was five months ahead; by one year later, five years ahead. He and Coach flew to Las Vegas, then Germany, to play his first major tournaments. He won.

After that, we stopped training together.

Nicklas's father moved them back to Austria.

Rahul's parents wanted him to play cricket instead.

My grandma failed her driving test, and it was too far for me to go from school.

Even before we quit, Coach made it felt that we were on our way out. After Rahul lost to a younger, newer kid, he said, "Someone has to be overtaken."

As each of us left, we felt fall away the virtues we had not even known he provided: Nicklas's precocious if jaded circumspection, Rahul's comforting credulity, my bland implacability. The collective spirit Coach had cultivated through togetherness and scapegoating, love and fear, an invisibly humming force field over us, could only truly be felt when it chipped and broke.

New boys took over Court One.

The second floor of the club was renovated. We never saw what used to stand there. Maybe nothing, only a blank gray floor across which A/C danced tiny, plaster-dust devils.

Alvin left after Rahul and before me, but he and Ryan stayed friends at school. Years later we saw them at Rahul's homecoming. Alvin was dating a girl at Rahul's high school.

"Snuck this guy away from *practice*," Alvin told us, punching Ryan in the corsage. Ryan's face of indifference had become his adult face. Now he was the strongest-looking, and shorter than only Rahul, who'd shot up. "Guys, guess what he won last week?"

"A ride on your mom?" Rahul asked, nervously.

"No, pervert. Under-21 at the California Open. Bow down to your homecoming king."

"They don't even know what that is," Ryan said. His tone said that what we thought or knew mattered less than ever.

"That's cool, man," one of us said.

Through a series of events funny and serendipitous, Rahul was invited to Alvin and Marcy's wedding and brought me along. They were only twenty-three; all of us were only twenty-three. The wedding took place in November in the South Bay. Rahul had just started his new job in Cupertino, thirty minutes by bus from Coach's club.

Ryan was there, at a back table with a pretty girl. She was making his hyperfocused expression, even more intense than his.

He had just gotten back from Germany, Alvin explained, drunk, when he ran into us at the bar. No, wait, he left Germany a while ago, but recently returned to the Bay. Did we remember that Austrian kid? How had *I* ended up at this wedding, anyway?

"He's my plus-one," Rahul said.

"Good man, Rahul," said Alvin. "You were always—you tried to get me down from that roof. Remember? When I climbed out of the window?"

"I didn't really . . ."

"No, I remember. You had the ladder. You guys were so scared of Coach, oh my god, you ran back *literally* pissing, but you tried to help me."

"You were always gonna get down."

"Do you think?" He looked toward Ryan. "D'you think *he* thought that?"

"Of course," I said.

We were just kids, we said.

"Like hell," Alvin said. "Look. Watch this."

He marched toward Ryan, choking a bottle of champagne. He loomed above the couple, talking, stabbing the air with the gold foil cap. He pointed to a ladder at the edge of the room, which ran up to the catwalks of the Chinese Community Center auditorium, where, as good Chinese Americans, Marcy and Alvin were hosting the afterparty.

The pretty girl shook her head and chopped at her beauty-marked throat. Ryan slowly stood. He scanned the ladder, the labyrinth of walkways shading to black above the stage, unused on this occasion, a crosshatched mound of chairs piled in the wings, biding their time for more momentous gatherings, New Year's and election speeches and funerals.

Alvin waved us over. "He'll do whatever I say," he said. "It's my wedding. HEY, EVERYONE!"

The party kept rolling. Across the room, Marcy's head peeped out from her cluster of bridesmaids.

Ryan approached the ladder, tugged it appraisingly.

So that only we could hear, Alvin said, "Showboat. A guy never outgrows that shit, does he? Glad we didn't turn out like that."

"Marcy," Ryan called. The bride came over, dress bunched in both hands. She was a careful person. She caught his tuxedo jacket as it slid off his arms. Then he was airborne. For a few breathtaking seconds his legs free-floated, suspended by the strength of his shoulders alone. He climbed so gracefully, that by halfway up, even his pretty girlfriend's annoyance melted into tenderness, or at least admiration, which for people like them, I supposed, was the same.

"Great," Alvin said as he reached the top. Ryan kept moving along a catwalk and squatted directly above Alvin's head. "What's up, jackass?" he called down.

"Awesome," Alvin said. He raised a thumbs-up, arm quivering, overextended. "You can come down now."

"*Hey*, man, you can come down."

"Oh, no," Rahul breathed.

Ryan made a hand signal. It could have been deuces or the middle finger, or some mysterious sign he learned abroad. In the shadows of the ceiling, we couldn't see his face. He stayed up there for a long time.

2007

KAGIN

Kagin wouldn't have called a time-out while leading two sets to one, but maybe that's the kind of thinking that keeps him unexceptional: Regional Umpire who gave up competing after a year, stagnated analyst at a tiny accounting firm in outer Chicagoland. Taker of the dumb, easy way.

The kid taking said time-out has probably played since his fingers could close around a paddle, like those three-year-olds on YouTube who toddle at sawed-down tables, muscles too soft to fully stop at the end of each stroke. The kid, Ryan Lo, has been competing long enough to rock a swaggering anime haircut, headbanded and parted down the middle so it brushes his forehead, suggesting he could drop into a breakdance anytime. (Kagin thinks of Johnny Fu from his fourth-grade class, perched on a ledge outside the science lab, flanked by cronies in sweatpants and basketball shoes, doling out favor in the form of Donkey Kong stickers.) His coach, jowly and squinty, speaks with a German accent, which makes Kagin perceive an un-American stillness to him, legs and torso rooted perfectly upright. No sign of a pulse.

In tournament photos, Kagin is always crimped in his blazer, one shoulder dropped like a broken marionette's. Taking the National Umpire exam—which requires him to be here officiating US Nationals, the largest domestic tournament, a hundred courts filling the floor of a vast Vegas convention center—is his first major effort to lift the crushing weight of self-doubt. In the grand scheme of things, becoming National Umpire of a third-rate sport, a title held by over fifty dilettantes and retirees, is nothing. But you cannot begin by considering the grand scheme of things. He can earn this small token. He *will*.

Ryan Lo flexes one foot then the other, calves cleaving, alternating arms as he wipes his forehead with his sleeves. The coach holds out a towel. Ryan shakes his head. The coach pushes down his arm and drags the towel along his nose.

"Time," Kagin calls. What did the coach instruct? To serve shorter, more to the middle? To move his opponent to the backhand so he can hit into the open forehand court? This match has surpassed his ability to assess, though perhaps an aspiring National Umpire should simply let the details of matches wash over him, as he imagines the particularities of cloud formations wash over seasoned pilots. Returning to the table, Ryan slaps his thighs and grunts, "Come on, come on." From behind the scoreboard, Kagin smells his sweat cut with powdery wafts of deodorant, and from his opponent, Dennis Ouyang, the sour musk of a forty-six-year-old man facing destruction.

Ryan zings a serve down the forehand, forcing a weak return, then flicks into Dennis's backhand. His coach claps so long Kagin considers a yellow card. 9–9. The winner will advance to the Round of 16 in Men's Singles, and from there, potentially, onto the finals; and maybe, they are surely wishing (without thinking, since thinking is fatal), to a victory that will crown them National Champion. The players wipe their hands on dead patches of table beneath the net, too nervous to go to the towels draped over the courtside barriers, and Kagin examines his indifference toward the outcome, turning it over in his mind like a carpenter his neatly sawed plank. Only recently has he mastered neutrality—not just to stop rooting, but to annihilate even the urge. He is the surface on which matches must evenly stand.

Especially because he will be randomly observed for his exam. Like the players, he cannot let himself want it.

"Nine–nine," he says. "Serve, Ouyang."

The kid smashes Dennis's first serve into his shirt. He pushes the second, which pops up—no spin; Kagin misreads it, too—and jumps back in time to counter Dennis's loop with a loop of his own, the ball clipping Dennis's shoulder as it ends the match.

Kagin permits himself a smile. *Cho*, he mouths, the sport's meaningless word of celebration. For one year, he was Dennis's student; having shown no affinity for the sport, despite his love of its style and tactics, he quit and began umpiring. For three years he has worked Denny's semiannual tournaments, but Dennis still mispronounced his name at check-in. *Fuck you*, Kagin thinks during post-match handshakes, a slightly silly round of *thanks coach, thanks coach, good game, good game*. Ryan's shake is perfunctory, his eyes glassy with victory. It reminds Kagin of the samurai masks Johnny Fu doodled in his notebooks, the shading and anatomy more terrifying than impressive back then, harbinger of an unfathomably wide world.

Coach Gao sidles over as he packs up the scoreboard. "How's it going?" she asks, leaning on a barrier and buckling its thin metal frame. "Learn anything?" She introduced herself yesterday while Kagin sat alone at Concessions. At first Kagin wondered, foolishly, if she wanted something from him, but as a two-time Olympian and one of America's top coaches (her students comprise half the Women's Singles bracket), she's accrued sufficient influence. She knows all the officials and knows he's new. She's taking pity.

"I'm too old and slow for this sport," Kagin says. He scans the empty bleachers and tries to recall the faces of spectators. He won't know until afterward which match was observed, nor which National Umpire observed. If he does well and passes the written test later, he'll join their ranks. Gain sufficient standing to buy them an unselfconscious beer.

"They weren't watching," Gao says, and winks. Of course *she* knows who it is. "And you're not too old, even *I* still play. You find ways to run less."

He's flattered she thinks he competes, and that she would put them in the same breath. "I'd love to watch your students compete," he offers.

"Anabel's starting now. If you mean it."

His next assignment is after lunch. Suppressing a desire to hide away with the umpire's handbook (over breakfast, he recited the first ten pages verbatim; *you're ready, fool,* he tells himself), he follows Gao to table eleven, where a girl snaps a pink elastic around the thick base of her ponytail. Her face lifts at the sight of her coach, then squints skeptically at Kagin.

"This is Kagin," Gao says. "Don't look so excited, he's not umping your match."

Anabel Yu shrugs. Kagin recognizes her from last month's *USA Table Tennis*. It made a deal out of the fact she "only" started when she was eleven. Her parents are computer scientists in Central New Jersey, and on weekends she stays with Gao above her club in the state's northeastern corner. Outside of table tennis, she likes the manga *Fruits Basket*. Kagin, who's read his share of manga, can't imagine her ingenuously scanning the twee illustrations. "He can watch," she says, "if he stays quiet as a mouse."

She doesn't smile—not after the small wisecrack, which Kagin identifies as such too late; not during the match; not after she wins a tough tiebreak, 18–16 in the fifth set. She plays close to the table at a relentless pace, windups short and wrist snappy, always clicking the ball onto empty pockets. Envy tightens Kagin's shoulders. Of all unadmirable emotions, it is his most tenacious predator, and this tournament has given it many opportunities: the officials' meeting last night, where everyone knew each other; morning call, where everyone but him wore National Umpire pins; watching his peers—no, superiors—swagger into the coliseum of

Courts One and Two to adjudicate key matches with state-of-the-art electronic scoreboards. He could never play like this teenager—had disdained, while he *was* playing, to "play like a girl"—and yet. He excuses himself while Anabel and Gao debrief, in the post-victory euphoria that makes it easy to say difficult things ("Why d'you *sit* into backhands, Anabel? Want me to set you up a lawn chair?") and reveals, more starkly than any coach's box or spectator section, who was really in the world of the game. Gao is the rare coach who fully lives her student's exertions; as Kagin walks away, she's fanning her sweat-drenched armpits.

The officials' booth stands empty. Kagin straightens a stack of clipboards. The other umpires have gone out to spend their measly lunch stipend. At Concessions, he meets eyes with one of the loners at last night's meeting. She waves, fingertips brown with barbecue sauce. An unpromising lunch companion. Just a snack from the vending machine, then. Pretending to be needed elsewhere, he strides along the perimeter, toward the untrafficked bathrooms in the back where, before his first assignment this morning, he lightly slapped his face in the mirror. Beyond the walls of the Mandalay Bay Convention Center, he imagined, the city struggled against the red desert, potbellied men shot sawed-off guns, gazelles keeled over in toxic green springs; the world was huge and powerful and strange. It is a cleansing abnegation to shut it out.

"'There is sometimes a tendency to pay most attention to aspects that you find easiest to check,'" he rehearses. "'To offset this tendency, a short summary will remind you of the aspects of a good service.'" Ready yourself with a steadfast mentality, the handbook says. The best an umpire can do is make a good call fast. The second best is to reverse a bad call fast. Then the cascade of now-intuitive rules: eleven points to a set, win by two; best three of five sets; serve tossed six inches above the surface of the table, alternating every two points during the game and every point during deuce; towel breaks every six. Speak to the coach only between sets. Upper surface of the table 2.74

meters long and 1.525 meters wide, lying in a horizontal plane 76 centimeters above the floor. He's known it all for three years, and if he still says it with any shade of prayer, it's without expectation of a reply.

He's half-consciously raised his hand, step peppy, prepared to deliver another bracing slap, when a door swings into his path. Ryan and Anabel emerge from the family bathroom.

"Hi," Anabel says, unlacing her fingers from Ryan's. The freed hand balls up. Ryan faces Kagin squarely. Kagin can't tell if he remembers him from an hour ago.

"Hello kids" is all he gets to say. Then Ryan's coach overtakes him in the aisle.

"Hello, Anabel," the coach says. "Congratulations on your match. No mercy, hm?"

"Thanks . . . thanks for watching." Anabel eyes the gap between the coach and the barriers. Ryan tucks the hand she was holding into his pocket.

"We were talking about my game against Dennis," he says.

Kagin ducks into the vacated bathroom and shuts the door. Through it, he can still hear, between coach and student:

"Have you had a long enough break? Or were you having problems in the bathroom?"

"No."

"You're not losing focus, are you?"

"No."

"Are you?"

". . . No."

"No?"

Kagin flushes the toilet and turns on the faucet. He doesn't want to see or hear them. Can't. It might affect his judgment. The mirror is the fancy light-ringed kind, displaying his mild distaste and impatience in high, porous definition.

After what seems a reasonable amount of time, he slowly opens the door.

In the nearest court, he sees the coach's back, horizontal as if in a plank. The kid lies beneath him, arms akimbo, foot on the coach's shoulder. The bottom of his shoe, its rubber a clean flesh tone, floats by the coach's ear. The best sense Kagin can make of it is that they are stretching. The veins down the back of the coach's forearms bulge; his triceps stand out. Something shifts and the coach's torso sinks lower.

"NOPE!" Ryan shouts. Screams.

"Breathe. Just breathe."

The kid's splayed fingers twitch at the knuckles, joints spasming, twenty independent nodes of discomfort.

From the floor, he meets Kagin's eyes.

The coach turns, and beside his indifferent expression, Ryan's shoe on his shoulder becomes a terrible second face.

Kagin stumbles back. The door slams. DO NOT FLUSH FEMININE PRODUCTS DOWN THE TOILET. Earlier, the coach toweled the kid's face too hard—didn't he? Or had it been a loving wipe, like scraping chocolate from a toddler's face?

A kid like that wouldn't say no often. You had to give yourself over. Not even Kagin, who has achieved the palest facsimile of success in life, really says no. Yes to the boss and the head referees. Yes to the dinky tournaments that invited him for gas money and a motel stay.

But players also shouted *no* out of motivating rage. He'd seen it during the 2004 Olympics, back when he still watched to learn. As if he had anything in common with gold medalist Ryu Seung-min, or even the kids here.

The court is empty when he emerges again, stomach fluttering, feet hot in their dress shoes. Confronting the lifeless expanse of red floor, he can't say he wished the coach and boy were there so he could say something; can't even say he wants to tell himself that lie.

Why, oh why, did he of all people have to see it?

The officials' booth is packed again. The barbecue sauce woman chats with two others, who, by their flushed faces, have loosened up over lunch. The head referee, famous for cracking a joke after umpiring the 1993 World Championships, offers Kagin two leftover biscuits, squashed flat between grease-soaked napkins. So everyone noticed he wasn't there.

A deputy ref informs Kagin that he's on Court Eight at two o'clock.

"Not Court Five at one thirty?" The assignments have been out for weeks. He memorized his timetable on the flight from Chicago.

"We'd like you to switch in. It's a two-man."

Kagin checks the draw and taps the kid's name. "I umped for him earlier." There's no rule saying he can't ump for the same person twice; still, he asks, "No bias concerns?"

"You don't seem like you have favorites," the deputy says.

He tries taking it as a compliment, to sever, as his first slam of the bathroom door did not, any attachment to the boy. For twenty minutes he sits in a corner of the booth, head bowed, bringing the plank of impartiality down again and again.

Thirty-five minutes before the match, he approaches the head ref.

"Sir," he begins, "I saw—"

"Just Arthur, please."

"Arthur—I'm not sure what, but I saw . . . I'm not sure what to make of . . ."

Arthur perks up, gray pupils glinting through rheumy corneas. "Anything that might affect the tournament should be reported."

"It was a coach and his student, I think. That is—it *was* his student. Over there. The student, I know the, uh, Ryan Lo, I believe—"

"Ah! And Kristian. Of course. Kristian and Ryan." Arthur rocks onto his heels, avaricious old bird waiting to be fed. Last night, as everyone dispersed, Kagin heard chatter about on-court tantrums and petty emails, complaints to the USATT chair, even a seduction attempt. Is what he has to report mere salacious trash like that?

"I . . . no," he chokes out, "sorry. I didn't realize it *was* his coach. I got confused about the rules, if the coach can, well . . . yes, never mind."

Arthur's eyes dim. He peers at Kagin's clipboard. "Better tighten up before the match," he says, and turns back to the draw sheets pinned helter-skelter across three bulletin boards.

A more confident man would reengage him. Does knowing this move Kagin any closer to becoming that man?

His co-umpire comes up, already excited about the match; Arthur summons another umpire to reassign him; the opportunity is lost. Kagin thought it would be easier to approach the court as a duo, but the more his co-ump talks, the farther away he sounds. Kagin has to be told twice that he'll lead, making the calls.

Like this morning, Ryan and Kristian check in half an hour early and warm up on the adjacent court. Neither of them looks Kagin's way. Anabel sits on the highest courtside bleacher, hugging the railing. The net is the correct height and the tabletop wipes easily clean. Everyone arrives on time and Kagin catches the coin on his first try. Ryan chooses the side of the table facing his coach.

The game is evenly matched. Ryan is fast over the table and aggressive on serve returns, his opponent, the former Olympian Barry Chen, powerful behind the baseline and tenacious in rallies. Barry plinks a short serve to the middle, Ryan steps in and flicks, Barry leaps back and countersmashes; if Ryan's block lands, Ryan outspeeds Barry in the rally. Ryan slices a Tomahawk serve to the baseline and Barry either whiffs or booms a loop past him. They take turns serving cautious underspin to the backhand, setting up for a push the opponent sometimes hooks at an awkward angle, into their elbow or far to the side, hoping to force a push back. It's a better match than Dennis's. Their feet scuff and stamp terse music on the polyester. Kagin feels a wind off their swinging limbs. The click of each contact, ball ringing on the racket's sweet spot, thrums in him from wrist to wrist; inspires his fingers steady around the scoreboard cards, despite his anxiety.

They trade three points at a time. You can tell beforehand who will take it—if Ryan doesn't close in the first three touches, the advantage tips to Barry. It's Chen 2 to Lo 5, 7–7, then first set to Lo at 11–9. The next set drags on, 3–3, 5–5, 8–8, 10–10, 13–13. 13–15, to Chen. The third set is close, too: they end up at 9–9, serve, Lo.

"Injury time-out," says Kristian. "His leg." He points.

Kagin can't see the boy's face. He's turned toward his coach, legs planted shoulder width, hips tilting as he settles into a slouch. The match is tied, one set apiece. If Ryan takes a break, he'll probably win the next two points, then the set, then almost certainly the whole thing.

Injury time-outs are for damage sustained during the match. They do not apply in cases of cramps or exhaustion. Or whatever Kagin saw on the floor by the bathroom.

"What's hurt?" Kagin asks.

"His leg," Kristian repeats.

Maybe he did hurt himself and Kagin missed it. Ryan does not turn to confirm. He shakes out a leg, but not in an exceptional way. He's not making an effort to seem injured.

The best an ump can do is be right fast.

"Denied," Kagin says.

Kristian rises.

"Sir, please," says the co-ump. "Stay in the box."

Sweat tickles the nape of Kagin's neck, though it's December and the convention center—is this a Vegas thing?—runs A/C all day. He points toward Ryan, palm extended flat and fingers aligned, like he's practiced so often in mirrors. "Serve, Lo."

"You can't be serious," Kristian says.

"Please," Kagin tells Barry, who's holding the ball, ambivalence pulsing the vein in his broad rhino's forehead, unsure whether to take the high road or the advantage, "pass me the ball."

"He's injured." Now Kristian stands over Kagin. He's wearing pomade, citrusy and foul. Kagin looks anywhere but into his shadow. The raftered ceiling, a yellow balloon deflating between its beams; the bleachers, where the barbecue sauce umpire has joined Anabel.

He reaches into his blazer pocket and extracts the yellow card, its plastic matte from daily cleaning.

"Please sit, sir," the co-ump says.

A few seconds later, the nylon of Kristian's tracksuit rustles away. The coach sits. Ryan loses the set. When he returns for the fourth set, he looks stricken, like he's been slapped. He does not meet Kagin's gaze once as he loses. The rest of the match goes smoothly, really, because Kagin is no longer thinking. Maybe thought is the real vice. The thought that Barbecue Sauce is his evaluator and he's fucked it would paralyze him through his remaining matches. So would overthinking after he shakes hands, or when, packing up the scoreboard, he sees Kristian standing with his arms around Ryan as the boy's shoulders heave. If the point was to show Kristian he's onto something, it's been for naught: the coach meets his eyes unflinchingly. The worst an umpire can do is double down on his mistake. Kagin has done this, Kristian's expression says, but, as the bigger person, secure in his competence and importance, he will let it go. Kagin can't touch him.

He's hurt the boy, though. The weeping boy.

"You made the right call," Kagin's co-ump says. "Nationals is Bullshit Central. Especially for hotshots. They think they're exempt."

"Oh."

"Really. He was out of line."

Does Kagin feel better?

At least he can breathe again as Ryan and Kristian walk away.

Laughably—or maybe poetically—his next match, at three thirty, is Anabel's. Kagin sets up alone. Anabel's playing another young girl, with whom their exasperated, lightning-fast warm-up belies a long history. Kagin calls two edges the girls fail to report, and both times, the offender brazenly scowls at him. Otherwise, it's a standard match. At least he has stopped sweating. He rolls his shoulders back, like Dennis always reminded him in lieu of more helpful advice.

More shaking of hands. Kagin's barely closes around Gao's before she launches herself at the opposing coach, singing praises, gesturing vociferously, whatever interest Kagin held for her overruled by this higher order of relationship. Anabel, waiting patiently with her towel across the back of her neck, grants him a friendly nod and totes her duffel off to the next court.

Once again he is on his own, with an hour until the written exam at five thirty. He finds a cracked chair beneath the outermost ridge of bleachers, releases his back from its erect umpire's posture, and tries to visualize the testing area. A big gray conference room like the ones he frequents for his day job, outside this subterranean world. No, too nice. A school desk beneath a hot spotlight. He took his Regional Umpire test alone at his breakfast table, a mug of creamered oolong muddying atop the handbook he laid out as motivation, and like then, it's a relief not to be looked at or spoken to. He could just as well sit unlooked-at and unspoken-to at his breakfast table, in the privacy of his work cubicle, or in his favorite corner of the bed, and not in this relentlessly public sports arena. Perhaps he is not needed here. Perhaps he is not suited.

He's been sitting for twenty minutes, socked heels resting on the stiff collars of his shoes, alternately reciting the most esoteric passages of the handbook and contemplating going back to his hotel room and not emerging until the flight home, when the kids approach.

Anabel speaks first: "Do you wanna play?"

Kagin tenses and jams his feet forward; forces himself to recline again, left foot awkwardly pinched. They're just kids. "So I won't call your edge balls anymore?" he says.

"For fun. Coach told me you were testing for NU."

"Of course she did."

"It'll relax you." She looks to Ryan. "He thinks. *I* find practice stressful."

Ryan smiles. It's like a film over his face has been pierced, brushed away. He appears a more normal boy, emotions straightforward and apparent, but whatever Kagin saw in his eyes from the floor has been obscured by this clarity, a dark pit occluded by surrounding lights. "You can use my spare paddle," he says.

Kagin's not canny enough to glean their ulterior motives. To assuage his fears? Of what? "You know I can't do you any favors, right?" he says. "Even if I feel bad for ruining your game today."

"I lose to Barry every time."

"You weren't going to."

"He'd figured out my serve."

"Come *on*," Anabel says.

"Coach is buying us dinner," Ryan says. "We gotta play before the food gets here."

Coach is buying them dinner—nothing could be wrong, right? At least not so wrong he can't take Ryan's spare paddle and join for a bit.

First he plays Ryan alone. The boy returns all his erratic shots to the forehand. Then he starts moving Kagin, left-right, left-right. The stiff seams of Kagin's blazer restrict him, but he shrugs up the shoulders and lets sweat run down his collared shirt.

"Tell him to keep his shoulder low," Anabel says quietly from the sideline.

"Keep your shoulder low," Ryan says.

"I can hear you both," Kagin pants. He drops the shoulder. His stroke flies smoothly from hip to forehead, a faulty joint snapped back into place.

"Runaround," Anabel says, stepping onto the court. She serves the ball to Ryan, who hits it back for Kagin—exhausted, but still limber enough to leap and swing—to hit to Anabel, who's run around to the other side of the table. Then Ryan's running, and Kagin, and Anabel, circling like crazed puppies, hounding the ball. In this game, they almost appear equal, Kagin's loose stroke as good as Anabel's machine precision.

His watch shows 5:00, 5:10. He could have played like that forever. He could simply stay at the table. But then, hitting back to the boy—who shouts, plants a hand on the table, and launches himself to catch Kagin's poorly aimed shot; who doesn't want the ball to drop but also does not want Kagin to feel bad—he imagines Gao telling Anabel, telling Ryan, that the new Regional Umpire no-showed his exam. He imagines faking a departure to the kids' faces, and the shame briefly deafens him. At 5:20, he catches the ball and bids them farewell.

"Good luck," says Anabel.

Ryan says, "Don't need luck if you have preparation," and raises a fist.

Kagin whispers to himself as he crosses the hall: "'Many players will show emotions—happiness, disappointment—and these kinds of emotions are part of the game.'" The tables stand empty but for a few lingering enthusiasts, rallying and fooling around, just like he was. He can't see daylight but imagines he can feel it shifted, low and mellow, ochre flung softly over the earth. "'However, if emotions are used against an opponent, a match official, a spectator, or brings discredit to the sport, the Umpire should be ready to respond immediately.'"

When he turns for one last look, the kids are on the floor, Ryan on his back, Anabel crouched over him, levering his leg in a hamstring stretch.

Of course. That's what he saw.

The test is in a spacious room overlooking the Strip. Kagin and the other Regional Umpire sit at a massive U-shaped table. Barbecue Sauce and Kagin's co-ump proctor. Sun off the glass Luxor pyramid pricks Kagin's eyes. He waits alone in the windowless hallway while the two National Umpires grade. Barbecue Sauce, who emerges first with the papers, informs him kindly that, while his written score was good, he miscalled two edge balls during Anabel's match.

He has to laugh. "I thought I botched the men's side."

She wasn't evaluating then, she says, she just wanted to watch the match. But he made the right calls.

He passes the exam the following year. Working the 2014 US Nationals, he will be one of the last people to see Ryan play before he leaves for the vaunted Bundesliga. Despite practiced impartiality, he will watch with tears in his eyes, because he was wrong, so wrong.

2011

ELLEN

As soon as Ellen accepted her invitation to play the US–Canada "friendship tournament" (a friendship that must be very strong or very weak, if table tennis was key), her mother posted it to WeChat. Ellen did not have an account, but logged into her mother's whenever the iPad sat unattended; which, as her mother bustled around their apartment in a blitz of purses, lipstick tubes, and chiming Baoding balls, was often.

So proud to represent the US of A!!! her mother had written, beneath an action photo of Ellen at age eight, when her stance still looked competent and sure. American flag emoji, handshake emoji, Canadian flag emoji, *So much hard work.* This was targeted at Ellen's father, who thought Ellen didn't improve fast enough. Ellen had overheard them arguing on the phone—the only way she heard from or about him, besides her mother's stories. All her mother's WeChat posts were really meant for him.

The post omitted that Ellen was substituting for another girl at her club: Anabel, three years older and six hundred USATT rating points better. Anabel was staying in New Jersey to help direct their club's big tournament. Anabel was also busy with her lab internship, which would probably get her into Princeton. Anabel was tall with eyebrows like delicately shaded helicopter seeds and wafted the scent of coconut. Anabel maintained an Instagram grid tastefully populated (every fourth photo or so, up until last month) by the face of her handsome boyfriend, fellow table tennis star Ryan Lo. The two girls rarely spoke, since Anabel trained among the club's elite, with whom Ellen, who appeared younger and worse at table tennis than she was, was not invited to play or hang out. But speaking, Ellen was sure, could only emphasize the insurmountable gap between them. You could not feel like Ellen, like your joints were made of cracked crab shell, and play table tennis like Anabel.

She had little choice in the matter: Coach Gao had jogged out to the car during pickup and asked Ellen's mother directly. "How could she not go?" Ellen's mother said. "Wow. Thank you, thank you. Thank you!"

In the backseat, Ellen rolled up her window, but Gao's smug smile cut through the tint. Peeling into the street, Ellen's mother said, "And of course, your *father* never took us to Canada." She wanted to go—*needed*, as soon as she learned of the opportunity, to visit that mythic country up north. Since Ellen's father had left them for Shanghai six years ago, her mother saw every decision as reparations for his wrongs, no motivation pure and noble but her willfully lived life. So Ellen would suffer it. For a month she sulked in her room, storing up facial stamina for all the fake photos and fake conversations her mother would instigate, and memorizing the itinerary emailed by Coach Kristian, the delegation leader.

That was the most exciting, or simply least dread-inducing, part: meeting this minor celebrity. Ellen expected him to be eccentric like Gao, who propped her metal Buddha statue, in his tiny crochet cap, on a caddy to "watch them play," and sometimes showered them in candy or blasted K-pop during conditioning. Occasionally irate and blustering, shouting invocations to Heaven and Guanyin bodhisattva, but never boring. Maybe, Ellen found herself speculating, he would see something Gao didn't and fix her stagnating game.

The Americans were arriving two days early to hike around a glacial lake and practice. Vacationing beforehand made no more sense to Ellen than the tournament's premise, but her mother wasn't going to miss a photogenic outing. They were flying alone from LaGuardia, silver lining to a brutal dark cloud: the other kids were traveling from a Ping-Pong Diplomacy showcase to which Ellen had not been invited; like Anabel, they played at much higher levels. And the lining dulled to almost nothing when their flight was delayed, leaving them to navigate the shuttles alone with three Louis Vuitton suitcases. Ellen never bothered suggesting her mother replace them with something subtler and lighter, just as she held back any suggestion that the hiking gear bought for the trip—pants, boots, and jackets in clashing shades of olive; bucket hats with beavertail neck flaps and mesh panels—would never be worn. Waiting for her mother outside the Edmonton airport bathroom, Ellen tapped into the pink iPad to see a picture of crossed legs, a hand loosely cradling two silver Baodings, sneakered feet coy before a wall of LV print. *Love to travel in comfort with #AirCanada and #LouisVuitton #LouisVuittonGirl*, her mother wrote. *Off to the competition!*, flexed bicep emoji. One like (Ellen's aunt), zero unread messages.

Ellen knew shame wasn't pure or noble, either, but at least it told you how to make life less difficult. It was harder than it needed to be not having a father, attending a predominantly white school she had entered in the seventh grade, playing a sport in which she fell further behind her peers by the hour. But no one saw that: they just saw her lose, lose and cry beneath the cover of her plain white sweat towel. She didn't even have a sponsor to give her a branded one.

They arrived three hours late to the upscale "inn" at the base of the mountains. During the hour-long ride from the airport, her mother, ignoring fellow passengers' pointed looks, alternated between complaining about the distance and photographing, through the shuddering windows, snowcapped peaks and firs packed tight as toothbrush bristles; low clouds that clung to the treetops like cotton candy wisps, associations that brought childhood vertiginously close, like the murky outlines of rocks beneath the rushing green ice melt.

Kristian sat in an armchair by the lobby fireplace. Surrounded by guests in rain puffers and shoes like ugly rocks, wearing a sweat-wicking polo and nylon track pants, he looked, with his alert and subliminally discontent fox face, like the essence of a table tennis coach. Beside him slouched Ryan Lo, feet planted firmly, one hand resting sphinxlike on each knee. His face looked broader, brows tenser, than in Anabel's selfies, and the details of his undepicted body—long hairs hanging from calves, fabric bunching at armpits and waist, under-short darkness encircling his thighs—felt too immediate, a strange hand hovering millimeters from the skin of Ellen's throat. Before she could wave, or otherwise make herself known, her mother had engaged the attendant, a young East Asian man who smiled patronizingly but refused to switch to Mandarin. While he informed them breakfast was served from six to ten, provisions could be purchased at the strip mall across the street (Ellen's mother glared at the giant metal bowl of chips and apples on the counter behind him), and there had been bear sightings (he gestured toward the taxidermied specimen by the door) so they should hike in groups and speak in moderate voices to give bears fair warning, Ellen pretended not to have registered Kristian or Ryan's presences.

But she had already stared too long. Kristian stood and took a few steps toward them. Ellen grabbed the fingers of her left hand and squeezed until a knuckle popped, praying he would neither leave nor come any closer, nor feel put-upon to hover, waiting.

"How many bears?" her mother demanded.

"Five, maybe six," said the attendant. "I apologize for the inconvenience."

"Is it safe outside? What are we supposed to do?"

"Mom," said Ellen. Kristian had now waited an unconscionable amount of time. "*Mom*. C'mon, the coach is here."

The attendant slid keys across the counter. Ellen grabbed them and tugged her mother away.

"Okay, okay." Her mother gathered the suitcase handles. "Who is it?"

"Miss Xu?" Kristian had a slight German accent. "Ryan, come welcome the young woman from New Jersey."

Ryan drummed his kneecaps, rose, ambled over—Ellen felt herself holding her breath—and extended a hand between Ellen and her mother. Ellen's mother grabbed his hand and pulled it nearly to her breast.

"Ryan Lo," she cooed. "So excited to meet a national *champion*! Let's take selfies."

The pink iPad ascended; a bangle soared down Ellen's mother's arm and caught on the swell of her bicep. For what felt like minutes, the camera clicked, loud and wet like a sucking orifice, so long Ellen had to release her left hand, because the pain was reaching a bone deepness that forewarned permanent damage. She didn't want to understand where her mother was coming from, but even if she had not known who he was, she would have done a double take in the lobby: even in a surly mood, Ryan seemed assured, poised, tapped into a level of understanding—of table tennis, of his surroundings, of his own body—far above Ellen's; all the things she might have expected from Kristian's protégé and Anabel's professed "inspiration." Not belonging to the cliques of superior junior players who stalked the big tournaments, Ellen had never been this close, but just remembering the sight of him practicing with Anabel, their yelps of laughter as they circled a court like mating birds (Ryan launched himself airborne; Anabel giggled and skipped sideways, the ball flying back past her, irrelevant), and her own awe as she watched him dance around the court, running a lesser boy in and out of the table, unwittingly melded with the other spectators' in one suffocating hot front of covetousness, she blushed. He smelled like the fashion magazine her mother bought in the airport.

It was Kristian who finally clapped his hands—Ryan recoiled as he brushed the hem of his *Naruto* T-shirt—and said, "Better get going, then. We hike at eight."

Ellen's mother smiled at the grid of new photos. "Will we climb many mountains?"

"Just one. The nearest one, to see the glacial lake. You see, around now the ice melts, because it is getting *warmer* here, due to summer and *global warming*—that's an aspect of climate change—and then flows *down* the valleys, because, as you could see on your way here, they are very *steep*; and then that makes a *lake*, an aggregation of water."

The longer Kristian talked, the more evident it became that he meant the condescending tone. The longer she let him talk without interrupting, hands clasped rapt at her chest, grunting assentingly, the more evident Ellen's mother made it that her sycophancy toward Ryan, already uncouth, also extended to Kristian—about whom, during the weeks before the tournament, Ellen had never heard her speak! Of whom she didn't even know until ten minutes ago! And who, Ellen could already tell, was nothing like the noble elder she had envisioned, from whom she might receive kindness or guidance; neither lovable, attractive, nor funny, not even harmlessly bland.

Ellen looked to Ryan. All around them, normal, friendly interactions took place. Two lanky ponytailed men tied their boots. A Sikh family clustered around a rafting brochure, quibbling about which level of difficulty to brave. Ryan caught Ellen's gaze and, as if to say *You really want to do this?*, bore down on it.

"What?" he finally said. It was to Ellen, but Kristian paused.

"What, 'what?'" he said.

"I was talking to Ellen."

"And I was talking to her lovely mother."

Ellen said, "They have brochures about the hikes, Ma." She tugged her mother's wrist; her mother tugged it back.

"Yes," Kristian said, "good idea. We'll see you early tomorrow." Arms arrogantly swinging, he disappeared into the stairwell. Before he followed, Ryan said, to Ellen's surprise: "We're hot-tubbing at seven thirty. You can come."

Ellen helped her mother subdue the suitcases, their handles sliding and clacking off each other, and wrestle them into the elevator, narrowly avoiding the foot of an emerging guest. A bit faint in the wake of Ryan's cologne (*Las Vegas 12/16/09!*, she recalled Anabel's captions; *Chicago 10/12/09 < 3, Cary 7/5/08*☺, her complexion lunar and serene in every tone of light), she heard her say: "I hate that man. Stupid short man. Short, schnitzel-eating man."

"Uh-huh, yeah. Wait—what?"

"I said," her mother said, "that is a stupid, short, schnitzel-eating short man."

Ellen snorted, surprised. "You can't really say things like that," she said, but added, "Also pretzels. And sauerkraut."

There was a glow of solidarity; then her mother said, "Sow-ler-clout?" and embarrassment past and prospective snuffed it out.

"Never mind," said Ellen, "he's just an asshole."

"He is also a big, famous coach. They need to be assholes." Her mother went back and forth with herself as she shunted their luggage down the hallway and around the small room, which faced the mountain ridge; emptied her main suitcase into the plywood dresser; set her cosmetics along the bathroom counter; reapplied her day-to-night moisturizer; checked the location of the hair dryer and bemoaned said dryer's weakness as she clicked it on and off; rattled all the wooden coat hangers before hanging up her puffer; circled the room searching for a nonexistent USB plug; changed her underwear without warning Ellen, who sat on her bed thumbing her lock button, watching minutes go by; and, finally, wedged herself beneath the taut comforter with her iPad, a historical drama playing across her thighs.

"Kristian *is* mean," she sighed conclusively. "But because someone was mean to him."

Ellen eyed her lone duffel and decided she'd just leave her stuff inside. "*Who* was mean to him?" she asked.

"Could be anyone." Her mother waved her hand. "You don't know everyone mean to you."

Ellen did, actually: kept a list her mother often topped, ahead of boys at school, Coach Gao, and her worst imaginations of her father; but she only nodded and, kicking her feet in a performance of indifference, asked if she could hang out with the other kids.

"Ah." Her mother sank deeper into her pillow pile. "Sure. Could you pass me the quilt?"

Ellen rushed to get ready before her mother could change her mind and scurried out in her travel clothes, room key in one clammy fist and her mother's bathing suit in the other. Her heart had thumped as she reached into the drawer, but her mother didn't notice. She paused the show once before Ellen left, only to check her phone and shout, "Hike at eight, okay?"

In the lobby bathroom, Ellen discovered that her mother had packed a black string bikini. The air felt slimy against her genitals, her nipples, the glands beneath her armpits she still remembered her fifth-grade teacher explaining during the puberty unit. Despite its dry cleanness, she sucked in through her teeth when, with one tug, the bikini bottom buried itself between her legs. Her period had started a year ago, the collapse of childhood's final bulwark, and she'd had to fight to get tampons. The bikini top strings took minutes to untwist and tie, the back knot a precarious bunch. Ellen replaced her jean shorts and shoes before realizing how mortifying it might be to remove her pants in front of strangers. She untied the shoes, slipped out of her shorts, and darted down the hallway, a squirrel clutching her soft bundled nut.

Here she was again, putting herself through discomfort, probably to be let down. Hard to feel optimistic about the tub situation, though it *was* optimism that brought her. Ryan *had* invited her, and even knowing that someone like her could rarely hurt the feelings of someone like Ryan, she did not want any chance of him feeling let down.

Yeah, I know Anabel, she mouthed. *Yeah, I know Anabel. Yeah, I* know *Anabel.*

The sauna, tiled claustrophobically in brown and gray, rang with splashes and murmured teenage nothings. Through the frosted window, Ellen counted three shadows: Ryan; Lola Cheung, who had beaten her seven times over the last three years; one other thick-torsoed boy. She tried to forget everything she'd unwittingly learned about them at tournaments. Then she pushed through the glass door into the chlorinated cool, panicked, and reeled off all their names and home states.

"What's up," said Denny Ouyang from Indiana. "And you're . . . ?"

"Ellen," said Ryan, pedaling his feet through the water. "Thought you guys should meet her."

The boys sat side by side in T-shirts and navy swim trunks, dipping their feet. Lola held onto the ledge beside Ryan, cheek resting on her folded forearms, floating so the pink of her tasteful one piece blurred up through the surface; rolled her eyes as Denny scanned Ellen's body. Her hair had been cropped since Ellen last saw her, a blunt bang and bob that swished across her cheekbones when she tilted her head, two oversized barrettes—same color as her swimsuit—pinning back flyaways. With a girl like Lola around, there was no hope of extra kindness from a boy like Ryan. Even that goofy name suited her, made her more interesting. Ellen wished she were an Erica, a Michelle, or a Tiffany, like the rest of them.

"Anyway," Lola said, nuzzling the back of her hand, "I think this should've been in Toronto."

"We weren't arguing with you, Lo," Denny said.

"I'm just saying. It's environmentally irresponsible to fly so far. And I bet tourism's bad for the animals. Like, bears are vulnerable when they come out of hibernation."

"Lola knows everything," Ryan told Ellen. "She got a thirty-six on her ACT."

Lola glared. Ryan's tone was one amplitude short of kindness, knocked off course somewhere between brain and mouth. Still: Ellen thought she'd like to hear Ryan brag about her, even if sarcastically. "Congratulations," she said.

Lola pulled herself out of the water, legs emerging coquettishly crossed. "It's only what they expect of people like us."

"Asians?" Ryan said, mildly.

"Yes. Quiet and good at tests."

"Yeah, well. Last week Haesun threw up doing suicides, and you know what he did?"

"Ate it?" said Denny.

"Ew, dude. No. Just chucked sand on it and kept going. So maybe they've got us pegged."

"They're sure not getting it from *me*," Denny said. "I'm slow *and* dumb." He thunked the top of his skull.

"Your loss, Denny," Lola snapped. "And yeah, Haesun is like, *Asian* Asian. That's different." She turned to Ellen. "What's your ACT? Since they're targeting women here."

Ellen could imagine Kristian looming over her in that terrible lobby bathroom, his presence sufficient to bring up her airplane lunch. If she thought hard enough, she could imagine Gao managing the same, though she would have apologized and helped clean up the mess. And Lola, definitely Lola. She might make Ellen throw up right now. "I . . . I haven't taken it yet. I'm a sophomore."

"But you must've done a practice test," Lola insisted.

"Not yet."

"She's probably a genius," Denny said, "just like you, Lo."

Lola slapped Denny's shoulder. "Literally, shut up. What's your rating, Ellen?"

Ryan rolled his eyes but didn't meet Ellen's frightened gaze. Denny was watching his underwater feet. They were used to being surrounded by greatness.

"Seventeen hundred," Ellen admitted.

"*Seventeen hundred?*" Lola was rated nearly 2200, which meant she could beat Ellen with a five-point handicap every set. Ryan was over 2500, Denny in the 2300s. The lowest-rated Canadian woman would be 2000. Comforting, at least, that Ellen could expect to lose without reservation. "Ugh. Why didn't Anabel come?!"

She looked to Ryan, but Ellen caught it too late; blurted, "She's busy with school."

"Like the rest of us aren't?!"

"She takes hard classes," Ryan said.

"Like what?"

"She's in seven APs," said Ellen.

"I'm in eight," Lola said, "big effing deal. *Actually* why isn't she here, Ryan?"

Ryan shrugged. "She didn't tell you?"

"She left me on read." Lola sniffed. "*Not* that I'm holding it against her."

"You know who never leaves me on read, Lola?" said Denny, half-heartedly. "Your mom." Lola lofted a palmful of water onto his shirt. He yelped and brushed at the dark spot. Lola said it was payback for upstaging her Thursday night. Ellen's knees went hot with gratitude: her hazing was over. She sat dazed on the edge of the tub, calves submerged, leaned back with her stomach sucked in, and drew paths through the grubby static of the stucco ceiling as the others bantered and gossiped about players at the showcase. When she'd made it from the upper-left corner to the lower right, she said she had to go back, her mother had given a curfew.

"Bye," droned Denny. Lola waited until his echo dimmed to chirp, "Have a good night."

There. She had done what was expected. Ellen stood, shorts and hiking shoes scooped against her ribs. Ryan withdrew his legs, too, unfolded upward and shook out his calves. "I should go, too," he said. "You know how Kristian is."

"Tell Anabel I say hi," Lola said.

"I will," Ellen said, the same time as Ryan; flushed at the misunderstanding and again as Ryan's arm extended toward her, as if to high-five, only to burrow into his black hoodie. As he followed her to the door, his breath tickled her bare shoulder blades and a thread of heat ran up her back, so that out in the hallway all she could manage was "Um, I'm taking the stairs?"

Ryan flattened his damp bangs and squinted up, cross-eyed. "Hey, um—did Anabel say anything about the tournament?"

"Like what?"

"About, I don't know. Me, or Lola. Or . . . Coach."

Anabel sometimes nodded encouragingly when Ellen happened to hit a solid shot, or let her ahead in the water line, but she would never have shared anything intimate. "Why are you asking me? Isn't she *your* girlfriend?"

"We—not really. Coach made me break . . . it wasn't . . . agh. We stopped talking."

So that was why he had invited her to the tub. In Anabel's photos, he looked sleepy with contentment; on his profile, he only posted photos of her. Through Ellen's ridiculous, selfish disappointment—of course he wasn't interested in *her*—sounded the sharp squeaks of Anabel's shoes against polyester, her pained grunts as she rattled a thousand shots into the white-painted corners, the thwack of water bottle targets knocked to the ground, violent efforts to which Ellen had never truly aspired; whose relief in the form of an ideal romance was, she now realized, an impersonal source of comfort, like her mother's soap operas.

"She never mentioned you," Ellen said.

"But—"

"Sorry, I need to change." She speedwalked away. In the empty lobby, the dead bear still yawned, slack-limbed. Poor, dumb, lonely bear. She slammed the bathroom door and dropped her boots; the left one ricocheted and coughed up its sock. She sat and yanked the rough wool over chlorine-sticky feet, toilet seat chilling the insides of her buttocks, muttered *Shit!* when she realized she'd put on shoes but not shorts. Walking upstairs in her suit—she could not bring herself to step in and out of the shoes again—she allowed herself a shiver of triumph that she had been right about people this time, and a pulse of sorrow, a tightness deep in her ears, that even the best-made things fell apart.

On the third floor, she could hear her mother's voice from the end of the hall. It did not pause or falter when Ellen entered.

Her mother did not even turn in the bed, where she had cocooned herself, phone pressed between her head and two pillows.

"Why would you say that?" she said. "No, I don't. Yes. No. Obviously!"

Ellen exhaled through her nose. Her mother turned, teeth crookedly bared, eyes focused beyond her daughter. "No. Yes. I already told you! We need to go to bed. You'll see. I'll send you pictures—no, yes, I will."

She dropped her phone on the rumpled bed. "Your father," she said unnecessarily.

"Cool," Ellen said.

"He's excited for you to play this tournament."

Ellen smiled wanly. Her mother watched her compete at every New Jersey tournament. Even against people her own level, she played uncertainly, destabilized by the slightest disturbance. She was a three-legged table, functional but shaky, waterlines trembling. She had been that way since her father left, though she hated admitting this and would never yield an inkling of it to her mother. In the six years since, he hadn't started a new family. As far as her mother knew, he wasn't remarried, or even dating. (She claimed this was an intuition, into which Ellen, like all women, would age.) He had not left them for a better option. They were simply not enough, and nothing Ellen did would change his mind. Even at her tender age, even with earlier memories of their family going watery around the edges, she knew that.

Before she fell asleep, nestled against her mother's back, she revisited Ryan and Anabel's Instagrams. On Ryan's page, Anabel still rested chin on fists beside an empty US Open court, tight-lipped smile pushing her eyes into crescents, the sleeves of Ryan's black hoodie swallowing all but the pale tops of her fingers.

On Anabel's profile, the photos of Ryan had disappeared.

•

Ellen slept deeply and woke to her mother's warm back and chiming mandolin alarm. Even after her mother made them late—shucking her hiking gear in favor of acid-washed skinny jeans, a pilled pink-and-white striped sweater, and Coach sneakers; staying in the bathroom for fifteen extra minutes—the overcast morning seemed one of gentle promise, the roads empty, hikers clicking like mild mantises along the shoulders. The mountains were clean cut-outs steamed atop a base of dense blue sky.

The trail started at the end of the log-building strip across the street, past a sports equipment store and an Indigenous art gallery. Kristian, Lola, and Denny stood around the trail sign, all in hiking boots and San Francisco baseball caps. Ryan sat apart, staring listlessly across the lot, hands curled empty in his lap. He and Ellen turned their heads to avoid eye contact. Kristian plucked a piece of lint off Ryan's hat, then clapped his hands. "Listen up!"

In the early light, against the everyman affability of his outfit, his face looked craggier and meaner. Ellen flinched at the phlegmy croak of *up*. Lola rolled her eyes toward Denny. Kristian distributed four holsters of bear spray—one to Ellen's mother, who smiled as she took it; two to Ryan, who wrinkled his nose but tucked one into each side pocket; and one, after a "No thanks!" from Lola and reluctant shrug from Denny, to Ellen—and explained, using the fifth can, how to release the safety on the canister, how to spray in a zigzag with both hands, and how, to alert bears of human presences, they should talk in low to medium tones. "But," he concluded, "they say no one has ever used the spray."

"Oh goodie," said Lola.

Ellen's mother stamped her foot and grinned. "Goodies! Oh, yes, I have some. Take some goodies." She cocked her arms painfully backward and yanked two fistfuls of snack bags from the side of her backpack. "Important to stay energetic, run from bears. Ellen, help me, one in the top pocket . . ."

Denny, lips happily pursed, plucked a bag of pretzels; Kristian barked, "We shouldn't eat on the trail—ESPECIALLY not chips!"

"Denny, get me the Bugles," sniffed Lola. Ellen recognized the snacks now, from the bowl behind the front desk. Her mother hopped backward, shunting her backpack into Ellen's face, and said, "Take something."

"These were for the *staff*, Mom!"

"No, sweetie, I ask and they give them to me. No? Tsk. What about you, Ryan?"

Ryan stared at the ground between his feet. Of course he'd leave her in the lurch. Kristian snatched the remaining bags and crunched them into his jacket pockets. "No," he said. "Let's go. Someone take the lead."

Lola pulled Ellen forward by the handle of her backpack, jingling Coach Gao's '08 Olympics ornaments. "Go on, fearless leader! Take us to gold!"

"Go, Ellen," her mother said. "Lead the kids." She was still watching Kristian; still wanted to ingratiate herself.

A coil of cold burned in Ellen's chest. The hike to the glacier was two thousand feet of elevation. Like at the upcoming matches, she would have to find a way to endure. Her father once told her that he passed long flights across the Pacific by walking the streets of Shanghai in his mind, populating them with infinite staircases, lost friends, unicorns, aliens. Her mother countered: "He just counts money on his laptop." Back then, Ellen had protested this as slander. Now, she'd probably side with her mother. As Lola's coltish legs bounced impatiently at the knees, Ellen thought about lying in her bed at golden hour, the house empty, the lawns outside unmolested by mowers or sprinklers or the churning feet of children, at peace. Peace. It was fine. It was fucking fine. She'd been through worse and would go through worse soon at the tournament.

She pumped her arms through the first flat mile alone. She hopped across tinkling, loamy creeks; brushed past fir trees grown slanted as if gossiping with their tree friends across the path, their needles glossy as liquid caramel. Then the ground tilted up at a forty-five-degree angle, switching back overhead. She leaned forward, then back. She took longer strides, then shorter. Either way, her breathing would not slow.

Behind her, Ryan's voice called, "Hey!"

Ellen tried to speed up, but the piney air seemed to be gluing her lungs shut, so she turned tail and jogged back past Ryan, through the acrid cloud of Denny's aftershave and Lola's protest at being brushed aside, panting, "Sorry, gotta see my mom." Her mother was a hundred meters behind, forefinger sliding around her phone, trying to upload photos. Kristian waited beside her, arms crossed. The silk of the Baoding box flashed red from his backpack's mesh side pocket. She had probably taken out the balls to relieve her fangirling nerves; he had probably confiscated them, irritated by the clanging.

"Cell service so bad," her mother huffed. The brightening daylight exposed the density of her makeup—harsh carnation-pink eyeshadow like beetle wings, outer edges cracked, a hastily blended fingerprint trapped in her second layer of blush. None of that was any use, Ellen wanted to tell her.

"You can do that at the hotel," she said. "C'mon, Mom."

Kristian patted her mother's shoulder. "Maybe your mother needs the rest, Ellen. It's a hard hike for sedentary people."

"She's not sedentary."

"How are you feeling about the tournament? A big step up, yeah?"

"Yep. Mom, stop checking WeChat."

"It's okay if you lose," Kristian said. "This is only an exhibition."

"It *is* okay, right?" said Ellen's mother. She lowered her phone, letting it dangle from its wrist strap. She smiled at Kristian, toothless and simpering, yellowed foundation bristling in the long creases around her mouth. "That's what I told her father. He is always so demanding about winning this, winning that, no appreciation for what you have. That's how you give up easy, you know, give up and get a divorce. We were divorced seven years, on Tuesday."

"Well," Kristian said, "it's always *preferable* to play well. Not to make a fool of yourself."

Ellen tilted her face toward the sky. She imagined herself as a satellite dish, receptive and steel-smooth and incapable of feelings. "Mom, come on . . ."

"Why don't you go talk to the others?" Kristian said. "Ask them for tips. They're used to these big venues."

So Ellen walked back again, furious. Why did she keep trying, anyway? She caught up to the pack in five minutes and broke into a jog to pass them. Lola ignored her, but Ryan repeated, "Hey, Ellen, wait!"

She jogged until she couldn't stand straight, which was not long: she had always been slow in conditioning drills, slower than even the little kids who tried to sneak soda past Coach Gao. To her right, spindly saplings shaded a narrow tributary path, marked only by its topcoat of yellow pine needles; she followed it onto a parallel trail, sat on the nearest boulder, and rested her hands on the bear spray. Her heartbeat slowed.

"I'm not a bear," she said. "I am a human. No bears, no bears for me. Please, leave me alone. I am a harmless human. No bears, no bears, no bears."

Five minutes passed, then ten. Her breath evened. A trio of chipmunks skittered around in the undergrowth. A squawking magpie rocked the hedge behind her. The landscape turned her senses inward, casting her forward into the tournament. She would lose the first set respectably, eleven to seven or six, but in the second set she would begin to make unforced errors, slicing her serve into the net, shuffling left when the ball flew right. Such mistakes were easy to fix. As Coach told her, you just had to slow down and breathe. But Ellen struggled to breathe. Her opponent before her, her coach and mother behind, were like steel plates inside her rib cage. Always, she was caught between: Ryan and Anabel, her mother and Kristian, her mother and herself; the desire to quit and to keep going; the grubby riotous claustrophobia of adolescence and the smooth, airless claustrophobia of what she could glean to be adulthood, the very few things that came to or were permitted to matter.

Sometimes she missed her serve on purpose, missed her cue in lunchtime conversation, just to take a side, just to reassure herself that the worst case was also bearable. Said a mean thing to her mother. She tried her best not to, though. She really did.

Something rustled behind her. She turned to watch the dappling beneath the trees shiver, and through it a denser thing rush toward her. She raised the bear spray.

Ryan cohered out of the shadows.

Ellen lowered the canister. Her fingers were numb. "I almost sprayed you!"

"Roar?" He raised a loosely clawed hand. "You need to unholster it first. Come on, your mom's worried. She said to bring you this." He held out a granola bar.

"Yeah," Ellen said, "of course she did."

"It's nice she watches out for you."

"She is my *mom*."

He lowered the bar. "And? It'd still suck if you got eaten by a bear."

"She's the only person who'd care." She hopped off the boulder. The heaviness of her legs bided poorly for the tournament.

"And?" Ryan said.

"If you got eaten, you'd have Anabel, and Kristian, and—"

"Kristian would be mad I let it happen. Anabel wouldn't care. Anymore. Are you not gonna eat this?"

"Have it if you want."

Crumbs scattered the path and the chipmunks froze, nostrils flickering, as Ryan gnawed into the granola. He was, Ellen thought, just another handsome boy who'd had everything his way; who was stopping at the first steep face of adversity. He had never been bullied at school. He had never watched a parent crumble. He had no idea how far and painfully care could stretch, from Livingston to Shanghai; how much time one could waste trying to communicate it through time and indifference. How could he just send away someone who cared about him?

He was, at least, helping her mother, and he ate so sloppily that Ellen felt the icy lattice within her loosen, ever so slightly.

"It wasn't your choice to break up, right?" she said. "I feel like she'd get it."

He swallowed, eyes watering. "She'd never let Gao tell her what to do."

"Coach Gao would never ask something like that."

"Well, she's not the best in the country."

So? Ellen heard Coach say; could picture her, arm propped against the cinderblock wall of the club, one ankle crossed over the other, dragging her jade Guanyin pendant up and down its red string. ". . . so?"

"*So?*"

If her father had his way, Ellen would train in China every summer, far from her mother. Now that she knew Kristian, she could finally imagine that in its full misery. "I'd rather be bad at my club," she said.

"That's crazy. But I guess I respect."

"Anabel is doing fine, right? Maybe Kristian's the crazy one."

Ryan toed the edge of the path and kicked up a clump of moss. A green seed clung to the corner of his mouth, and as he brushed it off, Ellen thought a knuckle kinked up to dab the corner of his eye. "Always takes one to know one," he said, hand dropping beneath a sad, dimpled smile. "But maybe . . . maybe. Want the last bite?"

She let him drop the grain cluster into her palm, warm, shamelessly pliant and sweet. Before she could eat it, or further articulate the thought that maybe it was silly to refute a man to whom Ryan was living testament, who made clubs run, planes take off, and nations come together, but there had to be something besides that, the stuff of life teeming beneath the frozen surface of power and attractiveness, well-spokenness and respectability, there had to be!—her mother screamed, just far enough away to alarm.

In the two-room urgent care where they rushed Kristian, Ellen would learn that her mother's phone had conjured a photo of her father with another woman, his first-ever post. Ellen's mother had screamed at that; then at Kristian, who scolded her for scaring the wildlife.

For now, a dark shape approached. Even as she unholstered the canister and flicked the safety away, Ellen knew, not far beneath the surface of her mind, that it would be Kristian, not a bear, who stepped into the crisp orange zigzag of pepper spray. That Ryan would laugh before running back, past his teammates, to find Ellen's mother, who was perched on a rock above the ice melt, despondent but dry, her reflection steady and true.

2012

RAHUL

Rahul sees Ryan and Coach again outside the supplement store. There's a clearance sale and his parents, who distrust Western medicine, are away on business. Most Saturdays they sleep in, and Rahul has to tiptoe around the kitchen or stay put on his bed until his father's satisfied groan tides in a day of stilted company. Today, he got up at six thirty; ate three sesame bagels out of their plastic sleeve and kicked the seeds beneath the trash can foot pedal; played an hour of Fruit Ninja and a few pump-up tracks on speakerphone; biked four miles downtown to the tune of sawing bugs in the roadside vegetation and the rush of passing cars, under a flat satin sky, its opaque powder blue expanding and contracting with each downward dive bomb and belabored ascent. His parents don't let him drive, and over the years, after one joke too many from the other table tennis boys (though not Ryan, too busy training with Coach and Haesun) that he smelled like a bus toilet, he has invested much of his allowance into this bike.

Since quitting table tennis six years ago, Rahul has seen Ryan only on social media, at a random homecoming, and in a local newspaper his father flapped in his face before crumpling it around a stack of smartphones he was pack-muling to India. Now as then, Ryan is ahead, ten feet from the frozen sliding doors, hair damp because he and Coach have practiced already. Rahul recognizes their orientation: Coach, arms crossed, tilts toward Ryan on all the tiny muscles in the front half of his feet, which they used to strengthen at the end of practice, gripping the glossy weave of the red polyester floor and imagining themselves as monkeys; peers as if for a secret floating behind Ryan's head, though always, the secret was Ryan himself. And Ryan, hip cocked on the verge of impatience, talks to Coach without looking, eyes scanning the sidewalk cracks. When the door rattles, their heads turn in hawklike unison.

"Thank fuck," groans the guy behind Rahul, stashing his phone in his pocket, and Rahul—fighting the urge to take out his own phone for a quick game of Fruit Ninja; it would still be mortifying for Coach to catch him loafing—applies himself to their collective forward shuffle. The line comprises men at all stages of ill-set adulthood: bodies hunched and stiffed, bulging and striated, obese and patting at the jiggling excess pieces of themselves. No one with Ryan's lithe athleticism and very few beanstalks like Rahul, who only started lifting weights three months ago. That day, he woke up with a cough, caught his watery eyes in the mirror as his bony torso spasmed and his neck veins flared against the cartilage of his throat, and felt a self-hatred so intense it burned his airways clear. His parents were away, so he did fifty push-ups in the hallway, tapping nipples to wood. He watched five hours of tutorial videos and signed up for a trial at the gym behind the supplement store. He went twice, drifting between clusters of equipment in the wake of a young Indian guy who looked how he knew he should dream of looking, muscles clefted and back swinging stiffly as he walked, imitating his motions with furtive glances. Then he started sneaking into the football team weight room during lunch and drinking protein sludge brewed in secret beneath the bathroom tap. His parents think weight lifting is dangerous.

Inside the store, DMX booming off rubberized walls, there's a frenzy around two-dollar bins at the front, hands plunging and resurfacing like the hands of knife-bearing assassins. Rahul gets hold of a random tub before he's jostled away. The desolate metal shelving has been picked nearly clean. He sees Ryan and Coach through a shelf, framed by two strips of a sloppily torn-off poster, fragmented grayscale triceps and calves. Ryan looks past the tub they were reading and says, "Hey, man." And in one of those collapses of time that always caught him at the table, ball back in the opponent's hand when he just saw it leave the dusty red surface of their racket, Rahul finds himself stuck with them in the checkout line, Coach having offered, with his insidious mild disdain, to pay for Rahul's hard-won creatine.

"Wait, so, you don't have a program?" Ryan says. He's offloaded his tubs to Coach, leaving hands free to prop disbelievingly on his hips.

"I mean, kind of . . . I work out different parts of my body, like. Split them up."

"That's nice," Coach says, and smiles wanly. He seems to remember Rahul, the way you remember a funny sign by the highway.

Rahul says, "And you're still, like, training and stuff? Are you going to the Olympics?"

A stupid question, one any oaf in the store could have asked; but amazingly, Coach says, "North American trials in three weeks."

"Oh wow! Congrats!"

"Haven't made it yet," Ryan says. "Only the top three go to London. Come watch, it's in Sacramento."

Rahul imagines getting up on a Saturday and telling his parents he needs to be in Sacramento. For leisure. *You haven't talked to that boy in years*, his mother would say, selectively knowledgeable about his friendships. *What do you care what happens to him?* Coach doesn't approve of the invitation; he sighs, shifts the tubs against his forearms. "Maybe you could learn something," he murmurs, "*maybe*." Rahul feels a sour trickle from the old well of self-doubt, which Coach dug into them all. Still, beside Ryan, it's bearable.

"Yeah," he says, "I could. That'd be cool." His creatine slips from his grasp; Ryan catches and pretends to shotput it.

"Pay attention," Coach hisses.

Out in the midday sun, Ryan holds up his phone, and it takes Rahul a beat to realize he's asking for his number. Hot in the face, he taps it in.

"Cool," Ryan says, "see you soon, then."

There's no safe way to bike back up the hills. At least not by his parents' standard, both hands and butt cheeks on the frame. Rahul tucks the tub beneath his arm and steers one-handed, helmet strap weightless across his throat, foam lining an affectionate touch on his forehead, and pumps his legs as if he could outpace Coach's car pulling away up the northbound roads.

•

His parents extend their trip to India by three days, then seven. The indulgence of a trash-littered kitchen and unmade bed has turned on Rahul. He cleans up everything, but this both leaves him with a sense of desolation and reprimands him for the remembered neglect. He goes to school and the grocery store and comes home, does his homework and texts his friends. He does fifty push-ups, sit-ups, jumping jacks, and squats every hour. He hits the leaderboard in Fruit Ninja and, with a few items from the school woodshop, rigs a basket for his bike. One morning, more to prove that he exists than anything, he jacks off into a chipped glass from the back of the kitchen cupboard and holds it to the light, as if to discern the microscopic movement of sperm; failing that, spikes it with mouthwash hoping to see their dying throes. When he cruises past the supplement store again, five days after seeing Ryan, it has already been emptied and stripped.

A message from Ryan arrives on the sixth day. *Hey coach wants to know if u need a ride to Sac?* The text box descends into Fruit

Ninja, above an exploding watermelon. Rahul accidentally clicks the thread and sends *jjjllll*.

It's ryan btw

"Shit," Rahul mutters. *LMAO sry was playing fruit ninja LMAOOOOO not fruit ninja*

Not allowed to have video games . . . my dad. . . . .

Oh, right. So u need a ride?

His thumbs hover. It's cool Ryan remembered. Right? It's cool he gets to ride his bike around town, spending his time and his parents' money how he likes.

His phone buzzes again. A screenshot of another Fruit Ninja screen. *Why this ish so addictive tho*, Ryan writes. His scores are much lower than Rahul's. With a surge to his head, like remembering an answer in the last thirty seconds of a test, Rahul adds him.

yeah i'll take a ride, he replies. *Thx*

Two days later, his mother calls to say they'll be staying yet another week. "Big opportunity," her scratchy voice says, "we're sorry to leave you but want to send you to a good school debt-free, you know."

He invites *hhlmx81o_mn* to 1v1. Top-bottom split screen. Ryan starts with a combo of three tangerines. Rahul circles his finger to hit a cherry, two peaches, and two grapes. There's some transference of skill from table tennis: the perception of speed, the ability to hold in your mind many disparate elements. But while, at the table, Rahul could not simultaneously manage ball speed, racket angle, and distances between the edges, on his phone he feels ten pieces of digital fruit at once, as if they were growing from his fingertips. By the end, fruits are not so much falling as boiling, exploding so thickly they obscure their still-whole brethren. TIME UP!

He beats Ryan by two thousand points. The RETRY apple turns above his home button. He needs to enjoy the win; surely Ryan will get him next time. He's panting like he ran miles, their old two miles to the yellow house and back, but without Coach waiting oppressively in the background.

He sends another game invite. Ryan accepts.

•

He knows Ryan practices after school, so he sends Fruit Ninja invitations starting at 8:00 P.M. Four days in a row, they play between three and thirteen games. Rahul's arms are sore from the push-ups, but he creates an ergonomic position from which to swipe and slash, nested among couch pillows with a comforter beneath his arm. He wins every game but the last. Halfway through, the pace accelerating, tightness gnaws his arm from shoulder to elbow, making him groan and twist against the pillows. Two dozen cherries fall through his screen, while on Ryan's side metallic lettering shouts: COMBO! AMAZING! SUPER RARE!

Ryan swipes RETRY and Rahul texts: *sry man need a sec*

The internet says he might need more protein. He's out of smoked turkey slices, out of peanut butter, out of the gray-pink chicken thighs he defrosted on the counter then sluiced around a panful of olive oil. There's half a head of broccoli shedding yellow water and two scoops of bran cereal. The cramp has subsided, but a deep ghostly ache remains. A material, rather than spiritual, explanation for his loss, undeniable as how speed and oxygen-burning capacities explain others' victories.

It's unclear now when his parents will return.

U got anymore protein powder? he writes.

lol like loads. why

Getting cramps. Not enough protein

Been lifting more, he adds.

where r u

home

w h e r e

Rahul texts his address, then sticks the dirty dishes in the washer. Not because there's any chance Ryan will show up . . .

An hour later, the sliding doors to the backyard shudder. Suctioned to the glass, a single sweaty knuckle, haloed in mist. "Damn," Ryan says over the squealing rollers, "you live far as fuck." He's in jeans, a polo, and a black cotton hoodie, his face pink from the night. In one fluid motion he heel-swivels, tips his backpack onto the kitchen counter, and kicks off his checkered Vans. "Stuff's in there."

"Stuff?"

"Powder."

"Oh," Rahul says, "wow, yeah, thanks. I mean, I could have gotten it myself, but—"

"Is that a NutriBullet?" Now he's in the kitchen, twisting apart a blender, a gift from his father's client that sat untouched for years beneath the drinkware cupboard.

"Uh. Probably."

Ryan turns it so Rahul can read the lettering, NUTRITBUB. Close enough. The granite beneath is dusty. The room still smells like chicken. Ryan extracts the tub of protein from his backpack, measures with a baking implement Rahul didn't know existed, fills the plastic capsule with ice and water from the fridge, screws it back onto the base, laces his fingers over its pointy alien head, and yanks down. To the secret rhythm of the scream, his head bobs and his lips move around the lyrics of some song, cutting off when the noise does. "Got honey?" he asks. In the cupboard above the fridge, which Rahul is surprised to find he can reach now, there's a bear-shaped bottle crystallized into yellow-white foam. Ryan microwaves it, then shoves a knife through its plastic chest and suspends it above the blender to bleed thin, sweet squiggles. The mixture goes into two glasses from the dish rack.

In unison, eyes fixed to the bottom of their glasses, they chug, chug, sigh, and burp.

"Your arm feel better?" Ryan says.

Rahul had forgotten about it. He swings it around. "Yeah."

"Maybe you jack off too much."

"I don't—"

"Just messing, man." Ryan opens the fridge, thuds around, holds up two tangerines and an apple—weeks old, surely stale and airy inside. From the woodblock of knives (Rahul's mother bought them off a door-to-door saleswoman but kept using her twenty-year-old knife from India), he extracts the two longest blades, tests them against the apple, and extends the narrower one to Rahul. Through the sliding doors, Rahul sees light in the back of the Sheehans' house. They don't care about him. They won't hear the whistle of steel through air, the thud of fruit against freshly swept hardwood, the trickle of juice down cabinetry. He takes the handle.

"On three," Ryan says, raising the apple. "One—two—"

•

Six nights in a row, Ryan shows up. They play Fruit Ninja and count pull-ups, done on a bar Ryan finds downstairs beside a stationary bike still swaddled in cling wrap, yellowed thank-you note stuck to its handlebars. Rahul manages six; Ryan, twenty-five. The record in the Bundesliga, the professional German league where Coach played and Ryan aspires to play, is fifty. After the Olympic trials, perhaps after the Olympics—"After the Olympics," Rahul says, "definitely"—Ryan will play a circuit of European tournaments, aiming to secure a spot on one of the Bundesliga's twelve teams. Fifty people selected from all over the world, a group small enough to fit in half of the supplement store.

During the day, Rahul bikes to school, sits through classes, does push-ups and sissy squats and lat pull-downs. He drinks a protein shake in the morning and another at night. He finishes his homework at his father's glass Costco desk. Sunset possesses him to perform aimless rituals: he gathers pebbles from their backyard, tiptoes to the property border, and sprinkles them in the Sheehans' grass. At the melody of the red bird outside his parents' bedroom window, he stretches his arms upward and lets loose an echoing croak.

They are some of the happiest nights of Rahul's adolescence. (He has no way of knowing they will take hold in Ryan's memory, too; but they do.)

On the sixth night, Ryan's backpack yields a PlayStation. They play on the flatscreen in the unused living room, a samurai game that involves hunting ninjas in a dark Japanese village.

"How do you even get here?" Rahul asks.

"Call a car," Ryan says. His dad's in the OR every night this week, he explains, and his mom never interferes with his plans. She feels bad his days are so busy, that he never sees his dad.

Rahul's not good with the PlayStation controllers. He shoots at a ninja and misses, takes a shuriken to the face. His half of the screen flashes pink. "Does Coach know you're here?"

"Why would he?"

"Because, he like"—the joystick jerks the wrong way and the controller bucks as an arrow impales him; intricate lines of fletching waver above his gasping, ruined chest—"runs your life?"

Ryan's samurai sneaks around a stand of pines and slits the throat of Rahul's killer.

"I wouldn't say it like that," Ryan says coldly. Two more squelches as he dispatches the remaining ninjas and stalks up to the warlord villa to complete the mission, leaving Rahul's corpse in the dirt.

"Sorry," Rahul says. "I mean—you're going to the Olympics. It's not like, a bad thing."

"Haven't qualified yet."

Stab, stab. An arrow flies from Ryan's bow and the game follows it through the eye of a woman crouched in the second-story window. She plunges onto the curved roof below, clutching at a grainy red triangle above her white kimono. Rahul's not sure she was an enemy. Ninjas materialize from every corner of the screen. Zing, zing, zing. Stab, stab. Video games rot your brain, Rahul's parents insist. When does Ryan have time to get this good at them?

The screen shakes as an arrow finds its target, raising a pink veil of blood. "Shit!" Ryan mutters. The buttons keep clicking, combos of rolls and stabs and slices, but they're being overwhelmed. Splat, splat, splat. He's in the main hall now, looming red pillars and braziers. The boss stands at the end of the long red carpet, helmet feathers quivering.

"Here," Ryan says, and shoves his warm controller into Rahul's hands. "Finish him."

"What—"

Shuriken. Flaming arrows. *Bzzz bzzz bzzz*, the sticky plastic in the heart of his palm.

Rahul watches himself crawl forward and unplug the console. He tries to toss the controller back in a casual way, but Ryan lets it bounce off his thigh and cartwheel across the rug.

"What the hell, man." Ryan runs a hand through his hair. His forehead is the sticky yellow of last week's honey.

"Sorry. It was stressing me out."

He's upset at Ryan for one-upping him again. Of course. He imagines envy as a rug of purple smoke rippling toward him from the door jamb, imagines fanning it back with great heaves of neutrality and maturity. He sits a few feet from Ryan, farther than when they were playing, hugging his loosely crossed legs. Why did he ask about Coach? Ryan never asked about his parents. They're irrelevant, obviously. Obviously.

"My bad," Ryan says. "Should've brought something chiller."

"No, it's not, it's—"

"Coach gets less intense right before a tournament, so he wouldn't care I'm here."

It's a relief to remember this from the hazy past: easier practices and shorter runs, leading up to a dreaded Saturday. "For sure," Rahul says. "Yeah, that makes sense."

He follows Ryan into the family room, where portraits line up above the unused fireplace. His father's college graduation portrait. His mother's college graduation portrait. Their wedding. His birth. His first day of elementary school. Ryan lifts a knuckle as if to rap the glass over Rahul's father, then lowers it. "D'you like your dad?" he asks.

"*Like* him?"

He feels the house hold its breath. Like if he gives the right answer, it might finally deliver something good. His parents have stopped updating him daily. Every other day, third day. The trip drags on; big opportunities. Last time, their spoils took up all the counters and a couple shelves in Rahul's closet—rearview decorations, tiny plastic Ganeshes with circles of blush on their elephant cheeks; phone chargers and stands; spatulas, butter knives, scallop-ended forks and spoons; bottles of ibuprofen and vitamins; rolls of silk and sari cloth in fuchsias, periwinkles, seafoams; yards of twill, linen, flannel, wool; coils of beading and lace; bracelets, nose rings, earrings like pyramids of gold droplets; brown leather Jesus sandals, black leather motorcycle jackets, leather backpacks and duffels; leather-bound volumes of Dickens, Kipling, Tagore; cricket bats and badminton rackets; toothbrushes; Levi's; sheets. Will that be it this time, too? Will that be all?

"Do you think he's a good guy?" Ryan asks.

Rahul thinks longingly, for the first time, of the adults one door over. Their dull, closed-off lives, which they would probably open up to a scared teenage boy, if only they knew how scared he was sometimes. Inside, he still feels six.

"Sometimes," Ryan says, "it is too intense. Not training or anything, or even if Coach, like, hits me with balls or whatever."

Hit him with balls? "Just like, how can this be my life forever. Or like, maybe my life is run by—just, run. You know?"

Once in the streets of Delhi, Rahul's father sent him to haggle with a sari salesman. Rahul was six, the Tetris-board table of textiles level with his nose, cloth must tickling his nostrils. For days since touching down he had been coughing and wheezing; that was the first morning enough mucus filled his head to stop it. If he didn't manage it, Rahul thought, he would be left there, he'd have no choice but to stand beside that table, in the exhaust and roar of scooters, until the sinister man who pretended not to pay him mind turned his attention on Rahul and asked something far worse of him; the inscrutability and strangeness of whose desires frightened him more than any demand his parents could make, and seemed forevermore to spring at him from the enemy pitcher's glove or the mocking, featureless laughter of another child . . . But he can't share that with Ryan. That's probably not the kind of thing he's talking about.

"When's it like that?" he asks instead.

Ryan laughs. Without a reciprocal insight, Rahul realizes, he won't respect him. "You're still coming to Sacramento, right?" he says.

"Yeah."

"'Kay." He frees the PlayStation with one succinct yank of the console, all the cords popping easily free, sinks it into his backpack, and slips his hands through the straps to cradle the console in front of him like a mother kangaroo. "I'll see you then."

●

Early on the morning of the trials, Rahul watches an episode of *Shark Tank*, his father's favorite show. *You see, Rahul, when they ask you a question, always answer optimistically.*

Isn't that lying?

No. It's telling a truth you intend to make happen.

A couple stand, fake smiling, shouldering duffels made of scrapped firefighter uniforms. The judge's every uncomplimentary verdict lands as a flicker of their TV-primped eyelashes, but the smiles stay put. Rahul's father would ask what they used to stuff the bags. Paper? Foam? *That tells you a lot about someone, beta, what they do when they think no one's looking. Why you need a bag that big, anyway?*

Rahul imagines himself riding in the duffel, head popped out, fingers grasping at the zipper tape. He sees his head and Ryan's side by side, grinning from beneath the woman's arm. He thinks of his father, a Herculean version engorged on spite and whey, whipping them round before smashing them to pulp against the sidewalk.

His phone pings; the rideshare to Sacramento, paid for with his mother's credit card. He figured Ryan needs the time alone with Coach, who didn't want him there anyway. The highway north is remarkably clear, the sky movie-set blue. Downtown Sacramento looks small and staid; according to his father, people live there when they lack the imagination and grit to stick it out in the big city. He dangles his hand out his window, sampling the air of flat wide residential streets more densely populated than his, with more apartment buildings and empty fields. The venue is a windowless brick groundscraper at the end of a long drive, past an artificial pond in a broad bowl of freshly mown grass. As their car passes, two geese burst up from the stalky reeds.

In the endless gray lobby, everyone wears red lanyards, showy clean sneakers bobbing atop the carpet's erratic purple polygons. A gray-haired woman at the front desk, guarding the doors to the tournament floor, squints when Rahul tells her he's spectating. He's in jeans and a cotton quarter-zip tight beneath the armpits. He didn't want to wear anything sporty enough to imply he's a player. Then a real athlete steps in, giant and mohawked, and claims the woman's attention. The corners of a Canadian flag patch strain off his tracksuit, as if to flee his impressive chest. Rahul has never seen him, was never important enough to attend the kind of big tournaments he undoubtedly frequents.

"My dad will come get me later," Rahul offers, to no one.

Inside the hall, four tables stand empty. A couple faces swivel in his direction as he enters, eyes unseeing dark slits. He hesitates at the edge, barely breathing, until a distant hand swabs a welcoming arc. Coach. He's atop the farthest bleacher, wedged into the corner railing, one leg extended along the bench and the other propped on the foot plank. Rahul lowers his gaze as he passes the assembled players. He can't remember the last time he was alone with Coach, who still wears the tracksuit of his Bundesliga team, vowels flaunting double-dot crowns. Rahul tries to remember the name of the dots; something rich, close-lipped, smoked meats and high mountains. Below them, the relentless click of cellulose balls begins, and he feels a primeval, fearful tightening in his hamstrings.

"A pleasant surprise," Coach says. He probably expected Rahul to forget about or lose interest in the tournament.

"I don't mean to bother you guys. I don't have to—"

"No no, sit."

Rahul perches beyond Coach's feet, leaving a person's-width for Ryan. Across the arena, two women do jumping jacks.

"You look strong," Coach says. "The science does not support creatine, but surely it's encouraged you to adopt healthier habits." His arm rises in a noncommittal, perhaps mocking, bicep curl.

"I'm actually using protein powder," Rahul says. "Ryan brought me some."

His old tattling habit: *The drinking fountain broke 'cause Alvin kept hitting the button. Nicklas dropped the caddy.* He wants to slap himself. Coach raises an eyebrow.

Stupid. Stupid.

"I was passing by. Biking."

"From where?"

"The—the Sawyer Camp trail."

"The six-mile loop?"

"Yeah, I like, ride it a couple times every weekend." He had, once, six months ago.

Coach sniffs. "I admire the dedication."

"I'm really slow," Rahul says, savoring the deprecation he hopes will end the conversation. Coach hates negative self-talk. "I'm uncoordinated. And out of shape." To cover his mistake, he'd happily admit that he sucked at cricket when his father made him play, that push-ups still wind him, that the last night he saw Ryan, he punched the pillow trying to dissipate his indignation; and that when his parents return he will feel encroachment rather than relief, that only when they are compromised can he find the spiky edges of self that stamp others so distinctly onto the world. No one so much as Ryan, who now emerges, to Rahul's relief, from the men's bathroom at the end of the hall. Two-thirds of the way to them, he slows. Because he's seen him, Rahul knows, but does not want to believe until Ryan stands before him, frowning like the world-weary help in his mother's Bollywood melodramas.

"Don't be nervous," Coach says.

"I'm not." Ryan flexes his hand, inspects its pale palm—thirty-four muscles, to be strengthened by farmer's carries and wrist curls—and chucks it up for Rahul to dap. The creases of their fingers briefly grip. Rahul shuffles farther down the bench, sliding one butt cheek off, and Ryan takes his place beside Coach. As they confer, Rahul digs his tailbone against the ledge; peppercorn prickles of pain awaken his lower back. His calves and thighs are sore from squats and mountain climbers. He wishes he were at home doing crunches on his mother's old yoga mat. If she were home, she'd be frying up dosas for him to eat, erasing the afternoon's progress in five greedy bites. Coach and Ryan set their provisions along the bleacher, three bottles of jewel-toned liquid, three bananas, a single foiled square of what appears to be dark chocolate.

Nervous, Rahul slips his hand into his pocket and finds his phone is gone.

Stupid. Stupid!

The tournament will proceed from round-robins into two rounds of single elimination. The top three men go to London. The indivisibility of this number strikes Rahul as cruel. To lose a semifinal and be forced to fight again, bloodied and desperate, for the last slot. Ryan jogs away down the bleachers to sprint and grapevine along the aisle. Coach follows a minute later. They stay down there, in a player's box, through all six round-robin matches. Ryan's closest match is 3–1. It's hard to return to the feeling of watching Ryan when they were younger: back then their bodies and rogue movements still left gaps between the seen and ideal, craggy fingerholds for the other boys' ambitions and Coach's corrections, but in these matches, Ryan clearly superior to his opponents, it's like watching a variation of something he's experienced over and over, viral fall videos and planes crashing into skyscrapers, men and women in armchairs on bright stages conversing in a cadence he could replicate before a mirror or with any one of his peers, the three hollow notes of the red bird outside his parents' window. There's still uniqueness to Ryan's movements, a syncopation and smatter of microsteps in his footwork, a speed and lowness to the forehand flick, but they feel like a stylistic indulgence. Even if they both drank the plasticky honey protein, even if they both slashed recklessly at the fruit, Ryan is fully formed and Rahul is not.

After the last win, Coach ushers Ryan down the aisle, hand hovering behind his sweaty back, counseling. The women's half plays on across the adjacent tables, and more so than when he was ten, something in Rahul's chest vibrates, plastic and pathetic, with the relative emptiness of the arena, and the plainness of the people filling it. The players still look resolute, but their coaches, teammates, parents, and children blink wearily out of purposeless faces, gulp sterile air through slack and colorless lips.

And when Ryan returns to the table for his semifinal, it's like something of this observed plainness has tainted him. His opponent, the mohawked Canadian, returns his warm-up loops almost motionlessly, hips and legs clicking a few degrees left-right, left-right, like the timer on Rahul's mother's slow cooker, foreboding its dragon's belch of steam. Rahul is sweating well before the coin winks above the impassive referee's hand, before the Canadian takes the first serve and they stalk a circle around the table so Ryan can take the side facing Coach, before Ryan hops in place, knees flying to his chest, the scant fat in his cheeks bouncing itself pink and mottled. The Canadian blows into his racket-holding palm and crouches to serve without shifting his soles from the flooring, back muscles pert through his shirt. His hunched shoulders block Ryan from view, though Rahul can imagine him on the other side, knees bent, eyes level with the net, lower edge of his racket millimeters from the neon-white end line paint. Compacted. Small. The first serve flies at brutish speed, sidespin cutting vicious toward Ryan's elbow; *boom* stomps the Canadian's foot. Ryan's return, a stunted forearm swipe, sails short and limp over the net, and with a huge languid stroke—a baseball stroke, a lacrosse stroke, a movement from some sport Rahul would never dare attempt—the Canadian punches it through the empty corridor of Ryan's backhand. Ryan skids short; he knows it's lost. The rafters echo a few hollow claps. The Canadian blows into his hand again. Ryan nods and prepares to receive once more.

It's possible for someone of the Canadian's stature to be unsubtle, drunk on his wingspan and eager to back away, opening wider angles to exploit. The Canadian exhibits no such faults. When Ryan softens his strokes, he waits patiently at the baseline and blocks or countersmashes. When Ryan drills into one wing, he hunkers in the corner and returns with different speeds and spins. When Ryan stays close to the net, refusing to open or offer an opening, he drops underspin shorter and shorter until Ryan's the uncomfortable one, then shoves it deep into the fabric of his shirt.

Coach's voice rises set break by set break. Ryan goes down two sets; ekes out the third, in which the Canadian misserves and three of Ryan's smashes clip the edge. Then Coach talks with his arm around the back of Ryan's neck, their foreheads touching or nearly touching, Rahul can't tell: they're superimposed, Ryan a thin border around Coach, breaths synchronized. Even with minute-long set breaks, with electrolytes and water fresh in his system, Ryan struggles to catch his breath. Rahul slumps lower as the devastating fourth set ticks along, the unique nightmare cadence of an uneven match. Even with closed eyes Rahul must hear the stilted short rallies, the killer smacks off the Canadian's racket against the rushed soft defense off Ryan's. Serve, return, kill.

For a couple points, down five match points at 5–10, Ryan regains the golden, levitating air in which Rahul's memory wreathed him. The Canadian serves short; he reaches in and swipes it away. Two aces and it's 8–10. Coach stands, claps, shouts. But the serve goes back to the Canadian and everyone in the hall—they all watch—knows what's coming. Half tighten their crossed arms, grip the floor with their toes, and open their eyes wider. The cowardly half, to which Rahul belongs, looks down. The rally is decently long, *click-clack-click-clack*, grunt, stomp, four-legged scuffle, the delayed descent of balls lobbed far behind the table and a gasp at a virtuosic loop; but then the ball kisses the floor, *hiss*, and it's over. The Canadian sounds a deep bellow. He's still pumping his fist when Rahul looks up. Ryan stands deep in his side of the court, hands on hips, breathing slowly and staring at his feet. Maybe playing the counting game, which Rahul suddenly remembers: one-three-five-seven-nine-eleven-thirteen-fifteen-seventeen-nineteen . . . all the way up to fifty-one and back . . .

Ryan raises his racket, as if to hurl it.

"*No!*" Coach shouts.

A few rows below, a cluster of players whispers about the Canadian's recent victory in the Bundesliga. He's already a pro. That information should reverse the effect losing has on Ryan, correct the perspective like an eye doctor's glass wedge, but Rahul can't help placing Ryan's defeated posture among the supplement store men, their statures distended and reduced. Ryan's footsteps shake the bleachers, but not as much as Canadian Mohawk's. Not as rightfully. With less beauty. At the corner of his mouth, a pimple noticed for the first time. Rahul saw warnings online that too much whey could worsen them. It's something his parents would believe in an instant.

There's still the playoff for third. Ryan could still make it.

Rahul extends a hand. "Don't worry, bro, you still got this."

"What do you know." Ryan's towel flies across the aisle. "Fuck!"

"No," Coach said, "what do *you* know, Ryan? Your attitude is shit. Your footwork was like a maimed pig's. Don't talk to yourself or your friend like that."

"It's okay," Rahul says, "I don't—"

"I'm sorry," Ryan says. He makes eye contact, even looks contrite. It's worse, like it'd be worse if Rahul's parents apologized every time they left him in the lurch. The pipe that exploded, the bugs that swarmed their newly planted eucalyptus, scattering with a collective hiss as Rahul ran screaming out of the sliding doors, two kitchen spatulas flapping above his head. Worse and worse; it probably takes the wind out of Ryan's sails for the playoff, too, which he loses. It's a close fight on the scoreboard but lifeless on the court: the opponent is inferior to Canadian Mohawk and Ryan— Coach says so, more and more stridently as the match drags on—but Ryan moves with the grace of a foosball figurine. Every time the ball zings past, Rahul sees the video-game arrow exploding the geisha's eye. The pixelated knife through a cherry's heart. Splat, splat.

Afterward, Ryan sits limply, reeking of BO. Coach zips up his racket, unlaces and pries off his shoes. "There will be a lot to learn from that tape," he says, quartering Ryan's towel and tucking it beneath the flap of his duffel. "Get the tripod. Can you manage that, or are you still feeling too lazy?"

Rahul steps between them. "Can I get a ride home, Coach?" He'll never draw the same vitriol from Coach as Ryan. He used to be jealous of that. He sees it all now, in its latecoming irony and relief. "I . . . my parents have a last-minute business meeting, so they can't get me."

"Sure," Coach says. This second, lesser incompetence relaxes him. His voice softens and he nods as Ryan zips the camera bag. Then they retreat to the bathroom for a long time.

Stretching his legs onto the lower bleacher—inexcusable in front of Coach, but his calves are sore—and staring down the giant overhead lights, Rahul recalls how loss operates beyond time, how it forms a solid sphere of noxious gas around your head, half-life unknowable. He, for example, might always be a loser.

When his hamstrings go numb, he begins to worry. What are they doing?

From the image of the firefighter duffels, it comes: Coach makes Ryan do punitive push-ups on the piss-sticky floor, maybe sitting on Ryan's back. He forces Ryan's face before the mirror, by a handful of hair, and lectures him with a stabbing forefinger. He slaps him, one cheek then the other. He kicks him. He just stands outside his stall as Ryan tries to squeeze something foul out of himself (the nausea of the last match, the red electrolytes), voice issuing through the crack like the finger of damp wind Rahul's father claimed ruined his back when he was at school in Delhi, sharing a draughty room with five other students.

"Let's go, Rahul." They're standing over him. Coach has returned fully to his peacetime demeanor. He sounds sated, rather than annoyed, as he says, "Your parents should know better."

Rahul stumbles after them down the bleachers. The night is scratchy with crosswinds and yard lights of clashing whites and yellows. In the window of a house at the end of the long driveway, Rahul sees female figures dressing, talking. Coach speeds toward them, profile unblinking, perhaps seeing only the nightmare of the afternoon. Ryan slouches in the back with Rahul, middle seat between them, darting phone light fragmenting his slack face. Fruit Ninja? Rahul wonders, then registers motionless forefingers, two slugs in the antifreeze light. He looks out the window and tries to recreate the morning's journey—water tower, vineyard, reservoir, big sign marking his school, long boulevard with a palm-planted median and low glassed-in homes reflecting pink sunset—but he's lost until Coach says, "Ryan, we'll drop you first."

"All right," Ryan says. Then, "Wait—where are we?"

"Your house." Coach turns right and accelerates uphill, weaving with one hand on the bottom of the steering wheel. "Then I'll take Rahul to his."

"I thought—"

Rahul's flung sideways as they roll into a circular driveway, before a two-story house of white stone. The windows are dark. Violet light stains the spaces beneath the orange clay eaves. The car stops and the doors click.

Looking straight ahead, Ryan says, "Come in, Rahul. My mom wants to see you."

"Isn't she with your father in Hong Kong?" Coach says.

"She's—"

"I'm sure Rahul's parents are worried."

"Call them," Ryan says. "Tell them he's staying."

He shoves his door open and hops out; juts his chin to indicate Rahul's door. So now he wants something again. Rahul curls a finger around the handle. The night chills his shoulders through the window. It wasn't his fault Ryan didn't make it to the Olympics. He hadn't done anything to merit disrespect, this time.

"They'll know," he says. "I can't lie to my parents."

"It's not a question," Coach says. "You two can sleep over some other night."

"We need to finish the game," Ryan says. But Rahul has withdrawn his hand from the door.

"I didn't like the game," he says.

It's not the slam of his door that feels final, but the anonymity of the roads Coach takes, Rahul promoted to shotgun with air-conditioning blowing up his nose. Ryan's mom drove him home once. It was rare to see Ryan's parents, but he'd been waiting for the bus so long he texted the groupchat *Lol guys i'm never getting out of here!*, and fifteen minutes later a silver convertible appeared over the hill. She drove with her hair loose, Medusa tentacles slapping her freckled face, and by Ryan's laughter in the passenger's seat Rahul knew it was for his amusement. Ryan lived between the club and Rahul's house and he pointed out the turn as they passed, inaudible in the wind but arm sticking up confident and proud. That was the high point of Rahul's month.

Then he forgot about it. Another joke about the bus, another shitty scrimmage. But the roads they're taking now are not the ones Ryan's mother took. They're empty, dark, and narrow, closed in by dense vegetation. Rahul can barely see the yellow lines.

They pass a white cube of a roadside store, window dark and door light shivering gray. "Wait," Rahul says. "I need to pee."

"We're almost there," Coach says.

An oncoming car blinds Rahul. When his vision clears, there's a black triangle cleaving the tree-dark to his right. A valley, a cliff, light-studded only far, far below. The whoosh of the car past guardrails is like a machete through air.

"Let me out," Rahul says. "Let me out. Let me out."

Another car passes, headlights sweeping the windshield, tree trunks, and Coach's forearms ramrod at the wheel; the dark in their wake shrouds his vision like death. Wordless, Rahul lashes at the forearms. The double yellow line seems to bulge. He crashes into the door.

"Stop." Coach's struck hand thuds back onto the wheel. The car recenters itself. Rahul's back rejoins its seat.

"I'm sure there's a reason for your outburst," Coach says. "I'm sure it's difficult, with your parents. But you need to act your age and collect yourself."

Rahul cups his elbows, rough and cold, and holds himself still. If he starts rocking, or any such melodramatic motion, Coach may leave him on the side of the road.

"I shouldn't have come," he says. "I'm sorry, I'm sorry I came and ruined everything."

Coach waits out his trembling. He waits out his ragged breaths. It's remarkable how normal Rahul suddenly feels, feet from a darkness that might plunge to the bottom of the ocean itself. Coach was always saying you could get used to anything with enough time. Less oxygen, steeper hills, faster balls. Maybe he should have promised them that once in a while, it would take what seems like no time at all. That without your noticing it diminishes from a burn across your chest to a dull stretching sensation beneath the armpits. From admiration to indifference, to a similar dull ache as he recognizes the gas station at the next intersection—how close he was to home, how he suddenly wishes to be elsewhere again.

2014

ANABEL

The difficulties at Nationals began as soon as they reached Austin. There was one restaurant open for dinner within walking distance of the hotel, a greasy-tiled, antler-mounted diner across the empty eight-lane road, and the next morning Anabel woke to a burbling stomach. Her teammates Kevin Chen and Kevin Wang lay peacefully nose-to-toe on the other queen bed, their team captain, William, in a cot against the door. Fucking Texas. She hated competing here. The girls were cliquish and the water poisoned her.

On the toilet, she checked her phone. Last night's message to Ryan—*You here?*—was unreplied to. She could have written something wittier, but his text from three weeks ago, breaking three years of silence, said only: *Nationals?* It had been a shock; though Anabel saw him on UC Davis's roster—she could not help but look; she had also learned that he just signed a Bundesliga contract—she assumed he had let the team register him to boost their rating. The collegiate tournaments themselves, a closed system with no bearing on rankings domestic or international, seemed beneath him.

Now she drafted and deleted in the text box as her thighs pimpled and blued. What could convey that she forgave him for how things ended, but as a matter of time and principle, not so he could act as if nothing had happened? Even if, really, she would prefer to act that way. Though—what would that look like?

Her bowels wouldn't empty. She traced the edges of the Buddha sticker on her phone case and said one of Gao's irreverent prayers to Guanyin. *Listen, old lady, please magic this shit out of me today.*

"Doing all right?" William asked through the door. "Nervous?"

"What would I be nervous about, Will?"

She flushed and pulled up her shorts. The faucet emitted a mineral reek. To the mirror, she flexed her face in a passive-aggressive smile, trying to look as scary as Coach said people found her. She would see old friends and rivals soon. Maybe even Kristian. She needed the reps.

"Nothing, you're invincible, sorry for doubting you. Can I please pee?"

As they passed in the doorway, he clapped her bicep and said, "You'll crush it."

That was how Gao talked to her, too: *You'll kill them. No one can stop you. You lost this match, who gives a shit, kick their ass next time.* A senior studying computer science, William reminded Anabel of sweet boys at Coach's club, steelier qualities hidden behind rounded shoulders and hair shorn a single unfussy length. Last semester, he knocked on her door every day asking her to join the team. Between classes and her own training, she barely had time, but she could not turn him down. She would help him break the school record (a modest tenth) and go back to her normal life. That, as she reassured Coach, was her only goal. *Not* to see Ryan.

Kevin Chen sat up, hair mashed in one direction along the back of his head, and mimed swinging a hammer onto Kevin Wang's head. Anabel chopped a hand across her throat. Kevin suppressed a giggle and settled for poking Kevin's butt. "Rise and shine! Winning time!" The Kevins were another reason she hadn't refused William: after just one practice in the dinky rec center, they started commenting chains of fire emojis on all of her Instagram photos and running up behind her in the library, knocking her against the edge of her carrel desk with delighted thumps to the back. She couldn't let them down.

The gray slab of tournament hall was a short walk across the hotel lawn. The Kevins stopped to photograph parakeets on the roof, but Anabel plowed ahead, so fast she nearly slipped on the damp grass. The hall itself could have been anywhere she had competed, Tokyo or Mexico City or Shanghai: twenty large courts, an arena for Courts One and Two and practice tables in the corner; a mezzanine on which players and spectators had stationed themselves, eating egg sandwiches out of clamshells balanced on their knees; the arid perfume of industrial air conditioning, sweat, and glue. Swiveling on a heel, William took a panorama photo.

"Anyone have Tums?" Anabel asked. Coach used to pad her duffel with gallon bags of medication—painkillers, antacids, vitamin C, Tiger Balm. Now all it held was her equipment and a travel pack of tissues. She had packed distracted by thoughts of Ryan: the last time they saw each other was the 2011 US Open, when Anabel tried to quit for the first time. There had seemed no opportune moment to tell him; she did not want to taint the minutes they stole in the hotel stairwell and corners of the tournament hall. On the last day, they snuck up to his room while Kristian was in a coaches' meeting, kissed standing in the middle of the floor, laughed, fell dead serious, and fell onto the bed. Anabel rolled up Ryan's shirt and pressed her lips, tight with nerves, into the divots between his pecs and abs. She trailed her clammy fingers down to his waist. When they reached his waistband, he raised his hips. His pulse fluttered in the translucent skin of his groin. He asked if she would take off her clothes, too. He was the one who fumbled a condom out of the pillowcase. Anabel was the one who asked, "Are you sure?" He nodded, eyes damp, chin lovably doubled. As she pressed him into her, she rested her face on his neck and felt the beauty marks there soft against her cheek.

Then, they had to fumble on clothes and walk around the Strip as if they'd been there the whole time, secretless beneath the flashing lights. When, still dazed, Anabel finally told him it was her last tournament, Ryan said, "Wait, are your parents making you quit?"

They were on the MGM sky bridge, parting a stream of women in sequined pants. "No," she replied, addressing the Strip traffic, "it's just insane to keep going. And, what, drop out of school? Go pro in Germany?"

"Guess I'm insane then," Ryan said.

"Not you. The rest of us."

"You're not 'the rest of you.'"

They'd both known it was over then, even if they kept messaging. His last message, from a month later: *sorry but I can't anymore.* This after several outbursts about how he was sick of Coach. He never heeded Anabel's suggestions that he was drilled too hard, spoken to too harshly; that Kristian pushed him to satisfy his own vanity. *Gao's not much better*, he often said, which devolved into meaningless comparisons. He never stood up for her against Kristian, either—not when he said things like *I'm glad Ryan has such a great fan*; not when he appeared at her matches, impassive expression willing her downfall but standing far enough away for plausible deniability and disappearing before the match ended. If she'd had Ryan's potential, maybe she would have chosen her coach, too.

She did not reply, moved on with her life. In total they had seen each other less than a dozen times, which, sex notwithstanding, meant nothing against all the time they spent training in their separate corners of the country, traveling, doing anything and everything else. He had nothing to do with her increasing uneasiness about the hours in Gao's club and subsequent hours studying, the sleeplessness, the leaving tournaments battered and depressed even when she won. The tension between her and her parents. "It's like you'd rather *she* raise you," her mother once said of Gao, and while Anabel never regretted yielding her life to the sport, she could not convince herself it was enough. No one else seemed able to, either. Ryan had been miserable. Gao, nerves and digestion fried from decades of stress, often called from her empty apartment, because the club was all she had, and for years Anabel had *been* the club, its public face and champion. It could not work forever. And yet. In fateful 2011, she told Gao she was quitting, then played again two weeks later. She tried to quit again the next year. Instead, she found herself taking over assistant coaching responsibilities. At college, she avoided the club team through her first year, but caved this fall when William showed up, begging her help to qualify for Nationals (his greatest dream, a legacy he could leave as long-suffering leader). The unfortunate, intractable fact was that she loved table tennis—found herself restless on free nights, half-doing homework to a pro match on her laptop.

Now this shared love was about to reunite them.

As the hall filled, balls clicking and shoes squeaking, kids touching their toes and skipping across courts, despite the gurgle in her torso, Anabel sank into her tournament stupor. To break the school record, they needed to win two of their first three matches, and the steepness of the order—with only four people, no one could sit out or have a bad match—further calmed her. She led the boys in warm-ups and reassured them: we've got this, cock your wrist and take your time. She rubbed the Buddha sticker's water-pulped belly.

Her first opponent was Lola Cheung, to whom she had lost just once, and whose new willowy beauty Anabel took as provocation. She had not played a big tournament in years, and crouching to return Lola's first serve still exhilarated. The ball seemed to hang mid-air, big as an apple, and the concrete floor, normally hard and slippery underfoot, launched her effortlessly. In the first set, she walloped every chop. "*Chooo!*" the Kevins screamed. At the barriers, William handed her one of the dozen Gatorades he'd extracted one by one from the hotel vending machine.

"Eleven–oh her!" said Kevin.

"Amituofo, motherfuckers!" said the other Kevin.

"Kevin," William said, "that's literally sacrilegious."

On the far side of the hall, Ryan sauntered in. Save for one overly friendly boy, who extended a fist to bump, his teammates gave him a wide berth. Ryan returned the gesture with the impersonality that had intimidated Anabel back when they were kids, before she knew him—before he had approached her after a match, before the secret meetings in tournament bathrooms, their first kiss at 2007 Nationals, at first uncertain, Anabel conscious of the trash can coughing up stained tissues and tiles stinking of urine; then deep, and tinged with almost fearful surprise at the intensity of what had seemed a straightforward, titillating endeavor, inevitable after feeling an invisible wire connect them across all those halls.

Before they had been caught by Kristian, who now prowled in a few steps behind Ryan, club logo splashed across his jacket. No one else's coach would have followed him here, to a tournament that meant nothing.

Anabel swallowed a last mouthful of juice, its lemon-lime tingle answered by a twinge in her bowels. The Davis team stopped and strewed their gear around Court Five. Ryan hovered in the aisle, monogrammed duffel resting against his side. He had grown out his hair and kept running his hands through the permed top, which Kristian flicked away from his forehead.

Lightheaded, loose-jointed, Anabel finished off Lola 11–3, 11–3.

The Kevins' shouting did not attract Ryan's attention; he was returning Kristian's slices, stroke light and natural. Nor did Anabel's cheering and clapping as William won an easy match and Kevin Wang, coached back from zero sets to two, upset his better opponent; nor did Kevin Chen's extravagant bound atop his creaking chair, where he pounded his chest like a gorilla.

"One down," William said, "one to go."

"Hey!" Kevin Chen hopped down. "It's Ryan Lo."

"Oh cool," said Anabel. The twinge was traveling down her left leg. Her ankle trembled. She needed to stretch. Ryan had always been vigilant about stretching.

"I wanna watch," Kevin Wang said, and began skipping in Ryan's direction.

"Wait. Let's stay and practice a little."

She felt stupid for how different his presence felt here than in her mind, where she was suave and sure. A difference of incomprehensible width, across which not even her dullest imagined dialogue—*Hi, stranger*—could be projected. Just looking at him, now that she was no longer playing, felt like ogling sleazy magazines lining the grocery checkout, greased celebrity pecs and boobs holding her gaze as she helplessly, surreptitiously grabbed for a candy bar. Even seemingly innocuous memories of the stretches she had helped him with—lying above him with her hands braced on the matted floor, savoring the bite of polyester fiber at her palms and the warm resistance of his calf hooked over her shoulder, an obliterating, selfish joy coursing through her as he groaned in pain—returned to her accusatory, incriminating.

"I wanna rest," Kevin Chen whined.

"I think it'd be inspiring," William said. "We do need a break."

She made herself look again. Ryan was removing his hoodie. His bunched T-shirt flashed ribs and abs. How many times she had clapped for him after an extraordinary point that tossed up the hem of his shirt, cheered as if for that ripple of skin as he ran down a loop fired wide, left leg flung across right as he swung his whole body toward the opponent, or, pivoting to face the table, ten feet back, carved a backhand that arrogantly scuffed the opposite corner, unreachable; the muscles of his legs, shuddering as he ran, tensed in sharp relief as they rooted his celebration, long lines of quad mirroring the tendons of his wrist, fist raised toward the bleachers—for a few precious years, toward her.

She excused herself to the bathroom and splashed water onto her neck. She could not bring herself to use the toilet or dry the splatters on her collar. It felt like every effort she made, every desultory preparation, would be written across her face.

The boys were waiting outside, bags hoisted. She led them toward Ryan's court, where he now warmed up. They had as much right as anyone to spectate, she reminded herself, taking several extra turns to approach from behind Ryan. The bleachers filled. When she was close enough to count the moles on the back of Ryan's neck, winking among creases of tender skin, she felt an ominous pressure work downward from her tailbone.

"Here," she said, and pulled the boys between two stands. Ryan smashed the first serve down the line and nodded, brushed sweat from his brow. "Whoa," said Kevin Chen, mouth agape.

Ryan, it devastated her to confirm, played better than ever. His shots spun lower. His undersplin serves, cut sideways at meaner angles, dug themselves more ferociously into the net. Even the grotesque faces he made after lost points, tongue stuck out or teeth bared grimacing, expressed a deeper conviction in his game, the tectonics of muscles more deeply and nobly wired. The Kevins moaned "*Whoaaaa*" at each blistering loop. More and more spectators gathered, obstructing their view of his straight-set win. When he scored, everyone clapped, clapping that seemed to go on and on, renewing itself every few seconds from a different quarter. At 10–9 in the third set, the ball zinged nastily off the edge; Ryan dove and lofted it. The crowd gasped. The opponent wound up and smashed. Ryan, who had somehow scrambled ten feet back, lobbed again. The opponent smashed. Ryan lobbed, closer now. The opponent looped, a change in pace, smart, except Ryan had rushed the ball, hitting before it peaked. Point, match. Ryan ran around the court, sweat-Rorschached shirt fluttering, and everyone screamed. They were all here to watch table tennis like Ryan's. All three UC teams stomped their feet. A cluster of girls above them deliberated whether to go congratulate Ryan. Most people who thought they wanted to approach him never would—for a long time, Anabel had been one of them. Was now. But maybe, Anabel thought, as the boys rehashed the last few points, heads wagging, and the stands emptied into the aisles, they would step up and keep him occupied, preventing her from saying hi and thus avoiding the whole ordeal.

Then Ryan passed feet away in the walkway, slaloming passersby, swaggering pigeon-toed with righteous exhaustion. Without thinking, she stepped out from between the bleachers. "Ryan, hey." He did a double take. "Just . . . hey. Just saying hi."

"Oh. Hey." He spoke in his voice for tournament officials, interviewers, and Kristian, who was just a few feet ahead and now turned his frightening clear green gaze on Anabel.

"This is, um, my team." The boys came bashfully forward, shuffling their feet.

"What's up, guys." Ryan circled a fist to bump. Kevin Wang breathed *Wow* as he made contact.

"You guys know each other?" Kevin Chen gasped.

Anabel thought Ryan nodded; she couldn't bring herself to look higher than their hands. She couldn't seem to curl her fingers properly, and after an awkward, hovering, second, Ryan's hand dropped.

"Good to see you *back*, Anabel," said Kristian.

"I didn't leave. I just stopped competing outside Jersey"—already, she had said too much; patronizing reticence was his game—"because I was focusing on school."

"And how are your matches?"

"I've only played Lola. I mean, I've beat her a hundred times."

She could have punched herself; right away, Kristian raised an eyebrow and sneered, "Really? That's quite a few times. Your confidence is refreshing."

Ryan said nothing, though the hem of his hoodie sleeve bunched up, as if he'd clenched his fist. Maybe in embarrassment at her.

"Our next match is at twelve," William said. "You could come watch. Give us pointers?"

"But only if you want," said Kevin Chen.

"I don't think so," Anabel said, "he's really—"

"Wouldn't it be nice to help your friends?" Kristian said. "You're not playing at twelve, Ryan."

Finally, Ryan met Anabel's eyes. He wore a smile colder than anything she had managed in the mirror. Her stomach gurgled, she flexed a muscle deep inside her, and liquid filled the pocket of her underwear.

"We'd love that!" cried Kevin Wang. They were closing in on Ryan, all but reaching out to stroke him. "It's table eight," William said.

Anabel speed walked back to the bathroom. Her period wasn't due for a week; of course it came now. There was no tampon dispenser. The seams of her duffel yielded one crumpled pantiliner, dusted with shards of black lining. She rolled toilet paper around the crotch of her lime-green underwear, browned by previous leaks. The stain was an orange nickel with a burgundy pupil. It could be managed, she thought, her scalp tight with stress, the tip of her nose buzzing.

??? William texted. *Where'd you go?*

Give me a minute!!! Anabel wrote; deleted the exclamation points and hit send as she sat on the toilet, in case her body released more blood. Nothing came.

She took off her tracksuit and stalked up to Court Eight, paddle in hand. The boys sat flanked by Ryan on one side and Kristian on the other; again, she passed from behind and hopped straight onto the court. She was up first, against a random girl whose face she already knew she'd forget. Everything was blurred by her unfulfillable impulse to look toward the deadly row of faces. At every stroke a half second interposed between her paddle and the ball, her intentions and its movement; she stared at the empty space through which the ball passed, seeing the half second of Ryan's cold smile; and, as if the brittleness between them had shattered and shrapneled, her stomach clenched and her wrist pinged painfully. Airless, soundproof disbelief dampened her teammates' shouts and groans. Ryan and Kristian watched silently. What did he see of the past—her most elegant points or her clumsiest, or anything at all? They had played mixed doubles once, at a juniors tournament in Shanghai, and for years she would lie in bed, hands squashed beneath her butt so she wouldn't touch herself, and recall the collision of their shoulders as he fell on her from an impossible leap, the intimacy as they grimaced and rubbed at their joints, precious for their capacity to feel then recover from a shared pain. And now the finger that had sometimes slid between her legs seemed to give off an incriminating smell, a grubby purple aura. Maybe while, all these years, he thought nothing of it at all.

She smacked a tricky sidespin serve off the table, ignored William's fluttering hand signal to meet him at the barriers. For what? She stood in the far corner and drank metallic, lukewarm Texas water, finding respite in the solid weight of her head on her frigid shoulders.

At one set to two, warmth flooded her crotch again. She looked down, from the receiving crouch that suddenly seemed the least dignified of poses, crasser than even squatting to shit in a latrine, to see a red droplet clinging to the widest curve of her inner thigh, then another droplet chase it down into the dimple of her knee.

"Fuck," she said. The opponent's serve flew past her ear, and Kevin Chen's laugh-cough echoed its frantic clicking against the cement.

•

William found her sobbing in the hotel shower, sitting on the tiles.

"Anabel!" The bathroom door shuddered.

"I'M SHOWERING!"

"ARE YOU OKAY?"

His shadow darkened the crack beneath the door. She had planned to sit until hot water ran out, but now she felt guilty keeping him waiting. She conditioned her hair, lathered a second tiny bottle of body wash around her crotch, and, wrapped in two towels, slowly pushed the door against William's back.

"Hey," he said, scrambling up, "don't get mad at *me*."

At the sight of his preternaturally kind face, her jaw shuddered open. She tried pressing her chin, knuckling her cheeks, but the sounds kept coming. William guided her to her bed, stacked two pillows behind her, and pulled up the comforter. "It's really not a big deal," he said.

His obtuseness choked off her hiccupping tears. "Will, imagine—I don't know, peeing yourself—yeah, okay, imagine peeing yourself in front of a girl you like."

"Worse things have happened."

"A girl you've liked *for years*."

"You've liked this dude for *years*?" He shook his head and tsk-tsked.

Against her will, not by much, she felt better.

The tears rushed back.

"Hey, hey," William said. "He said he wants to talk to you."

"Yeah right."

He shrugged, warm against her neck. "Really." Beneath the blankets, her body was beginning to chill. She imagined shucking the towel and lying naked atop him, soaking up his heat, dripping blood down *his* thigh and knee. "But if you don't want to go back out or play anymore—"

"Why wouldn't I?"

"'Cause you can't get over it."

"Don't laugh at me."

"I'm not laughing!"

"What about the record?"

"It's not that important to me. I'm not like you."

For him, there were small pure solaces, incompatible with how brutal, all-consuming table tennis had taught her to be. "When's our next match?" she asked.

"Two thirty."

The clock read one. "I'm just going to sit for a second."

"Okay."

"Okay."

He handed her a wad of tissues and a sweatsuit from his suitcase. She blew her nose and held the clothes in her lap. "I'm gonna bleed on these," she said.

"That's okay. I brought a stain stick."

She could try and kiss him. That could be nice. A taste of a different kind of life. When her phone buzzed on the bathroom counter, he retrieved it and dropped it in her lap.

hey where r u? need to talk

"See?" William said.

Anabel sighed. Another buzz: *in the lobby*. She locked the phone and counted the hairs furred along her forearms. She cracked each of her toes beneath the sheets. She texted Gao: *Can we call?*

"You should go," William said.

Five minutes passed, then ten. Wordlessly, William left the room and returned with a handful of tampons. He lay back and scrolled, phone inches from his nose. Twenty minutes in, Anabel submerged herself beneath the blankets and changed into his sweatshirt and sweatpants. At twenty-five minutes, William sat up and said, "Go, Bel."

Had she been hoping for something to happen? For a moment, towel shucked and sweatpants halfway up her thighs, she had pushed her finger down to rest in the hair between her legs, considering—what? What could be?

"You're not going to leave it, are you?"

"Nope."

She shook her hair out of its towel, stuck her feet into slippers, and shuffled into the bathroom to insert a tampon. In the elevator, damp hanks splayed down her neck, she looked like a vengeful spirit trapped in the brassy wall.

Ryan sat with Kristian at a table in the lobby, clenched traps bunching the back of his shirt. Kristian was emphasizing some point, slamming the side of his hand against the tabletop, and didn't stop when he spotted Anabel.

I'm here, she texted. Ryan tapped at his phone. "She's here," he said. "You have to go."

"Okay." Kristian pushed back his chair and stood. He set his hand atop Ryan's head. "It won't be easier. But you can do it." Ryan's head bowed. *Sorry*, she thought he said. "Goodbye, my friend."

He walked away down a first-floor hallway. Anabel shuffled forward, arms crossed, and lowered herself onto a corner of his vacated chair. She did not want to feel the heat of his body.

The rims of Ryan's eyes shone pink. Pink striped his neck where he had rubbed it. He looked terrible. Still, she wanted to run a thumb along his full lower lip.

He cleared his throat. "Those your buddy's clothes?" he said.

"Buddy?"

"William. Wouldn't peg you for an *Evangelion* fan."

Anabel squinted down at the peeling insignia. "Oh. Yeah."

"Good guy."

She clamped her lips against another swell of feeling.

"Hey," he said, "you okay?"

"Oh, 'am I okay?'" Her knuckles ached beneath the vociferous air quotes.

"What?"

"You were being so weird!"

His fingers clawed in frustration, as they had done the first time he vented to her about Kristian's constant belittling supervision, at the concession stand in Houston's convention center, the day after his fourteenth birthday; she had bought him a Snickers to celebrate and he tucked it deep inside his bag to hide from *Coach*. "You didn't text me back."

"Oh, my god. Then what"—she stabbed the passcode into her phone; turned their thread toward him and pecked at her last text with a fingernail—"is this?" He sat back, presenting the full expanse of his chest and shoulders, which she had watched broaden year by year beneath their rotation of T-shirts and hoodies. She wanted to set her fist against the front of his jacket and push until her arm tired.

"Okay, yeah," he said. "Three weeks later."

"You—oh my god, Ryan, *you* ended it." Anabel slammed the phone facedown. She had leaned nearly all the way across the table. The backs of her fists lay millimeters from Ryan's. She thought she felt their fingers hairs brush.

"Maybe," he said, "I'm being stupid."

"Yeah, maybe!"

"I was, I just—forget it. I mean, I just needed to tell you—"

"If it's gonna make me feel worse, save it."

He shook his head.

"Your Bundesliga contract got canceled," she said.

"No."

"Congrats on that, by the way. You got someone pregnant?"

"When would I have time to do that?"

"You're right, silly mistake."

He was beginning to smile. Then whatever he had to say bent his mouth back down. "It was our last day," he finally said. "Me and Coach. It was, weird, yeah. I fired him this morning."

"Yeah right."

He rubbed his eyes. "We can't keep on . . . he just . . . he was gonna come to Germany, and he can't. He can't do that."

"Quit his club and move to Germany?"

"That's what he said."

"That's nuts."

He grabbed the plastic saltshaker and began emptying it into his palm. "It was still hard."

"I don't really want to hear it," she said, even as hope began to pulse somewhere behind her exhausted eyes, a small stony heart.

Ryan opened his mouth. His tongue worked circles behind his bottom teeth, bubbles of saliva churning and popping.

She brushed the salt off his hardened hand and held it, callus to knuckle. If she were Gao, she would have tossed the granules over her shoulder for luck. "You can always go back," she said.

"I can't. You were right. I can't." His face hollowed as he bit the insides of his cheeks.

If Anabel called Gao, she would pick up. If she told her about the period fiasco, Gao would reassure her it was all right, she had once hocked a loogie onto a gold medalist, and don't mention the number of times she had thrown up in public. Who would do that for Ryan now? Could she?

"You don't need him," she said. Was that true? All these years, some part of her had wished Kristian gone, but she did not know what came next or what was still possible. She would have to fill his gaps. She had first seen Ryan in the bleachers relacing Denny Ouyang's shoes, seated one row above his hysterically giggling friend, tongue between his teeth and fingers nimbly moving as he tickled Denny's ribs with an extended foot. She knew nothing about him then, but when she recognized him at the next tournament, waiting at a corner of her court, it was for that moment.

Unlike Kristian, she would do it all for his sake.

She stood and walked around to hug him, cradling his head against her stomach. The weight of it slowly sank into the hollow of her ribs. His hand on the table flushed pink, veins rising. One thirty, said his watch. One hour left—to stay or to go?

When he finally reciprocated her gesture, wrapping an arm around her, his fingers caught on the baggy hem of the sweatshirt and skimmed her bare waist. She hoped he would let them rest there, and he did.

2015–2016

HERR DOKTOR ECKERT

In the forty-eighth year of my life, twenty years after I retired from——Bundesliga team, I had the opportunity to counsel an unusual configuration of players: a father, Jun Qiu, coaching his sons, Han and Kay, alongside a boy who had been Kay's competitor and who eventually revealed a connection to my own past.

A bit more about my involvement: I had played for——from 1988 to 1995, prior to which I trained in its youth program. Jun Qiu was my teammate until he retired in 1993. During the '94–'95 season, I developed inflammation of the patellar meniscus—right leg, same as the Player's chronic injury—which proved irremediable. I retired and enrolled in a psychotherapy course. For a few years I worked at the university clinic and then, perhaps seeking the intensity whose absence sends so many former athletes reeling, a center for troubled teenagers. I was saved by my former coach and manager, Herr Dieter, who, with his typical magnanimous foresight, hired a team psychologist long before it became common practice. I believe I was the first in our sport in the Bundesliga, and as I signed my contract below the aegis of our letterhead, the red lion that had presided, from its tournament hall banner, over so much joy and agony, I could not but wonder if my psychological endeavors had been undertaken with a secret eye toward reinstating myself. For twelve years, I talked to our club's professionals and amateurs, prescribed them medication, and conducted surveys assessing their motivation, collecting data which every few years my manager felt compelled to cart before sponsors, but which, for the most part, accumulated toward what I dreamed might become a magnum opus.

By the time of this case, the team had been under duress for several seasons. Dieter died, bringing down an onslaught of would-be replacements of only slightly varied hubris and ineptitude. Jun Qiu, who declined the managerial position to continue coaching his sons, stood by while unfortunate bosses made error after error, losing sponsors and spurning valuable players. Regardless of blame, which is not mine to assign, the '15–'16 season found the team desperate enough—facing relegation and the imminent retirement of its oldest player, Mika; having lost a younger player to poaching; saddled with yet another impotent manager—to hire an American relatively unproven and recently parted from his lifelong coach, a circumstance which one cannot now help but interpret as a sign of troubles endured and to come.

At the time, it was a prudent decision: the Player had consistently defeated Kay Qiu at international tournaments and, supported by wealthy parents, agreed to not only play for slightly less but also volunteer-coach for the youth program. In June he arrived in our town, to a room in the Sporthotel, which every summer housed dozens of trainees and stood quiet for the rest of the year, whitewashed face like barred gates to the end of the world. At our first meeting, he reassured me he had settled into his spartan lodgings with "a hand" from Han Qiu, the elder son, who guided him around town to procure trappings of a "normal adult life." Though it is a common delusion among the young, I found intriguing this identification with "adult," since at twenty-one the Player hardly qualified; and Han, twenty-eight, occupying an identical pauper's room out of brotherly self-sacrifice when he could have rented a flat or at least lived at home with their mother, hardly qualified, either.

The only complicating matter—which, I told myself, need not be that—was the Player's connection to a former teammate of mine, a certain Kristian. When Coach Jun first mentioned the boy's affiliation, I realized I had assumed Kristian dead, in the metaphysical sense. His career had died and I had helped ship the corpse away, and now he sent an arrow flying through my eye.

Perhaps my double-consciousness regarding the situation rendered me overly sensitive when we began our sessions. It did not help that the Player, leaning expansively back in the chair across from my desk, right ankle over left knee, began by saying: So what am I supposed to be doing here, anyway? Later, I learned that that leg suffered from chronic tightness, to which I felt sympathetic, but in the moment, I experienced irritation that he was already asserting dominance. This might have piqued the asperity with which I replied that just as the trainer was there to maintain his physical health, I was there to maintain psychological health (surely they knew this in therapy-crazed America?) as related to his athletics (I neither overemphasized this constraint, nor, as managers tried to urge, tacked on *or anything else*); to diagnose and address anxieties and inhibitions regarding his performance and relationships with teammates; to develop salubrious habits; to manage pressure inevitably mounted by the external world; and, in order to do so, meet with him every week, though I remained available at all times. And then I said that since there was no reason we could not start right away, and since it might—*would*, doubtless—influence or at least cast a shadow on his relationship with his new coach, I was curious why (and I must have been hoping to get this out of the way) he had left or fired his old coach.

Because I saw him hit a kid, the Player said, entwined limbs moving not one bit.

Coaches, I found myself thinking, hit people all the time, for all reasons. Everywhere parents hit kids, teachers hit kids, experts hit trainees, and it would not have made sense for it to differ within our intensified realm of sport. Surely our very own Coach Qiu had drawn tears on more occasions than his sons could memorialize. More surprising was that the Player's coach—whether it was Kristian or the Americans' proverbial Joe Schmoe made no difference—would do something so retrograde in front of a pupil whose temperament he knew, surely, to take it unfavorably. The important question now, for us, was what to do with the Player's internalization of the event.

Did he ever hit you? I asked.

No, and I'd never seen him do it before. It was just the straw that broke whatever. You know.

That is quite a few qualifiers, I said. To this he only leaned farther contemptuously back, so I went on: Have you told anyone else?

No.

Why now?

Because you asked.

What does it mean to be telling me?

That . . . I'm really done with him.

Are you concerned he'll hit anyone else?

Will you tell me to report it?

I believe, I said, as I was trained to under duress, I could be professionally obligated to, in some capacity.

You *could* be obligated to in *some* capacity.

If your concern is whether it could be prevented, in the future.

It won't happen again, he said, it was to prove a point. He knew I was planning to quit—to stop being his student, I mean. It sounds crazy, but—

But it means something that you said it, I said. Thank you.

So do I need to tell anyone else? he asked.

No.

Okay. He stood in an impressive upward surge. I need to go into town with Han now, he said. See you next week.

Wait, I said, and handed him a freshly printed Sport Motivation Scale Survey, which I collected from each player before and after the season. In a minute, writing against the wall, he circled his responses. I had not recovered sufficiently to challenge his wanton speed, though such a challenge could perhaps be denied on the grounds that speed produces truth.

Skimming the Player's responses assuaged my nerves. It all made sense, I thought: at a life stage when he prized autonomy, any action could be grounds for breaking the last infantilizing tie, even if, surely, he had long since intuited that his coach was a man capable of such a thing. (I could not have testified as confidently about the Kristian I used to know; time and ambition warp us all.) I tromped down the hall to deliver my impression that the Player was your typical elite athlete. More motivated by achievement and self-realization than fear of failure, egotistical and domineering to a favorable degree. Warmly inclined toward teamwork, which bode well, with characteristics that classed athletes as action-oriented (focused on what to do) rather than state-oriented like Han (focused on how they felt). Jun took the assessment well, that is, unseriously—he made no secret of his skepticism toward me—and I was free to return to my office and conduct my own work, a series of articles I hoped to publish in a journal of sports psychology.

Through a window overlooking the practice hall, embedded in the hallway between our offices, I saw the three black-haired boys, the Player identifiable by his backloaded forehand, so unlike the punchier forehands of the Qius and of Kristian.

The Player attended our sessions punctually. Every time, I asked if he would like to discuss his coach and every time he declined; declined, also, my invitation to explore why not, though I'm sure we could have agreed our first conversation had cauterized the topic. In our four sessions before the season, he mostly talked about Anabel, a girl he was dating, who had encouraged him to strike out on his own. He made no further connection between her and Kristian, no suggestion she knew what he'd told me about my former teammate. Mostly, he worried about the distance of their separation and the infrequency of their communication. Moving abroad was not easy for anyone; he confessed that he had had some trouble sleeping (though Han said his snoring sounded through the walls) and his jaw hurt, ostensibly from grinding his teeth.

Nor did he say anything that suggested knowledge of my affiliation with Kristian, which in my mind was both shallower, emotionally, and deeper, psychologically, than casual observers might assume; than perhaps Kristian and I could have described ourselves. If it was not of concern to the Player, I told myself, then it would not behoove me to introduce the additional facts, the work of explanation and interpretation, the (ultimately false) sense of deception. No need to add to his troubles.

More telling about the Player was practice, which I observed whenever possible. On his first morning, the Player's stiff angled torso said he wanted to respect Coach Qiu, even defer to him, despite a contrary instinct. By the end of the day, it had lapsed into irreverent looseness. As early as the third practice, his eyes drifted around the hall whenever Jun addressed the team, widening and narrowing at the stimuli of player posters, old championship pennants, and rusted beams. He preferred to practice with Kay but talk to Mika, and in physical conditioning drills was so obviously racing Han that eventually, after the Player nearly ran him into the wall at the end of a suicide sprint, the older boy pulled him aside to have some words I failed to lip-read. To the manager, he paid the minimum due attention.

August arrived and everyone dispersed for vacation. The youths happily escaped my instruction on autogenic training and volitional pathways. Jun traveled with his sons to Munich for the European

Games. For a few days, Mika and the Player could be seen practicing, then Mika left, too.

I asked the Player how he felt about the imminent season. Would he miss his coach's guidance, which, no matter the reason for its termination, had been a lifelong constant?

If I have to talk about it, he said, *no*.

I found myself underlining on my notepad, so forcefully it must have suggested mockery: <u>NO</u>. (The players were supposed to keep notebooks. Han's was the most fastidious, while mine, I must admit, languished in illegibility, disorganization, and omission, rendering them, at least in this case, less useful than memory.)

Any other concerns? I asked. We've planned to get fresh air in the mornings, drink lemon tea before bed, ice your leg twice a day instead of once . . .

Could we get more chicken in the cafeteria?

I said I'd pass along the request, and that was that. On my way home, having stayed late writing, I saw, through the hallway window, the Player jumping rope and weaving footwork drills around two lines of tiny traffic cones he must have transported from the States. Only when he fell onto his back, forearms over eyes in the universal performance of masculine exhaustion, did I notice the weights around his ankles. Had he discreetly strapped those on before every conditioning drill? Or had he been running his own training for weeks, somehow unnoticed by us all? Or was this endorsed by Jun, who could have it both ways: the Player might improve, which benefited the team, or suffer, which benefited the Qiu sons by comparison?

Anxiety about my powers of observation coursed through me, but perhaps this session was a quotidian diversion from the summer doldrums. Or, perhaps, he recreated the grueling regimens of his childhood as comfort and defiance—"I can do this on my own!" The great tragedy of rebellions, that desire to be independent of yet recognized by the old.

I waited until he turned off the lights, then made my way to the tram, in whose ordinary load of commuters and university kids I took a solace dry and practical as communion wafers.

A week later, the Qius returned, and the season began.

•

In the first set of a match, astute observation is worth more than victory. A similar attitude is often taken toward a player's first season.

Last year, at fifteen, Kay Qiu ended his season with three losses and five wins. Table tennis blogs crowned him the league's most promising young star. In 2004, Han Qiu went 0–6 until his penultimate match, when he picked off an injured veteran who was retiring. Everyone focused on the pathos of the send-off rather than Han's performance, kicking off years of predictable deviance. Han tramped off to discos and Cologne, ignored Jun's calls, and sweated beer through Monday practices. By '15–'16, he had long since traded in his dreams for protective guardianship over his brother. Whenever Jun spoke to his younger son, Han could be seen listening, tensed through the arches of his feet, prepared to strike his omnipotent Vater like a vengeful viper. All three of their square faces glowed with anxiety and love-hate.

In 1988, Kristian Kaellenius was benched in the second half of the season in favor of his fellow rookie, Andreas Eckert, me. I ended the season 3–3. Kristian converted his resentment into a wordless, magnetic desire for proximity (some might have said worship) I felt compelled to accept as consolation to him, and perhaps as a sweetener of my own perceived superiority. At his urging, we were always running around the grounds, as I had seen Han and the Player doing back in July, up and down the hill behind the Sporthotel and all along the streets crisscrossing town, doing push-ups in public parks and shoplifting from kiosks.

All that to say: it was not strict cause for alarm when the Player, sometimes pitted against impossible opponents so that Han or Kay might win, went down 0 wins to 3 losses in the season's first few months. For only one match was he the deciding loss, and at 1–3 the team was a less-than-ideal but not unacceptable third to last. The Player tended to overplay, a common affliction among rookies, as I reassured Jun. Of greater concern was the panic attack he suffered before the second match; Han testified that he'd hauled the Player from the locker room floor and coached him through breathing exercises. Asked why I was not summoned, Han replied, No offense, Herr Doktor, but we didn't think of it.

The Player's answer: It's not personal, Doc, I just don't know you that well.

But that's the point of us talking.

Then talk to me.

I am.

Noooo, you're not. Tell me something. About you.

When I was a player here, I said, I injured my knee. We had no psychologist back then, and the prognosis was bad. And so—

You came back to do what no one did for you.

Not as *ironically* as you say it.

Not a very personal story, he said.

It was very personal to me! I took a deep breath and lowered my flexed elbows to their armrests. Anyway, I said, I'm your doctor . . .

Tell me a fun fact.

Um. My favorite American soft drink is Sierra Mist.

Kristian had introduced it to me when it became available at our local kiosk, on a stifling September day whose memory, for whatever reason, just then swathed my mind like hearth-warmed wool.

Seriously? the Player said. He named two other, ostensibly superior brands.

I've never tried.

That's crazy, he said. Have you ever had McDonald's?

I don't partake in fast food.

We touched upon several superficial differences between life in the States and Germany and the mood lightened, and though the Player declined a prescription for antianxiety medicine, we reviewed techniques such as box breathing. The next day, he brought me soda cans in several shades of green.

Another issue was the verve with which he threw himself into the youth program—coaching three times a week, sometimes drilling with the students after practice, a displacement of energy Han had also exhibited when he decided his career had reached its limit. I was taking a greater stake in the youth program, too, running talks for the students and parents, and I repeatedly encountered insights—aligning implicit and explicit incentives; eliminating negative affects; orienting toward action rather than feeling—from which I had not benefited in my day. This bestirred the old ghosts of regret, which made me overeager, perhaps, to protect the Player from his own. One night in early December, after youth program, I invited him into my office and took a harder tack than usual: I'm wondering, I said, if coaching siphons too much from your main task. Which is to compete well.

I like coaching, the Player said. It inspires me.

Perhaps it is an attempted rehabilitation of the relationship with your own coach?

Now you sound like him.

To phrase it more gently, I mean—

I get it, the Player said. Touché, Herr Doktor.

Over the next two weeks, he reduced his coaching efforts, and at the subsequent match won his first professional victory. He limped off court, albeit smiling, then had to be helped from the showers. The trainer went to work, but the Player, I was told, bore only the minimum of treatment and walked out tourniqueted in sports tape.

The injury would resolve before the season resumed. This is not one of those hackneyed narratives terminating at the broken body, though considering their prevalence, it becomes amazing, even disturbing, that anyone endeavors in sport. Or is it just a nobler way to confront the reaper rubbing his hands above us all?

•

It'll heal, the Player said in my office the following evening. Just in case, I had stationed myself beside the practice hall window, fearing to see him working the leg as a denialistic cure, but the lights remained dimmed, the diorama unpeopled.

It happens, he said, I'll be good in a couple weeks. But I wanted to show you this.

He slid his phone across the table, screen displaying an email. I failed to preserve the text of the correspondence, but nothing in it struck an impartial observer as fraught. There was an apology for being so long out of touch; an inquiry into the recipient's well-being and condition of his knee; instructions on how to rehabilitate (*I suspect you are overtraining; I had a teammate whose career ended for the same reason, affliction of ego; REST*); a belated congratulations on having made it so far, as had always been their dream; and some tweaks in technique no one on our team had suggested. There was a photograph, as well: a wiry, well-preserved middle-aged man, his face the color and solidity of a copper pot, beside a girl with a gold medal gilding the belly of her cherry red polo, captioned as having been taken at the California Open.

Ah, I said, a bit shakily. What does this mean to you?

I feel—better. Because he always knew what to do about the knee.

As opposed to our trainer?

Michael knows his stuff. But hearing from Coach that it'll get better . . .

So your feelings are largely positive?

No, he said. When I saw his name, I wanted to throw up.

Do you feel better having shown it to me?

Yes.

Will you take his advice?

He shrugged. I'd do the same without him telling me.

I thought of his extra drills, the kilograms of strain on the pearlescent lining of his knees. I was the teammate who overtrained, and yes, Kristian had urged me not to push so hard. I ignored him to my demise. The insane thought occurred to me that somehow, Kristian had seen forward through time and planned everything so as to send the boy as emissary.

Will you write back? I asked.

No.

Are you tempted to?

... No.

It's good you came to talk, I said. I suppose this marks a turning point in your relationship. Or lack thereof, rather.

I suppose it does, he echoed.

Is it sad to think you may never talk again?

No, he said, unconvincingly.

It's okay if it is. Even people who have hurt us—

He didn't hurt me, the Player said, and it's not sad. He stood, nearly knocking back the antique chair. I'll be good without him.

Thank you for entrusting me with—

Thank *you*, the Player said, and strode out. But for the knee brace, I would not have known he was injured.

Throughout the winter holidays (Mika in Sweden, Jun and the boys in Munich), days typing at my desk and drifting through the old town, taking in lights and cheer, and visits to family whose boredom should have been a balm, the words ran along the edges of my consciousness: *I had a teammate whose career ended for the same reason, affliction of ego.* Of all the evenings the accursed K and I wandered town centers, me sometimes feinting down an alley or zigzagging over a seam in the cobblestones as if to throw him off my trail, the one that stood out to me was in

Cologne before the holidays, when we encountered his parents in the doorway of a church. Their necks craned, baring their throats to whatever of the Savior glowed through the lancet window, their faces crisscrossed by its stark lines. They were only sheltering from the slush, which I had kicked toward the exposed ankle above K's low boots, but I would have believed, by the chilly greeting of his father—which K wanted to avoid, ducking away, too late to prevent his mother calling his name—that they were the most arid of Calvinists. A few words, obviously perfunctory, were exchanged about the possibility of K returning to Koblenz for Christmas. I was introduced. I had known something of the strained relations between K and his parents, primarily the father. I felt remorseful, as if my horseplay had incurred the demoralizing scene. In penance—which embarrassed me; it felt wrong-footed to invert our dynamic—I upgraded us from our drafty, foot-scented hostel to a room at the nicest hotel in the old town, where for a week's wage we shared a queen bed beneath the twin spires of Cologne Cathedral. In sight of God and the seven hundred years of labor that raised the immense, fire-blasted cathedral, I felt the bombastic tenderness (I remember thinking) of the whale with Jonah on its tongue; and then, as K's jaw slackened and his beer-soured breath blew over my face, that most human loving repugnance, that most repellent sign of closeness. In his sleep he shouldered me away and I shouldered him back, as equals, the muscled swells of our shoulders symmetrically firm and proud, but as soon as we returned from the trip I lost touch with those ultimately mawkish and unmerited feelings. Perhaps I had let myself feel them then so they would not plague me in ordinary life. I might have been even harder on him after.

Perhaps, sometimes, I enjoyed his constant, recurring defeats at my hands, the oaths of fealty he repledged day by day. But they had not had to do with *my* ego, only the impersonal and ever-present temptation toward power; had not been important enough to travel forward in life with me. If the Player had not provoked remembrance, I would have lived the rest of my days untouched by what transpired back then.

•

On the first morning of the New Year, the Player walked in without limp or brace. Frohes neues Jahr, Herr Doktor, he said to me, and pressed into my hands a beribboned, moss-green sweater from the Christmas market. He appeared restored, if waxy and pinched as winter renders us all. He had taken the time to solidify his technique and sense of the ball, so that when he could jump again, cautiously at first, it unfolded into the most efficient movements of his career, the extra steps cut, the showman reined in. In good form, having rested and taken the necessary prescriptions, the Player entered the year's inaugural match and won.

It was an away game to which we rode by train, on the outskirts of a city differentiable from ours only to inhabitants of one place or the other, by their air redolent of soot and metal or the quality of our light, issuing from lower yet farther out in the sky. Church after church glided along the train windows, the deep country brown of their spires evocative of a different, more frightening time. The opposing team had a new coach, supposedly in line for a position on the national team; new stands and sufficient fans to fill them; a new speaker system, so that the boys ran on court to a menacing electronica pulse.

Han, inhibitions relieved by a simple turn of the calendar, won.

Mika, packed with fresh stores of Swedish glycogen, won.

The Player vaulted the barriers and punched the air. The stands screamed. Kay, who had been benched in favor of the Player, gnawed his nails.

With admirable restraint, the Player's opponent contemplated his feet, scraping the polyester like a testy racehorse.

Heads, said the umpire, serve, Lo.

The Player crouched for a Tomahawk—beside me, I felt the team question the prudence of deploying his strongest serve right away—and, winding up sinuous as a cobra beneath its arcing flight, aced the ball past his opponent's backhand.

The stands murmured, stunned. A few drops of applause plinked round the hall. The "1" on the scoreboard clicked down. For the rest of the match, whenever the Player crouched for a Tomahawk, his opponent locked up. And unlike ever before, the Player stayed close to the table and controlled the pace, the mood. He had, during those weeks away, found something of his own. The email seemed to have pushed his performance over a threshold. The motivation to dominate once and for all his fallen father figure had aligned perfectly with extrinsic demands for an improved season record. After the last point, Han swung the Player round by his torso, Kay jumping at their backs like a puppy.

At our appointment the following week, the Player resumed the arrogant posture from his first session. So what do you think? he said.

Of what?

My *breakthrough*.

I'm quite happy, of course.

Think it has anything to do with Coach?

I would have to ask you.

I would have to say no, he said, because I'm sick of thinking about him. That's why I even came here. He won't ruin it for me.

Very fair, I said; willing, for the relief of closing the topic, to let lie the contradiction of joining a coach's old team to forget said coach. Nor did I take this third chance to venture information about my past. My false conscience was still far less important than his well-being, and the team's.

Excellence begets excellence, good results alleviate fear of failure: over the next two weeks, the Player won two more matches, putting him at a respectable 3–3 record. I ceased mentioning

Kristian, and the Player obliged me with more details about his personal life. How the better he played the more distance it put between him and Anabel, though she expressed only happiness, because he no longer counted on her for comfort, and the better he performed the longer his forecasted tenure in Europe, where she could not move due to school, training, and coaching. How his otherwise absent father tuned into one of his match broadcasts without warning him, an action interpretable as considerate, underhanded, and/or domineering. How he had lost interest in replying to the messages of his few friends in the States, all of who played or had played table tennis, because this modicum of success in the Bundesliga destroyed any illusion that they (even the ones who took it as seriously) had been playing the same game, in a way they could never comprehend, putting them on lower ground at two levels, which the Player found painful in a further isolating way.

All natural concerns, for which small steps in communication and intimacy could be taken. We discussed and agreed upon them; further agreed that they might be easiest after the season, when he was back in the States, so as not to disrupt what was becoming a crucial role on the team.

But then, in early February, shortly after his record evened, the Player lost a crucial match in a humiliating upset. He swung too wildly, ran too hard, shouted too loud; reversed, in short, all his progress from the winter. Coach Jun cornered me afterward to ask whether it was not "time to start worrying." In our next session, I felt grateful when the Player volunteered: You're probably worried about that last match.

Your performance did seem . . . aberrant.

I'm not following Coach's instructions anymore.

Coach Qiu?

The other one.

I'm not sure what you mean, I said. You aren't in correspondence with him, no?

No. But the improvements I made were based on his email, and I don't want to win because of him.

I see. But didn't you say you would have done the same, even w—

He emailed again.

Ah. That must have been upsetting, when—

The Player's phone clattered across the table, into my lap. The screen was zoomed, so that all I saw was Kristian's name and a postscript: *Send Eckert my regards.* This line I recall in its very font. The letters seemed to distend toward me, their serifs grasping hooks.

Coach used to talk about you, the Player said. I remember now. The first time I hurt my knee, he mentioned you.

I raised my own phone and tapped into *Spam* and *Trash*. Had Kristian found my profile on the team website? It was hardly hidden, I supposed.

Why didn't you tell me? said the Player.

I could not remember precisely what I had said about Kristian, and told him so.

Don't lie, he said.

My experience does not seem relevant to our discussion, I said.

What did you know about him?

In what sense?

Did he coach kids back then? What was he like as a coach?

I don't know.

Did you know he was coaching again?

I can only begin to understand how stressful this is, I said, especially right now in the season. Perhaps we should address your immediate psychological state—

Herr Doktor, come on—

—chronic anxiety, based on your nightmares, apnea, clenching, palpitations, hyperventilation—

Seriously? Herr Doktor—

I have an appointment, I said. I'm happy to continue this discussion in a following session. As if cued, a knock on the door: Frau Rastalsky, one of the more neurotic parents, there to discuss her son Alex's performance anxiety (though, she had simpered over the phone, perhaps I could enlighten her as to whether that was the right term . . .).

I plucked the relevant forms from my desktop file and filled, in my steadiest hand, a prescription for antianxiety pills.

I'm also out of pain meds, the Player said. He splayed his hands on either side of the prescription slip, encaging the worn gray surface of my stalwart desk, dorsal veins rising and pulsing as if to double the strength of the grasping, thick-knuckled fingers, which the manipulation of a table tennis racket had in no way prepared for real force; yet for the first time in my tenure as team psychologist, I felt a shiver of apprehension.

Please consult Michael, I said.

He won't give me more.

Then I defer to him.

You should help me. To make up for this . . . painful experience. Which I'd rather not tell anyone.

Two more knocks. Herr Doktor? warbled the Frau's neurasthenic voice.

Looking back, his threat sits empty as a husk; but I suppose I saw no harm in it, as Michael would probably have written the prescription in the end, and I remembered from my own recovery, even as my pen drew its requisite marks across the slip, pain's guerrilla tenacity, its unpredictable returns and constant retribution.

Good chat, then. The Player seized the papers, saluted me, and sauntered out.

After my dreary, recursive conversation with the Frau, which left me sweaty and dull-minded, with the wits only to scheme how fastest to procure a soda, I rushed into the night. The boys' windows glowed behind me for a dark half mile. I had nothing to hide, I testified to their triple eye. After Kristian left, I had not overly considered his fate nor my role in it. Maybe I roughhoused harder when we grappled in the locker room or played one of our countless stupid games in the dorms, drinking beers standing on our heads or spitting table tennis balls from our mouths at paper targets on the walls; had knocked him onto his back and smothered him. I was always much larger. But always, it was he who sought me out, he who did what he knew would further provoke me, clawing the soft flesh of my elbow or elbowing my head. After I bumped him down the roster, he seemed to almost crave subjugation, to confirm that he had performed no worse than his natural and inevitable place. If, based on my ingenuous behavior toward him, the only kind of behavior that could have been expected between young men in our environment, he had craved something else from me, some other form of companionship or consummation, it was not my place to assume or bequeath. And if, when he was abruptly dismissed by Dieter, in an atmosphere of uncertainty and paranoia where any rational man would discount the rumors circulated about his conduct toward students, my decision to refer him to an acquaintance in California was partly out of guilt, a sense I had created or exacerbated the sinister tendencies which led to his dismissal, then it was no larger part than of a concerned teammate, and of an impartial observer who thought he might truly have made a good coach.

●

Over the next few weeks, the Player lost two more matches. The second, against a reserve player, looked nearly thrown. Han lost his matches, too, and the team faced relegation.

The Player stopped attending our appointments. *Reports high anxiety about the season's outcome*, I wrote in my notes the first time. The next two times, feet on my desk, notepad mashed across my thighs, a finger of Korn in a tumbler on the windowsill, which reflected the queer metallic light of early March, I wrote, *Discussed more tactics for focusing on single points. Improvement in morale, though still lacking some confidence in technique. Suggested talking through with impartial third party, such as _____ (?).*

Two weeks before the season's deciding event, Han reported that the Player had suffered more panic attacks—one the afternoon of a match, another the night before.

And he's been taking my anxiety meds, he said, projecting with a glower all his fear and disappointment. I gave him the rest of an old bottle, but he should get a prescription. He might be shy to ask about it, but I know—

He has a prescription. He's been to see Herr Doktor Strauss.

I didn't know that.

And again, you didn't think to ask me.

We could have hashed through his motivations, rationalizations, savior complex, guilt, but I'd heard enough. I secured Han's vow of discretion and followed him back to the practice hall. What's up, Herr Doktor, the Player said, and pulled me into a fraternal embrace. His hand was more callused than the first time I shook it, days on the Soviet-era bench, always five kilos more than Han; their texture revealed nothing about the state of his mind, though a certain indolence obscuring his eyes, a dopey blankness that took over when he felt unobserved, could have been attributed to the influence of substances. He left practice without exhibiting suspicion toward me or self-consciousness about wrongdoing.

In my office, I flipped through our notes. *Send Eckert my regards*, I had written in a margin.

I would act the next day. One way or another.

The dome of winter had cracked, and spitting rain fell to the chortles of intrepid finches. Round the complex I paced, until dusk, then rerouted into town, along the tram tracks past the Lebanese restaurant where Dieter used to see each season in and out. Without my willing it so, the route became one I had walked with the accursed K, but the memories its landmarks exhumed made no connections to the present. It was like casting lines toward a ship lost a stone's throw away in pitch dark. Would that I could tell the Player anything meaningful! I considered our walks, our kicking of the frayed football that lived beneath his bed, the hours teaching ourselves to serve Tomahawks. During none of it had I bullied or pestered K beyond the norm. God knew I felt bad enough taking his spot in the lineup. No: if he had struck a child, decades after our last words, as parents and coaches continued to do at every second of every day, it had nothing to do with me. Nothing. And nothing to do with the Player anymore, either.

Send Eckert my regards.

Herr Doktor? Kay said, querulously, as I turned into the end of the Sporthotel hallway, breathless, eager to leave behind the uninhabited moonlit rooms below. I followed his gaze to observe leaves and grass wreathing the hems of my slacks.

I left something behind, I said. He was in his pajamas, elasticized at the ankles and wrists, toothbrush held loosely at his side. Even in brushing his teeth, we had discussed, he should focus on the integrity of the action. He seemed not to be succeeding.

Is your brother here? I asked.

They're out. Want me to call?

No! That's all right. I'll . . . I'll get to my office.

In the stairwell, breathing through my mouth, I waited, knowing with equal clarity my inability to brave the landing again, even if Kay must eventually retire to his room; the guarantee I would find pills in the Player's desk or beneath his pillowcase, somewhere obvious, because we all eventually sabotage ourselves in the most self-evident ways, fear of failure overpowered by fear of what comes beyond; and the dubiousness of any negotiation between us. I could have confronted him about the pills, tried to talk honestly about the inadvertent deception between us, but perhaps, I, too, ultimately craved the safety of destruction. Perhaps I should have reminded myself that the boy was *not* capable of true malice; that at most his rebellion was childish retribution for my failure to confess acquaintance with Kristian, a classic case of transference. But at the time, I still perceived my foremost goals to align with, my foremost allegiance to be to, the team, as best as one can yoke anything so saturnine as loyalty to the earthly vehicle of a sports franchise, which like Theseus's ship had had its human planks replaced year by year, so that perhaps all that remained to me was a salary and some liberties afforded to a batty veteran . . .

Yes, at that point in time, with my powers of discernment limited by urgency, the next match imminent, the only action that seemed to justify my life, to evidence any of the "personal improvement" I always urged upon others, was to call a meeting with Coach Qiu and the manager and express my concerns about our rookie's mental state. He had been abusing drugs and, on top of that, expressed, through his performance, a subconscious impulse to sabotage the team; and while I knew Kay was also fragile, giving him responsibility for our season could be just what he needed to overcome remaining inhibitions.

Asked, by Jun, whether the Player presented any other serious symptoms, I said no, nothing beyond the pale, homesickness and the loneliness of achievement, but nothing you could see as causal, which in cases like this could not always be found—in fact, definitionally lacked rational cause. People behaved irrationally in order to regain a sense of freedom, which I suppose I had also sought through Kristian's counterintuitive company. A sense of surprise.

Okay, said Jun, leaning back, with what I could see, in the careful stillness of his crossed arms, was bitter satisfaction. At the end of the day he did not like the Player outshining his sons, and now I had gifted him an irremediable defect. I must say, I had been thinking this for a while. It's tragic to see—

Very sad, said the manager, a promising boy.

—but we have to think of the team . . .

He is still promising, I said, let this not taint all he has achieved.

They told him right before the children's tournament on Saturday, in which Alex would compete. From across the hall—I had been summoned by Frau Rastalsky to observe, even coach, without a moment's thought about how such favoritism might tarnish her son—I heard his indignant exclamation.

Bullshit, he said, my record is better than Han's first year. Better than Mika's!

Perhaps it would be relevant to note, at this penultimate juncture, that I myself was dismissed from the team at the end of the season. The stated reasons were budgetary and philosophical—they felt the responsibilities of psychologist should, once again, fall to the coach, whose high salary warranted their burden—but really, I felt, for my role in and reminder of the entire episode. After nearly twenty years, put out to pasture, where my studies and musings alone must sustain me, in addition to work at a private practice to which Jun, ever the diplomat, wrote me a very strong recommendation.

On the afternoon he discovered he would not play for the rest of the season, which led him, shortly after, to decline a contract renewal, the Player, action-oriented, quickly calmed himself. He scanned the hall. Right away, he identified my situation, Frau Rastalsky trying to coax Alex one more time onto the court, me presiding helpless and unwilling.

Here comes the Player, I said, let's see what he says . . .

As recommended, to inspire the youth, the Player wore his team jersey, representing all our sponsors and, in a smaller strip on the back, himself. From the young Alex's point of view, he must have cut just the golden gladiatorial figure he feared never becoming in his father's eyes, and this stopped his panicked hiccups.

Herr Doktor, the Player said to me.

Here is Frau Rastalsky, I said, whom you've met, and her son, Alex, whom you've coached. He could use your words of advice.

The Player crouched level with Alex and rested a wrist on each of his shoulders. The boy's limp arms sagged lower.

Tell me what you're feeling, he said. Yes, you can whisper, all right.

The boy leaned forward and, too guileless to even cup a hand around his mouth, told him something very simple.

You're afraid of not playing well enough? the Player said.

The boy nodded.

Here's what my coach told me, he said, in a tone of triumph. Imagine aiming the ball like a lightning bolt. Imagine destroying them all.

2016

SUSANNE

Susanne and Jonah met the kids at the three-table bakery by Central Park. Jonah loved the place, despite its impractical smallness, because it was owned by his high school classmate, who agreed to close early for their "business meeting." Of all his friends and acquaintances, all the actors, producers, editors, bankers, DJs, and sculptors, Jonah loved "self-starters" best—business owners and entrepreneurs, freelancers and hacks. Inevitable, really, that he took his own turn.

"I'm telling you," he said, clinking sugar into his third espresso, "they don't get offers this good. They don't even have managers."

"What a charming pitch." Susanne swirled her own espresso in its demitasse. The coffee was too sour for her. "'Work for us, you have no choice!'"

"No no, it's a compliment. Table tennis is the most underrated sport in America. We're going to boost its media profile, and the visibility of—"

"You're going all talk show, babe."

Anabel and Ryan were "table tennis Graf and Agassi": six national titles, four Pan American medals, and ten years of coaching experience between them. Ryan had just returned from the Bundesliga, the equivalent of playing soccer in the English league, Jonah said (which was also, he added facetiously, for Susanne's benefit, like doing Chekhov in the West End). He was drunk in the kitchen in his plaid bathrobe when he proposed hiring them, but he wasn't wrong: Ryan bore a resemblance to Daniel Dae Kim, Anabel to Zhang Ziyi, faces, blown up on posters, that could entice even the most harried New York pedestrian.

The business: a Ping-Pong social space ("a nightclub but without the *connotations*") staffed by professional players. Jonah had been inspired by the sight of two kids playing in Bryant Park, kids "you wouldn't have seen together elsewhere." Several of his friends had recently thrown themselves into "social ventures" and now he wanted to "connect people outside their comfort zones" and "tap cross-cultural potential" through table tennis. It was silly, whimsical—after a life of art-suffused wealth, his father a French movie composer and his mother a Korean model, a "career" as sometimes TV host and general showbiz layabout, Jonah was doomed to whimsy—and borderline nonsense. Susanne had already seen her fair share of table tennis: ten years ago, she played the mother in a Ping-Pong satire, thick Chinese accent and a thousand *AIYA!*s; the movie bombed and the director moved to Bangkok to start an "educational nonprofit" for women. It was the one poster they had mounted, ironically, among their tasteful abstract paintings and framed Kodaks.

Now, she wanted to do it *for* the absurdity. She was taking a break from big productions. Publicly, it was to focus on her health. Privately, it was to stave off the frost of indifference that descended every five years or so. It seemed to Susanne, who considered herself as grounded and pragmatic as an actor could be, impossible to prevent a sense of unreality, the sense that you could reach through any surface or feeling. ("I believe that's called privilege," an old friend said.) That was how her fitful charity work started: you could not reach through suffering; and often, Susanne discovered, suffering could not reach back. She could return from a village in China, where the streams ran with DDT and the little girls resembled her childhood photos, and pass out soundly in her downy king bed. Her parents were proud, at least. They didn't know that their smallest inconvenience touched her more than any noble cause. And since nothing seemed less noble than Jonah's table tennis fantasy, she had, in a giddy fit of perversity back in March, cosigned a lease on a two-level commercial space in Midtown.

The kids showed up in matching linen shirts. A breeze tugged cinematically at their lapels. The men performed an elaborate handshake. Susanne shook Anabel's hand, then reconsidered and hugged her. Their bodies felt eerily symmetrical, same height and densities of fat, muscle, bone. At Anabel's age, Susanne had done her first magazine cover, barely clothed, ribs airbrushed away, though the bob for yet another scientist role made her more Edna Mode than Anna May Wong. By now, at a permanently lean sixty, she had donated or thrown out all her sweat-browned Spanx of yore.

Anabel was not used to such attention, and certainly not its attendant money. When Jonah proposed a salary for coaching and promoting, her hand flew to her neck.

"And commission?" she asked.

"Twenty percent on lesson fees, and tips."

Ryan sat forward, shoulder brushing Anabel's. Susanne caught a whiff of cherries and leather.

"We'll just talk to Coach Gao," Anabel said. "About the schedule."

Heat prickled Susanne's shoulder at the spot where the kids' bodies met. It felt realer than anything—her three-year-old marriage, her projects and "projects," her hard-earned uptown brownstone, her parents happily retired in Singapore—had for a long time.

"Of course," Jonah said, "of course. You know how to find us."

As they left, their fingers drifted together. Anabel bowed her head, giggling, and Ryan bumped her sideways on the path.

Jonah lifted Susanne from her seat. Her feet hit two salvage-metal chairs as he swung her around.

"I think we got 'em," he said, in the flat gruff tone that belied his greatest happiness.

•

A week later, the tables and TVs arrived, occasion enough to invite "an intimate group" of investors and friends to an exhibition. Anabel was out with strep, so Jonah flew in a friend of Ryan's from Indiana.

"Not a single person within train distance?" Susanne asked.

"Come on, Sue," Jonah said, "have fun while we can."

"I'm having lots, *lots* of fun signing checks."

She did not speak properly with Ryan until midnight. The guests arrived. A goateed skateboarder type DJed atop the bar. Ryan and his friend stood ten feet back from the table. They dove, free hands bracing against the floor. The ball zoomed flat across the table, danced cunningly along the net, flicked itself off edges, torqued dust as it spiraled into the ceiling lights. The crowd *ooh*ed and *aah*ed. "We need a higher roof!" Jonah shouted.

Watching them play, Susanne began to understand his obsession.

After thirty minutes, the boys begged exhaustion and left the table, laughing as they walked toward the bathrooms, doppelgängers with their tousled black hair and slouches. Susanne shook hands and flirted, drank two highballs of Jonah's upsettingly purple "underspin punch," and perched on a stool to watch a replay from the Olympics. China versus Germany. The lights had dimmed to a vampiric orange; they should get that adjusted.

"Timo Boll's one of the greatest," Ryan said. He leaned against the bar, between Susanne and the rest of the room. Sweat glistened in the creases of his smile. "How's that drink?"

"Don't recommend," Susanne said. "And I know about Timo Boll, but I prefer Verizon."

"Oh, she's got *jokes*."

"The curse of leathery old women. You gotta be funny."

"You don't look leathery."

"But I do look old?"

"No no, didn't mean it that way."

Susanne pantomimed shoveling.

He laughed, rapped the bar twice. "Wanna play?"

"For your honor?" It was a famous line from one of her movies.

"'The only thing worth fighting for now,'" he quoted back.

Susanne had not played table tennis since drunken matches in college. (The Ping-Pong satire required only pantomime.) She struggled to land more than two shots. It did not help that an electrifying force held her spine and knees ramrod straight. Even when Ryan lofted the ball to her racket, she found ways to hit it into the net, more so when bystanders began to film on their phones.

Ryan shrugged off his jacket and Susanne followed suit, revealing a plunging wrap dress. Claps and wolf whistles.

"What's the score?" a spectator called.

"Fifteen to zero," Susanne said. Sweat slicked her armpits, a bead tickling its way down her left side. "I'm zero, to clarify." The audience laughed.

Ryan served. She returned a floaty shot. He let it fly by.

"Fifteen–one," he said.

Imitating him, Susanne bent her knees and waist. She prayed the dress would hold up. A gift from the designer. Her heels slapped the ground; a grunt burst from her mouth. Ryan let the ball fly beneath his arm, eyebrows flying up, Chaplin-esque. People chanted Susanne's name.

Jonah drowned out the last *SU-sanne!* "FRIENDS!" he shouted. "Listen up!" He was standing on a table, skin razed by harsh overhead light. "Listen y'all, I am so blessed and like, beyond myself with pure fucking joy . . ." Ryan caught the ball. Susanne, poised to follow it, caught herself against the edge of the table. "I cannot tell you how excited and grateful I am to be embarking on this journey. With Ryan"—pointing—"and with the love of my life, Susie."

Applause, a flurry of camera clicks. Susanne could not begrudge Jonah his eagerness to please, which had first sought the cruel and counterintuitive light of fame, then the perceived esteem of her approval ("Boy Toy!" the tabloids declared, capturing them on an early date, flash deepening the wrinkles around Susanne's laugh while smoothing Jonah's into naïveté), and now the guileless, frat-boyish warmth of someone like Ryan, a warmth that she, too, wanted to bask in longer. Dizzied and dehydrated by her all-too-brief exposure, she pulled her hair into a ponytail. The pose, arms raised, flattered her waist, and she pretended to be directing it at her husband.

•

Three weeks later, they visited Gao's club. A documentarian, invited by Jonah, followed their car to Newark, where a line of children greeted them, chanting, "Welcome to Canton Table Tennis Club, Susanne!" A little boy stumbled forward with a DVD case, plastic buckling over a photo of Susanne brandishing katanas. Ryan knelt and, placing a hand on the boy's shoulder, reassured him: "Susanne will sign it at the end."

Okay, the kid whispered, and hid his face against Ryan's shoulder.

They trained with Gao, who, like many stunt coordinators, found herself stumped by Susanne's lack of athleticism. Jonah arced his first shot onto the table and slapped his racket against his thigh, shouting, "Hell yeah!"

"Don't abuse your paddle," Gao hissed.

"Yes, Coach. Sorry, Coach."

During the water break, ecstatic from his superior performance, Jonah invited Anabel and Ryan to the night's cast party. Anabel protested that she trained early tomorrow.

"C'mon," Jonah said, "you can meet Jackie Chan's stunt guy."

"Not tonight," Susanne countered. "It's just my sitcom. Do what's right for you."

Jonah winked. Anabel sighed; looked to Ryan, who pouted; assented.

Sitting with Ryan in the backseat, Susanne let her knee hang over the center console. ("Leg!" the red carpet cameras were always shouting. "Show us leg, Susanne!") When they hit a pothole in the Lincoln Tunnel, it met Ryan's and stayed there.

The party was for the last show Susanne wrapped, an Asian American "dramedy" in which she played, again, the mother. Ten or even five years ago, she would have paid for a show devoid of martial arts and accents, but now, as her castmates playacted merriment across the set of her home (shimmying in the dark living room beneath state-of-the-art speakers, forty years of hits piped from Jonah's phone; drinking too fast in the kitchen, black fixtures daubed with light from Jonah's custom liquor cabinet; sitting, legs jumbled, in the middle of the polished staircase, smoking), still animated by the spirit of a script, laughing too broadly around the few white faces and lapsing into pockets of brittle tiredness among themselves, Susanne craved that pinprick of real, unconsidered touch. But she held herself apart; watched as Jonah monopolized Ryan by the kitchen island, refilling his whisky glass, tucking the dampened end of his cigarillo between Ryan's smiling lips, their faces mirrored behind a lattice of smoke.

Sometimes on set, Susanne seemed to fly into a hundred-foot tower, levitate above some vista from another life, and she ascended there now to try and see what she was truly desiring. Perhaps the same boyishness that attracted her to Jonah at a fundraiser for girls' skateboarding, though he had since substantiated himself through steady companionship, extended visits to Singapore and lily bouquets lining the foyer when she returned from late nights on set, patience and steadiness when she went to the ER after a drunken mandolining of carrots (Jonah loved carrot cake), walks in the park and nights drinking and laughing to their own filmographies. Perhaps the sense of purpose, his whole and wholesome world.

The simplicity of the fact that he had not moved his knee.

Around two, having danced, schmoozed, and regretfully declined coke no longer worth its lightning strike hangover, Susanne found Anabel in the den, asleep in the vintage skater dress she had borrowed, skirt smoothed meticulously over her thighs. Anabel, who that morning reassured Susanne: "It's okay. You're good at, like, everything else." Susanne sat beside her and watched every available clip of Ryan. The boy onscreen glided across courts, flashily pumped his fist and quietly nodded his satisfaction. There was something different in the one she glimpsed in the kitchen, who thumb wrestled a PA before the cyclops eye of a delighted Jonah's phone. The one who played with her at the club. *Her* Ryan, she already thought.

She watched until her phone died and, hand dangling inches from Anabel's in their side-by-side love seats, slept more deeply than she had in years.

●

You couldn't blame two bored older people for craving new company. It kept them energetic, versatile, freethinking; conversely, sweetened the goodness of their evergreen traits, the characteristics that could only develop over decades. Jonah's rapacious hospitality, Susanne's steadfast and self-effacing forbearance. There had been two emerging painters whose gallery opening they sponsored, twin acting prodigies from Susanne's alma mater whom she put up for roles in a friend's film, a husband-wife Romanian chess duo Jonah met at the symphony and flew to Greece to vacation with them. To none, however, had Jonah taken as much as Ryan, who stayed with them for seven Saturdays, after photo shoots, interviews, and lessons with sponsors; then whenever Jonah felt like inviting him, at first with excuses, meeting at the club before spiriting him around the city; then with a mere "Hanging out with the Rugrat tonight." After her first stay, Anabel never returned; over brunch, she had declared that she slept terribly in unfamiliar places, concealing half her face behind the shelf of her hand, the other half all dark circle.

Too embarrassed to admit the feelings that Jonah's solicitousness stoked—attraction toward an *even younger* man; yawn—Susanne did everything to encourage their friendship. She refrained from inviting herself or inquiring too deeply into their activities. Nights they went out, she took herself to movies, plays, drinks; put herself to bed, scooted over amiably when Jonah returned and, adamant about hygiene, nestled beside her damp from the shower, coconut body wash amplifying the traces of smoke in his scruff. She listened to him recount this ridiculous conversation with an old TV friend or that funny thing Ryan said to a sensitive musician, their hands clasped across the kitchen island, the morning-after ritual from their early socialite days, when Jonah wanted to be seen everywhere with Susanne. Despite the long nights, his training and management of the club invigorated him. More often than before, she woke in his shadow as he sat on the edge of the bed, reviewing a to-do list, his face shaven fragrant smooth. They still took their walks in the park. He still dampened her face with kisses and ran his palm lovingly down her side until she passed out, stuck sweaty to his chest, drooling.

Unadmitted, though, the feelings gathered force. They compelled her to make her way to the kitchen early on Sundays, while Ryan sipped an energy drink, or downstairs to do laundry after she heard his shower clank off, and to see as meaningful any number of gestures: Ryan cast an unguarded smile over his water-flecked back, droplets magnifying pale moles. He asked, "What's on your mind, Sue?" and peered intently over a half-liter can while she gave thoughts about an upcoming event. Once, while Jonah was in a meeting, he accompanied her to buy groceries. They split the list in half and raced around the aisles. If Ryan was watching something with Jonah, Olympics reels or a movie, he patted the couch beside him.

One evening, as they waited for Jonah to come home, he asked, "And what's your dream role?"

All the kung fu, the accents, the slurs veiled and open—her dream role, Susanne reflected, had long since lost its shape to her assigned ones. "How come it's always 'who do you want to play,'" she said, tone the ambiguous lightness Jonah would know concealed annoyance and pain, "not 'who do you want to be'?"

Ryan rested his chin on interlaced fingers, looked up through his dense, short lashes. "Okay. Who do you want to *be*?"

"The Dragon in *Balls of Fury*."

"Fuck off," he said.

"Who do *you* want to be?"

"World champion."

"*Outside* table tennis, silly."

His sigh tickled her arm, which rested on the couch velvet between them, fingers stilled so as not to distract. "One of those guys who goes around the park picking up the trash. Just making things nice, you know."

Jonah would have laughed and said the kid was being naïve, just as, by asking Susanne's help with the club, he had implicitly said her semi-retirement was silly; but of them all, only he had not earned the right to think so.

"Maybe," Susanne said. "But I don't assume more or less dignity in any career. Or any *stage* of our careers, right?"

Ryan smiled wanly and patted the back of her hand, reminding her that he must have been humoring her sometimes, just as on Sundays, when they drove him back to Jersey and trained at Gao's,

Anabel humored Susanne, guiding her through motions recently corrected. When she least expected it, one of them would say, "Bel says . . ." or "Oh yeah, me and Ryan always . . . ," deepening her shame.

She continued to attend meetings in conference rooms and cafés and bars, reply to emails, meet project managers and alcohol suppliers; return to the two-story space with the glass balcony, which filled with copper tables, ergonomic chairs, subtropical plants. Through Anabel and Ryan, they hired more coaches. The documentarians recorded more footage. Jonah and Susanne booked interviews with B-list magazines. No publicity was enough, where this sport was concerned. For all of their sakes, she wanted the club to succeed. Maybe then the fever would break.

•

It finally happened in the car. They were on their way to a friend's house in the Hamptons. Jonah sat beside the driver, another friend whose pay they would write off, along with the cases of scotch in the trunk and the salaries, room, and board of the photographer and lifestyle journalist who would join them. A red VW Beetle whooshed past and Ryan punched Susanne's arm. "Bug," he said, too low for Jonah to hear over his front seat laughter, some joke from a shared boyish past.

"No," Susanne said, "didn't see it."

"Scout's honor."

She rested her folded fingers against his arm. They were approaching the narrow neck of the island, the canal a needle of gray in each tinted window, skewering the moment. She ran her knuckles up his arm until she could unfurl her index finger into the opening of his T-shirt sleeve. The fabric was heavy and stiff, perfect for holding the color of a silk print figure that leapt across Ryan's torso. A cartoon, though not necessarily a child's; so many friends voice acted for adult animation. The cartoon man's forehead rose and fell with Ryan's breaths. On his thigh, over black cargo shorts, his hand turned to show its soft white face. She laid her free hand over it.

At her friend's house, she hung back as Jonah, the driver, and Ryan carried their bags up the brick drive and into the rooms. The air snapped and preened like the flag atop its driveway pole. Soon the island would close for the season; remembrance and biding would brine the shingles, leaden the breeze that now carried voices—Jonah, the driver, the hostess—out to where Susanne lingered, hand still resting against the warm metal of the SUV, one cork-wedged foot crossed over the other. In the most natural motions she had ever made, she crossed the house's threshold, holding her straw hat to her goose-pimpling chest, through the veil of tinted glassware shadows in the entrance hall, into the living room overlooking the bay. Dusky water lapped, fateful and coy, across the all-seeing back window. Ryan's gilt silhouette turned toward her, implicated hand in one pocket. She asked if he knew where her duffel went. On the longest couch, facing the sea, Jonah and the hostess were already conspiring, glasses of scotch exuding gay light and musk. Ryan and Susanne went undisturbed up the gray stairwell, brushing its silently quavering rails; down the glittering, polished wood hallway; into the master bedroom, the white bedspread like the geisha robe she'd thrown atop a smatter of cloth blossoms, many films ago, so that a warlord in a glued-on Fu Manchu could pretend to ravish her, actor's hairy nostrils whistling as he held himself over her on flabby forearms, except now she sat on the foamy duvet for real, the first and only take, running her hands down the sides of a man who stood there of his own volition.

"I don't know," he said huskily. Sweetly.

"Jonah won't come up."

He smeared a kiss across her lips, clumsy with indecision and maybe disbelief. Slowly he turned his head side to side, the bones of their noses bumping painfully, the grease of their brows intermingling; then stepped back.

"We need to go back," he said.

Everyone was in the living room now, the hostess's husband and the journalist, awaiting the exotic sports star. Ryan told them he had played a tournament last weekend. "First one in a while," he said, "and I lost to a total shithead."

"Once I lost a role to someone who ran an MLM," said the hostess. "Like, she went to jail."

"No fucking way," said Jonah. "The pirate flick?"

"Which pirate flick?" asked the journalist.

"Sorry to hear about the tournament," Susanne said.

Ryan shrugged. "Nah, I mean—I really thought I was done. I guess all this stuff with the club gave me a different idea, but I don't know. Some days it's like, is this the same sport?"

"It is what you make it," the driver said, "that's showbiz."

"But he's an athlete," countered the hostess.

"You don't need to tell me, I watch the Yankees like everyone else—"

"The *Yankees*?!" Jonah shouted gleefully, "this is a Mets household!" and as the conversation clattered around and away from them, blurred extras in the background, no trick could convey how much Susanne felt she understood the essence of his life. The ebbs and reversals, the hope, even as she readied for the hundredth take, that it might all end soon. Who better to be with him through this moment? Who else shared his experience, unburdened by the envy of common vocation or bitterness of failure? In a crowded room, he had shared this tidbit just for her. She dared to press a hand atop his knee and say, "One bad match doesn't change everything. Or if things have changed, that could be okay, too. That's life."

Amber light needled the wall as Jonah raised his glass. "To life!"

That night, after the pictures had been taken and the sound bites given, ankles chilled in the complicit sea and golden champagne sprayed into the golden haze of sunset, Jonah snoring on the sunroom chaise longue, he came to her.

•

At practice the next weekend, two weeks before opening, Anabel approached Susanne in the locker room. Susanne had hit twenty straight backhands, her longest streak yet. "Look at that torque!" Jonah whooped. At first, she thought Anabel was going to praise her. Instead, hand hovering at her neck, the girl presented a selfie of Ryan and Jonah in their underwear. Their torsos shone bare beneath the high-angled flash, Jonah's extended arm a beige smear. A pink bow tie lay wilted against Ryan's collarbone, matching cummerbund glinting atop a strip of black boxer. Jonah looked unrecognizably lean as he twisted to plant a kiss on Ryan's cheek. The stripes of a table gleamed in the background. Anabel informed Susanne that it had been an "informal sponsor event," with catering and a photo-booth and what Jonah had dubbed Naked Ping-Pong.

"Did you know about this?" she asked.

The photo dated from five days ago. Susanne hadn't known Ryan was in town. She had attended a friend's play, and the reception after. Jonah was smoking on the fire escape when she left and asleep when she returned.

"We'll do publicity," Anabel said, "but I didn't sign up for this."

"Yes," Susanne said, "of course. No Naked Ping-Pong in the contract."

"Ryan's always game, so he did it. But can you talk to Jonah?"

Susanne knew, from the high-up place, that she was hurt not to have known; that it was a defensive reaction, untrue to how she felt about the real Anabel, which was tender and a bit regretful (rather than her paranoid projection of Anabel—whom she feared, who would find her disgusting, whom she must best) when she said, "But it didn't bother him."

"He was wasted." It did tend to happen that way. Before her one full-frontal sex scene, Susanne had split a fifth of tequila with her costar behind the trailers, asphalt searing the backs of her legs, a burn that persisted through filming. Ryan had been sober last weekend, though, when everything happened. Anabel brandished her phone. "This isn't what he's supposed to be doing. It's a nice gig, we're really grateful, we'll do what's needed. But, the other stuff—he just needs to focus right now. He can still compete. He still wants to."

Then Susanne could catch hold of sisterly pity again. The poor girl, thinking it was so simple to steer a life like that. She couldn't remember what words she used to promise. She did not say anything to Jonah during the ride home, their afternoon break on the couch, their trip to the store, their cocktails at the kitchen island. She did not say anything, either—it would have given up her position, lost her the game—when Jonah set down his empty glass and said, "Let's see what the Rugrats are up to," as if it had occurred to him for the first time.

•

On the last weekend of October, the club soft-opened. They invited everyone they knew to the party and flew out several of Ryan's friends. The documentary would screen before it premiered at a minor festival. Jonah insisted they buy out two floors at a hotel across the street.

Ryan arrived with Anabel and a posse of young people. He ran onto the red carpet and tackled Jonah in a hug; encircled Susanne's waist and pulled her in for a photo. For a heart stopping moment, his fingers traced Susanne's collarbone. "Yay, Auntie!" he shouted. They had not been alone since the Hamptons, but there was only the night to get through. 1012 was his room.

Then he was pulled off her, Anabel between them. "We'll keep it together," she said, eyes narrowed by makeup, lithe in a clinging backless shift, bolder than Susanne expected. Before Susanne could muster the lie that she'd talked to Jonah, a stranger caught her hand and asked for a photo. The kids disappeared inside.

"I need to set up," Susanne said. "Later, anytime." But Jonah smushed a wet kiss onto her cheek, bade her do photos "for the team," and followed Ryan. She stood outside and obliged the stream of strangers, some who presumed to be more than that, until her gums ached.

Two minutes before the event's start time, she went inside to join the others. On the club's first floor, Jonah, Ryan, and Anabel stood with the director and producer at the front of the room, behind a podium someone had ferried last-minute from a high school debate contest. The space was finished, everything in place. Traversing it, Susanne felt the blue booths and metal bars, polished windows and matte table tennis tables—in what had turned into a festive room packed with people and conversation that would, in twenty-four hours, if all went according to plan, take over all the square footage and their lives, flow upstairs to the big dance floor and out onto the sidewalk—blur in and out of focus with the private, empty site it had been less than a year before, distant now as a Martian desert. A thirty-foot screen, which cost more than the documentary, whirred down from the ceiling. Jonah, self-possessed in a metallic blue suit, jaw sharp from all his training, ushered the documentarians forward. The din dropped to a murmur. The screen blinked to life. The director gave rambling remarks. The producer accepted the mic, only to roll his eyes and hand it back to Jonah. Jonah passed it to Ryan. Laughter. Behind them, Anabel, who had asked not to speak, beamed at her boyfriend.

"I am so grateful to be here," Ryan said, "and in this community. Huge shoutout to Jonah"—cheers—"and Auntie Sue"—quieter cheers—"for being my family. And to all my homies."

Susanne went next. The warm microphone was Pavlovian. Table tennis was a beautiful global endeavor, she said. To support it was to support people everywhere, with whom they would otherwise not be community. Just look at this room, she said. On and on. She had rehearsed it less than any other script; still it flowed, consonants crisp and vowels resonant, cadences varied and engaging. She felt something like disdain for the room as it cheered: for the obstacle they presented between herself and the reunion at the end of the night; for their necessary role in its eventuality.

The documentary was almost entirely predictable: slow-mo montage of Ryan and Anabel training; interviews with Gao and her assistants; home video-style footage of the club, kids blurring as they rushed the camera; a shift toward the stories of Ryan and Anabel, then Ryan alone. "Ryan's like family," said Denny Ouyang Junior, the friend from Indiana. Ryan's former classmates expressed astonishment and admiration. "Kids like him a lot," Gao said, eyes darting as she monitored drills taking place behind the camera. "Kevin, arm up!"

The first surprise was an interview with *Kristian Kaellenius, Ryan's Coach*, according to the caption. Susanne had never heard the name. "It was obvious Ryan would be the most talented student I ever coached," Kristian said. Like Gao, he was interviewed in his club. Behind him, two polo-clad bodies leapt around a court. The sound editor kept the ambience of squeaking shoes and rattling caddies. "It's been an honor to bring him up. As a coach, the most you can hope for is to identify and bring out a player's essence. I accomplished that with Ryan. Now that he's on the East Coast, I miss him dearly, but we will still see each other at big tournaments."

The second was Ryan himself, seated against a black backdrop. "Surprising?" he said. "Yeah, sure. It's surprising to be *here*, like—" He pointed to the camera, himself. "I guess it was always a very private, personal thing."

"Even on the world stage?" asked the producer.

Ryan's mouth hooked into a smirk. "Especially on the world stage."

"Do you miss it?"

The smirk hardened; the skin between Ryan's eyebrows tightened. "I was never out."

The screen went black. A few lines about Ryan's hopes for the future and Gao's club faded in. The filmmakers delivered more thanks, blinking into the spotlight that swung forward. Jonah bounded up to the podium and shouted, through a screech of reverb: "Thank you all! Be happy and pong!" Music thumped through the floor. Colored lights began to rove.

Susanne felt flung upward, to a painful distance from what she thought she'd understood. Around her, Ryan had never seemed so resolved. That Ryan was Anabel's, his coach's; had nothing to do with her. The camera could make strangers of people, but he had not seemed capable of such disingenuity. Before anyone could grab her, Susanne beelined for a table. On the sidelines, two phones rose to record. From on high she watched herself beat a stranger, throwing down her paddle as she won. She watched herself high-five the spectators and flex her bicep for a photographer, the flash tangible against her skin, unlike the wood of the paddle or the silk of her jumpsuit, which seemed props held by someone else's body. She had chosen an outfit with pants hoping to play Ryan again, but he was fist-pumping in a cluster of players on the dance floor. Jonah scrubbed at a damp table with his sleeve, people on either side smacking balls into the turbid half-dark. In the time it took Susanne to procure a drink at the mobbed bar, they had disappeared and reemerged together from the bathroom, Jonah shouting something into Ryan's ear. He pulled Ryan onto the staircase and rested a possessive arm above the boy's head.

Susanne hated him then, the helpless resentful hate toward those you love, a knife in an enemy's gut the knife in your own. Naked Ping-Pong. They were both pathetic.

She waited for Ryan to peel away and edged her way to him at the second bar, in the quietest corner of the room. He leaned against the dimpled metal counter, collar askew.

"Having a good night?" she asked.

"Yeah," he slurred, "sick party."

Susanne stroked his cheek with the back of a kinked finger. "We couldn't have done it without you."

"Didn't do much."

She snaked an arm behind his head, pulling their cheeks together. Ryan smelled like sugary vodka and, displeasingly, cigarettes, and beneath that, his usual cherries and leather, the kind of synthetic young man's scent Susanne had persuaded Jonah to stop wearing. Susanne rubbed her face back and forth. Their skin stuck together, Ryan's feverish. She wrapped her other arm around his neck and brought her body close. They could have been slow dancing. A few feet away, the bartender stirred and shook, tongue clamped between neon teeth.

Ryan shifted his face. Almost a kiss, his nose at her brow. Susanne tightened her hold. "I'd miss you, if you weren't around," she said. "Like your coach does."

He cleared his throat. The sound echoed at the base of Susanne's neck. His lips moved against her eyelids, soft with the years and tight with filler. "I didn't know he was going to be in it." His hands rose to cup her elbows. Prepared to pull her even closer.

Then she lost hold of him. Anabel's arm was around his waist.

"Think it's past our bedtime," Anabel said.

"I'll walk you back," Susanne said. They had almost dissolved whatever thin membrane remained between them.

Anabel mirrored her step forward. "Don't leave your own party."

She tried to lean in. Anabel shifted away. Her touch seemed to undo something in Ryan; he slumped against her, eyes hooded. Susanne understood. She had been in his position before. Anabel's feelings must be spared. She let the girl push Ryan ahead of her into the crowd and watched through the glass storefront as they revolved into the hotel, two bodies slotted into the same chamber. She counted to thirty and followed. The night was soft and blue with residual light, more like deep summer than fall. Women in dresses issued from a chain of golden cabs and blew petal-like down the sidewalk. The hotel lobby was bright and balmy. The whole time, Susanne felt that a second, sinister self mirrored her from above, descending foot by foot.

The besuitsed doorman's greeting, impersonal but warm, implying good intent in every guest it graced, briefly shamed her; in a last effort, she sat by the bar to loosen the straps of her shoes and tried to tell herself that maybe nothing would come of it. Then she saw Anabel in the descending elevator, a blue shadow trapped in the glass, bare arms crossed in a defensive pale line. She got up and went to stand outside the bathrooms, behind the elevator column, where she could watch the girl click-clack her way out through the revolving doors and across the street again.

Looking for her, to deliver retribution? Returning to the party? She didn't care.

She counted to sixty and went upstairs.

The tenth-floor hallway was silent and starkly lit. Susanne's heels caught on the carpet, which, beneath the frosted sconces, made it feel like the set of a cheap drama. That, more than anything, gave her pause as she passed the door and doubled back. She assumed Jonah's pose from the club stairwell, propping her forearm across the peephole, forehead brushing the dark wood.

"Ryan," she said. She lowered her arm and repeated his name.

The door opened. He was still in his blazer. Susanne smoothed the front of her dress.

"I wanted to . . . make sure you'd made it."

"Here I am." Even exhausted and drunk, he smiled with a rueful charm.

She didn't mean to peer too obviously into the room, she wanted him lead again; but his eyes followed hers, and he stepped wearily aside. Two suitcases lay on a bench at the foot of the bed, layers of neatly folded clothing showing through the unzipped sides. In the underlit wardrobe, a pink hoodie swayed on its lone hanger. Susanne fell into one of the armchairs between bed and window. Ryan sat in the other, legs straight and parallel, hands cradling kneecaps.

"Bel just went for air," he said.

"You feel okay?"

"Yup."

"I didn't know about your coach."

"Yup. Taught me everything."

"I had an acting teacher like that. Middle school. He was the first to tell me I could do it." Trapped by the chair's high leather arms and the contagious stiffness of Ryan's posture, Susanne could not move any part of herself closer to him. "And he's not around anymore," she went on, "because he was already old when he was my teacher, but he lived to be ninety-two, he was at *every* premiere."

"Hm."

"He had every one of my posters in his house."

"That's kinda creepy."

"Oh, no, it wasn't like that . . . though when I was young, I sometimes wanted it to be. You know how it is. Sometimes you think you want to be more grown-up than you are . . ."

He stood. "Water?"

"That's okay."

He leaned across her to pry the carafe from the coffee maker; separated two cups stacked beside the machine and poured.

"We drank up the mini fridge," he said, "but if you want something fun, there's leftover oxy . . ."

"No! No, I'm fine. I'm not saying—the doc just reminded me . . . I'm not saying anyone else feels that way about—"

"Yeah, no. What you're saying doesn't vibe with me."

He plucked a white pill from his shirt pocket and swilled it, water dribbling down his jaw and neck. The placket of his shirt rippled, flashing a crescent of stomach. Susanne heard shirt and blazer rub. Suddenly she saw him as if in that photograph, the gummy brown skin puckered over his abs, the vulnerable plunge of his underwear.

She stood. Her dress rode up. "I'm disturbing your rest," she said. "I should go."

"It's okay," Ryan said, but he slumped in relief. He offered the cup; she was already in the entry, grabbing at the handle, jogging in her heels down the hallway. The full-length mirror behind her suite door reflected a blanched face shedding cakey foundation. Fear and shame ran through her like a vengeful flu. She bolted the door, took a burning shower, and fell asleep naked, sausaged in sheets.

When she woke, alone and bundled, blinking in chaste daylight, cheek spit-encrusted, she was so glad to be rid of the night's fearful shadow self that she descended almost happily to the lobby to meet Jonah, who guided her to a corner table in the breakfast bistro, slid a cup of pale coffee before her, and rubbed her back. His curls hung over his forehead, adorably damp.

"Don't worry," he said, "they got me a spare room. For the better, I think, I was feeling sick . . . but how are you? What happened?"

"I drank too much, too," Susanne tried. "I forgot about the deadbolt."

"That's all? You're okay? I was worried. I didn't see you all night."

Concern creased his face with all the pathos of a sick boy on a fundraising poster. She imagined him holding court in their kitchen with his friends, laughing that his older party animal wife had blacked out and locked him out; his friends laughing, but not with him. "I went to find Ryan," she said.

"Right. Because you thought I was with him."

"I didn't think you were with him."

His lips pursed and relaxed. His jaw clenched and released. Susanne sat until, unexpectedly, he took her hand.

"I've been thinking," he said, barely audible over the swelling ambience of clattering silverware and chagrined morning laughter.

"We've gotten attached. I get it. But you heard him in the doc, right? He should be playing. Not wasting time with us. Right? Maybe that'd be better for everyone. What do you think?"

She saw the kids through the elevator glass as they ascended back toward their room, Jonah's chin atop her head and arms snug around her waist. Through the fragrant flutter of her husband's breath, she watched as they paused in the middle of the lobby, Ryan tried to take Anabel's hand, she batted it away and turned as if to storm out. Had he told her last night? Or this morning? The timelessness of the gestures depressed her, and she leaned into Jonah's warmth, his pulse against her back.

Whether you left or not, she would have told the girl, it made no difference: the consequences were scripted in you long ago.

•

Jonah fired Ryan for tardiness and unprofessionalism, which was not untrue: Ryan arrived for his first coaching session swaggering and unsteady, stinking of beer and (according to Jonah; Susanne kept her distance), given his possession of painkillers, possibly high. Anabel's bio sat alone atop the website's *Coaches* section for two weeks before she quit.

Two thousand people showed up in the first few days—many attracted, in the end, by Susanne's name, though she relegated herself to behind-the-scenes work.

Sometimes she missed the briny smell of rubber and glue, the ring of Anabel's encouragements. She felt an anguished pride when the club proliferated across the country. At Jonah's suggestion, they took tennis lessons, and attended the challenger matches of a few local players he'd heard about from his brother. She only googled Ryan's name once more. She read a blog post from the new club where he was coaching, with his friend Denny in Indiana, but even the shape of his name pained her, and she never looked him up again.

2017

THE YAOS

Another Thursday league night. They had spent the last three atop the bleachers playing chess on their new tablet. Their daughter bought them gadgets out of guilt: tablet, two tombstone-sized phones, Italian leather sports duffels, premium paddles.

Mrs. Yao was too old to be trying new things, let alone sports, but that's what happened when you fell: subjugation. She had warned her husband, she had sent the links for mats to line their stairs and bathtub, but he went ahead and tripped in the straight flat hallway. And now here they were, in Indiana—no one, not a single one of their friends, had opposed their daughter's idea to move them—at a recreational table tennis club.

How many afternoons they had passed watching televised games! How many times the names Liu Guoliang, Kong Linghui, Wang Liqin had flown in one ear and out the other, sometimes at gatherings with their neighbors in the courtyard, sometimes as they sat in their apartment, pipes humming with heat and the same match playing simultaneously in every apartment along the hall, buzzing in the gaps between flimsy wall and slightly less flimsy breakfast table, which they moved against the window, on one of their last nights in China, to watch a drunk man bike up and down the empty street, Mr. Yao clapping in delight when he finally crashed into the lone telephone pole; and now, in the middle of

America, from the nursing home where, despite similar density of living, she could barely imagine their neighbors as humans shitting and sleeping like them, their daughter sent them to play table tennis!

It was supposed to be good for her husband's condition.

They had stumbled and flailed through the first training session, under the tyranny of Coach Dennis Ouyang. After that, they refused to participate, though they also forbade Dennis from telling their daughter or denying them future admission. They were not old or pathetic enough for Dennis to spare his drill sergeant routine—"He l-looks at us," Mr. Yao said, "and sees his future and it . . . it makes him mad"—but still old and pathetic enough to twist his remaining sense of piety.

It was the fourth activity their daughter had foisted upon them. Zumba, watercolor, water aerobics. All they wanted was to be left alone, or better yet, returned to their apartment in Panjin. Nothing was even wrong with Mr. Yao's hip. Their daughter just loved to be in charge. She loved driving her father to his doctor's appointments and dictating his diet. Finally, the great seesaw of parent-child authority had tipped, launching her like Chang'e toward the sky!

Well, Mrs. Yao was not having it.

"Knight to D4," she instructed her husband. Chess was also good for his condition, though they were hopeless at it. Their daughter set their app to seek the weakest opponents, stupid computers and small children, afflicted old people like themselves, and still they found themselves at endless impasses, pieces gridlocked from A1 to H8. They would have been the worst at table tennis, too, if they descended into the melee underway across Ouyang Table Tennis Club's six courts, from the last of which Aleks, a lanky, perpetually grinning man around their age, beckoned them. (Their first night, he had tapped his sternum, "ALEKS," then shook his head, "no ALEKSANDR.") If you won at a table, you could move up; if you lost, you moved down. All the worst players quickly sank to table six, taking turns playing stuttering unskilled games; Aleks always arrived early to squeeze in some serve practice before the night's misery officially began. Once, with Dennis's begrudging help, he communicated that he came from Bosnia and had three children and ten grandchildren, most of whom live in a nearby city he showed them on his phone, the map so magnified it could have been anywhere. When he relayed a few questions about the Yaos, Mrs. Yao demanded, "Why does he care where we come from?"

"Please just tell him," Dennis said, "so I can get back to coaching."

Now Mrs. Yao returned Aleks's wave and vigorously shook her head. Her husband lowered a finger toward the knight icon, then hissed through his front teeth; he was shaking too much. Mrs. Yao tapped the piece into place and handed him a fresh bottle of water. It was crucial to stay hydrated, even while sitting and playing chess.

The rest of the players tossed their duffels down around the Yaos. A quartet of middle-aged men, former Chinese or European players all (how were there so many, and how had they all come here?), broke away to lap the practice hall, muscles tessellating their conical thighs, chatting and grinning and tossing their heads like vapid teenagers. They would spend the night destroying each other on the middle tables. In a loose cluster at the end of the bleachers, the real teenagers, who reigned on top tables, performed uneasy dances of allegiance and rivalry, emotions ringing clearly in their voices as if spelled for the Yaos in foot-tall Chinese characters.

At 6:59, Dennis, his son, and a new boy took their place before the bleachers for pre-match announcements. Always exhortations to play well, sometimes pointed comments about misbehavior clearly meant for the teens. (Dennis persisted in speaking bilingually on the Yaos' behalf, despite their boycott of practice.) He introduced the new boy as his assistant, Ryan, who had just returned from competing in the German leagues. "We're very lucky to have him here to share his insights," Dennis said, smiling so widely and tightly Mrs. Yao would have bet the tablet he nursed some grudge.

His son, on the other hand, looked thrilled, breaking his blank, shy stare to grin at his colleague. Friends, maybe even lovers; that could have accounted for Dennis's disgruntlement. Mr. Yao would have been happy to work alongside any of the nice young men their daughter discarded over the years. Ryan waved, head modestly bowed, ear studs sizzling in the harsh fluorescent light, then retired to the coach's corner by the water fountain, from which the Ouyangs watched and emerged to give pointers.

As the other players sorted themselves onto tables and, at table six, set paddle cases along the table frame to mark a place in line, the Yaos advanced their pawn to B4.

"Granny, Gramps, you need help with anything?" The new boy had ventured into their plebeian quarter and climbed their bleacher. He eyed the tablet skeptically.

"No thanks, young man," said Mrs. Yao. "Unless you know chess?"

Turning his head to take in the board, Ryan stood too close. As an athlete he was probably used to that—pushing up shoulder to shoulder, having your form corrected and muscles massaged, showering in a big room with your privates flopping, but especially since moving into the home, Mrs. Yao prized her space above all, and shuddered as she smelled the grease along the dense part of his hair. If he were her grandson, she'd have cut it for him.

"Sorry," he said, and stepped back. She hadn't expected him to notice; had not, of late, expected anyone but Mr. Yao to notice anything about her. Even when she stood in their paths, the nursing home caretakers nearly ran her down with their carts of food and linens.

"You could move your bishop here," Ryan said, and tapped. The bishop moved. "Oh, oops. Sorry."

"Good move," Mr. Yao said.

Ryan looked guiltily to Mrs. Yao. "Sorry I moved for you."

"What n-next?"

Mrs. Yao tolerated his presence until the end of the game. With Ryan's help, they won; or rather, Ryan won. Mr. Yao was ecstatic. Mrs. Yao wished he would have a little integrity, find it within himself to protest their first recorded win belonging to someone else.

"All right, all right," she said. "Ryan needs to go coach."

"I'll watch your matches," Ryan said. "You're waiting for this table?"

"W-we're not," Mr. Yao said as Mrs. Yao nodded.

"Why not?"

"We don't . . . play."

"What?" He looked between them, bewildered. Mr. Yao smiled radiantly and shrugged.

"We're here to pass time. Our daughter in . . . s-sisted."

Don't tell him! Mrs. Yao wanted to scream. Ryan did not seem to be under Dennis's thumb, as Denny Junior was. He might tell their daughter, who would then yank them away for gardening or cycling, or some other horrendous activity advertised on the nursing home bulletin.

"If you have to be here," Ryan said, "you might as well try it."

Dennis, tactless coward that he was, declined to meet Mrs. Yao's imploring glare across the courts. Before she could formulate a compelling excuse, Ryan guided her husband down to the floor. She could only follow and pull him aside admonish, while Mr. Yao caught his breath on the lowest bleacher: "Listen, young man, we really can't play. It will be humiliating, not fun. You understand the word *humiliating*?"

"Aleks will be nice to you."

"That's even worse."

"I thought Mr. Yao wanted to."

"He wants to humor you. Usually it's just the two of us, so when a nice young man invites him to play, he'll accept, though we'll see if he can get up. If he does, it'll only be because of you, and he'll be obliged to stand there and suffer until it's over. It's just like for our daughter, you know—we come so she'll feel okay about herself."

"I'm sorry it's like that. I don't need anything from you."

"That's nothing you *can* feel sorry for. The point is—"

But it was too late. Mr. Yao was standing in the court, jaw juddering, one hand gripping the table's sharp edge for balance. Mrs. Yao rushed back up the bleachers to retrieve his paddle. The boy watched from a corner of the court. He would see.

"Start," Aleks announced in loopy Mandarin. He must have made Dennis teach him.

"Start?" Mr. Yao echoed. "Start!"

"Start!"

"Hahaha! Start!" Mr. Yao raised the ball, tossed it, and swung his paddle through nothing. The ball was on the floor. Aleks batted the air, *no problem*, and jogged around the table to hand him another ball. Mr. Yao tried again. Again the ball dropped untouched.

"There are more over here, love," Mrs. Yao said, "I'll get them," but her husband crooked at the waist and began a painstaking descent. The two waiting players, six-year-old boys, watched horrified. Aleks held an admirably neutral smile. It took Mr. Yao a minute to pick up the ball, and four more tries to get it across the net in a semblance of a serve. Aleks lofted it back, so high and slow it seemed to rest mid-air. Across the other courts, players leapt, struck, shouted; hands were shaken and backs clapped; legs swung over barriers, carrying losers downward and victors up. Aleks and Mr. Yao managed eleven points before the latter, shaking and sweat-drenched, called for his wife.

"Not terrible, eh?" he panted as she wove an arm around his torso.

"Not bad, my dear, though you're not exactly Wang Liqin."

"But I *played*," Mr. Yao said. His fingers clawed her rib cage. Sometimes he underestimated his strength; she gritted her teeth and lowered him to the bleacher.

"You did," Ryan said. "It was great. You want a turn, Granny?"

"No," Mrs. Yao said. "I'm used to Dennis leaving us alone."

"He shouldn't," the boy said, triumphantly, as if he'd caught his boss stealing from the charity jar. The affliction of the younger generation: wanting to usurp, overtake, defeat. Their daughter, too, which was why she spent all her time at work. As if there was an Olympics of divorce court out there, waiting for her to storm it. Ryan leapt the barriers, sprinted down the hall, and rolled a caddy of balls from Dennis's court.

Mr. Yao pinched her ribs again, gently this time. "Wh-why you don't just try . . ."

They'd start with forehands, Ryan declared. Mrs. Yao sighed and squared up in what she knew was a poor imitation of better players. In their thin new table tennis shoes, her feet felt stiff, treacherous.

"Relax your shoulder," Ryan said. "Your elbow. Your wrist. Now hold it straight. Okay. Turn your waist right to left. Bring your paddle to your left eye." To demonstrate, he hit an arcing shot that blazed millimeters from the net and onto the backhand corner.

She swung and struck her forehead.

"Ouch! Are you okay?"

Black spots fizzled in the left half of her vision. "How'd it look?" she asked.

"Good . . . just stop next time."

"Next you'll tell me to breathe!"

He smiled and served. She swung and missed. The next ball clicked off the paddle's wooden edge. The next made contact, ringing up through her elbow. She'd remember that feeling, eight months later, when the plane took off for Ryan's funeral: it was the sudden weightlessness, the influx of morning light along the cylindrical cabin, the bright pink Pacific swooped into a dozen shapes as they homed in on Ryan's native peninsula. She'd weep hysterically in her aisle seat, hand hovered trembling above her face, as other passengers hefted their bags and pretended not to look.

"Better," Ryan said, "keep your shoulder down . . . aim for your eye . . . better, but look where you want the ball to go . . . okay, one second."

He came around the table and took her wrist between two fingers. "And then just . . ." One hand braced her left shoulder. The other guided her arm. It felt right. When they had trained with Dennis and Denny on their first night, both men seemed trapped behind the net, helplessly repeating instructions which, while similar to Ryan's, lost their meaning through the thickening haze of frustration. She repeated the motion; repeated it again as a ball flew toward her. It landed on the table.

"Hey! A natural!"

"I'm Liu Guoliang!" Mrs. Yao crowed. "No—I'm Liu Guoliang's daddy!"

"No," her husband shouted, "you're Liu Guoliang's g-great-great-granddaddy!"

Ryan surprised them by knowing who Liu Guoliang was, and laughing so hard he doubled over and couldn't serve properly. *Cho!* he taught her to shout after good shots, an exhortation she had heard on TV but never understood.

Ten minutes later, caddy emptied, she felt light and clean, ringing from pelvis to windpipe. Ryan unscrewed the lid of his water bottle so she could sip from the untainted rim.

"You are a better teacher than Dennis," she conceded.

"Thanks, Granny."

"Aren't there better places to coach?" She thought of their drive from Chicago to this town: Mr. Yao, exhausted, had slumped onto her shoulder, leaving her alone to contemplate the sky and cornfields and silos awash in what she considered American light, thin icy blue. Nothing like the Red Beach of Panjin, where, during a tour, they had seen broad tidal curls of crimson seepweed tinted green in the glaucous pre-dawn.

"Denny's an old friend. They gave me this job on short notice. Ready for backhand?"

For two more caddies, Mrs. Yao forgot to worry about her husband, to dread their return to the nursing home with its diseased yellow windows and hulking front desk nurse, its erasure of the past; because only energetic young people could resurrect the house of youth and strength around her, the buzzing of muscles unconjurable by memory, no matter how vivid or tender. She had once been like him, and he would one day be like her, and across these hypotheticals they met; right now, that was wonder enough to live on. She sweated and puffed unbecomingly, but what did that matter as she cheekily hit a ball down the line. During breaks she posed like Arnold Schwarzenegger, fists up. She posed like a CCP dignitary, arms stiff at her side. "I am dictator of the People's Republic of Table Tennis," she droned. She was Wang Liqin and Kong Linghui, Deng Yaping and all her ancestors. The advanced players hit furiously, some shouting on each strike, *Ha! ha!* like Shaolin monks, and she slammed the final ball into Ryan's body, flexed her biceps, and threw a domineering leg up on the bleacher beside her husband and Aleks, both applauding over their abandoned game of chess.

•

Still, the end had to come. Duffels and jackets were unzipped. Balls were scooped into minnow nets and sealed in Tupperware bins. Before heading out, Aleks curled Mrs. Yao's fingers into a fist and bumped his knuckles against hers. It would be a long time before she felt any desire to compete, but they could, at least, participate in the next practice.

"A good night," she declared. Their daughter had texted that she would be fifteen minutes late; her work event had run long. It gave Mrs. Yao time to properly thank Ryan, who, after helping pack the balls and straighten the barriers, stood with Dennis and his son in the coach's corner once more. Maybe they could even ask him for a ride home. Last week Dennis had offered, but he hadn't meant it. If Ryan said he was glad to, he'd mean it.

She gave Mr. Yao her arm and they shuffled across the hall.

Even in English, she could tell Dennis was berating Ryan. "No," he snarled again and again, the syllable of fellow nursing home residents denied exit at the doors, deprived of culinary pleasures in the cafeteria, the door of quotidian pain slammed in their faces. Dennis's son looked at his feet, hands clasped behind his back. A pacifist, evidently, a different kind of young man than Ryan, whose tensed neck signaled dissent even as he nodded.

"Is there a problem?" Mrs. Yao asked. Against her shoulder, her husband suddenly sagged with all his weight. He buried his face in the loose fabric of her jacket, a sign he felt more ravaged than he thought she could bear to see. Their daughter would reproach them for overdoing it. Anticipating this, imagining the exact phrases that would spike the black interior of the car as their daughter shuttled them through the starless night, turning at every red light to fire accusations more directly at her mother, Mrs. Yao felt her own limbs leaden and dread narrow her vision.

"No no," Dennis said, "I heard Ryan did a good job with you tonight."

"What was he saying to you?" Mrs. Yao demanded. She wanted to reach up and cradle Ryan's face, but her left arm was trapped beneath her husband. She made do with a hand on his shoulder. "Don't let anyone talk to you like that!"

"Granny," Ryan said, "it's all fine, don't worry about me," but as he reciprocated her gesture, resting a hand on her free shoulder, she saw tears in his eyes.

2017

DENNIS AND DENNIS

Dennis Ouyang Senior is dogged by fear. At least once a week since he left Hong Kong in his twenties, he has sat up in the night shouting. Sometimes for a relative, sometimes for a student; sometimes for someone he has not thought about in decades. Once he dreamt of his sixth-grade math teacher, a balding ginger Jesuit, falling into a construction hole, and awoke muttering the morning offering. *Prayers, works, joys, and sufferings* . . .

These dreams have led Dennis to believe he is fated to suffer immense loss. The astrologer he consulted implied it was residual pain from his divorce, but something so simple and obvious could not, Dennis believes, hold such sway over him. The divorce was as smooth as could be, and Dennis Junior chose quite easily to stay with his father. Now his mother has a family in Arizona and Junior visits them whenever he wants—which is, to Senior's gratification, never.

Some people say there's no point dealing in premonitions. Things happen or they don't. Dennis thinks you should exercise your utmost power to prevent the dreaded outcome. His house is organized and his work airtight. He follows his weekly training regimen to the last rep, and it's kept him strong and limber for thirty years. He helps anyone he can: the children whose harried parents don't know the club from a daycare and whom Dennis has stayed late many times to watch. The elderly couple sent against their will to a nursing home, who need a ride to the club every Tuesday and Thursday. The quiet high schooler Dennis eventually referred to a psychologist.

As far as he knows, as the person to whom Junior tells everything, no such fears plague his son. Maybe the curse is for Senior alone. Maybe, with his easier life, Junior is deaf to its nighttime warnings. Or maybe it's lulling them into complacency, winding up to strike one generation below. So when Junior asked to hire his old rival, Ryan Lo, a request at first galling (didn't Junior have self-respect?) but then auspicious in its generosity, and only slightly sweetened by schadenfreude (Ryan made it to the German league, as Junior never managed to, but didn't get to stay; went on to be the subject of a frankly humiliating, self-aggrandizing film, and was then dismissed from some dubious celebrity endeavor), Dennis agreed. Good karma never hurt.

Ryan arrives a few days after New Year's with three suitcases, which to Dennis seems excessive. He says to leave them in the upstairs den. "Maybe you boys can hang out there," he said. "Have some boy time."

"For sure," Ryan says. "*Boy time.*"

Behind Dennis, Junior stiffens. It's beginning, the self-consciousness, the degradation of self-worth only peers can inflict.

Senior pushes on: here are the guest mugs and glasses, the windows to keep shut, the days of the week to roll out the bins. He assigns Ryan the sparkly blue Donald Duck slippers, origin unknown (they'd never had the time or inclination for Disney World), rubber still gummy, seams scabrous. Ryan jams his feet in and strikes a bodybuilder's pose.

"Quack quack," he says to Denny. The boys laugh. Ryan buoys Denny in a way his father could never. Only natural, Dennis tells himself, only natural for young men.

He drives them to the club, where they'll start coaching in a few hours. When Senior retires, or dies, the club, along with the house and cars, go to Denny. They have it planned out, almost too well:

between seven days of coaching, fifty students, and seventy registered league players, there's no time for either Dennis to relax or properly train. Denny explains their scheduling app, all the surveys and calendar-syncing.

"You guys have done a sick job," Ryan dares say, as if they need to hear it from someone who—according to Kristian, who Dennis saw at Nationals last month and, in a rare show of personability, permitted Dennis to commiserate about his star pupil's decline—showed up drunk to work. He even flashes a thumbs-up from the passenger's seat. It's a demerit that he took shotgun from Junior.

They park in Dennis's reserved spot, shady all day during summer, buffered from sleet and snow now. Around them, extra flat beneath the featureless overcast, sprawls the town's largest strip mall. Dennis explains the facilities and Ryan nods before his sentences conclude. "Yeah yeah," he chuffs, "got it." Admittedly, there's not much besides matching keys to doors and learning to wiggle the toilet handle in the dank restroom, but it's Ryan's general impatience that irks Dennis, from the way he kicks at a rough patch on the floor to the way he lurches into a jog when walking would do. He's trapped because he's impatient, and vice versa. Unlike Junior, who is freed by his rootedness, his faith in inexorable, incremental progress. Junior takes the time to straighten crooked barriers and press down the loose corners of floor mats, which means he can take the time to pursue a ball past the corners of the table, to wait for a perfect attack. He may never go to Europe as a young star, but he will never have to come crawling home, either.

Ryan asks Junior to play. Ryan's game has gone off-kilter, strokes terse and shots heavy with a force he struggles to handle. Dennis lets them go until the first truly wild hit, a forehand for which Ryan runs through the barriers, knocking them across the concrete aisle. Then he says, "Better prepare for the students." His son relaxes and leaves the court. Ryan lingers, toeing the ground, hands curled into loose fists.

"Ball's slow in here," he says. He grabs a handful of shirt and scrubs at his collarbone. Not even an hour in and he's sopping wet, edging toward frantic. Dennis watched a few of his matches in the Bundesliga—that was his problem there, too.

"That's a Dragonfly two-star. It plays the same everywhere."

From the bleachers, Junior says, "It's the heating. We'll turn it off before training."

Ryan grins and shouts back, "The authentic experience!" The boys reminisce about some freezing warehouse in New Jersey, but Ryan grew up in the nicest club in the United States, state-of-the-art climate control and weight rooms. Even reticent Kristian nodded when Dennis declaimed, "And he has no excuse, he had every advantage with you!" Now Dennis dabs his brow with his quartered towel and wonders what possessed him to bring this upon himself. A bid for moral superiority over Kristian, perhaps. He should have known better.

●

Four days into Ryan's stay, groggily washing his face in the morning, Denny knocks Ryan's medicine bottles off the sink. Crouched on the tiles, sorting the scattered pills, he googles: antianxiety, antidepressant, painkiller. One disconcerting side effect of living with Ryan is the constant threat of seeing his flaws, his fallibility, the tics of just another dude in his twenties; and the possibility that some such tic will detonate between them. It's a hypothetical detonation, hypothetically blowing up the hypothetical grudge many (including Denny's father) assume Denny holds toward the guy who's beaten him in twenty-three of thirty-two career face-offs. Denny doesn't *feel* a grudge—he just doesn't think he's above basic human psychology. Thinking yourself above anything sends Senior into a foaming frenzy.

He reminds himself to tell Ryan, tactfully, that he should store his meds on their designated shelf. His father rarely uses this bathroom, but would hate a cluttered sink. Dennis Senior has already berated Ryan for cursing in front of the students, for letting them horseplay during breaks, and for wearing his permed shoulder-length hair loose beneath a pink headband. Ryan has also replaced the trash bag incorrectly (Denny caught and fixed this before his dad saw) and stayed up too late watching dating shows on the downstairs TV. After every reprimand, Ryan does as Dennis Senior asks. Yesterday, he trimmed his hair. Today is their first day off, and anticipating Dennis's low tolerance for adventure, Ryan downgraded their plans from a day trip to Chicago to lunch.

At the sushi restaurant Ryan found online, despite Denny's disclaimers about the low quality of local seafood (based not on his own standards, but on anticipation of Ryan's), Ryan says, "Respectfully, my guy, you're a martyr. I didn't realize you lived with General fucking Petraeus."

"You know martyrs are already dead," Denny says.

Ryan laughs and lowers the plumpest nigiri onto Denny's plate. Over Denny's protests, he ordered a party boat and a carafe of sake. "My old man's Type A, too. I admire your patience."

"Uh-huh."

"No, really."

Ryan drinks more than half the sake, one mouthful of which washes down a gray pill; turns the carafe upside down to shake out the last drops. Denny tries to relax. Not sloppy or undue ease, but receptive to what's next, broadly and graciously prepared. As kids, when Ryan was around, people stopped calling Denny daddy's boy. When he parroted Dennis's training tips, they actually tried them. When Ryan invited him to play an exhibition at a fancy club in New York, Denny, comfortable beneath the arm Ryan slung across his shoulders, spoke to the celebrity owners as casually as to the cashiers at the Asian grocery.

In Ryan's car, Denny smokes a blunt he's saved for months, wind whisking every curl of smoke up into the thin white sky. Ryan abstains, demurring, "One drug at a time."

"Man," Denny says, "it's good to have you here. This place gets boring as fuck." He feels himself resuming his young man's patois, like putting on cologne-doused party clothes. His last girlfriend didn't want to live in Indiana. Five months in, she left for Seattle. Senior had prophesied that she wasn't the one, and for a full twelve hours after the breakup Denny wouldn't speak to him. But then they had to teach, and Senior was waiting by the car like always. Like always, they reviewed coaching plans while Senior made his four decelerated hand-over-hand turns. ("My dad scored a hundred on the driving test," Denny once told a group of peers, to scathing laughter.) As consolation and apology, his dad took his chores for a month.

"Been dating since?" Ryan asks.

"No one to date."

"Apps?"

". . . I don't get matches."

Ryan extends a hand. Wasabi streaks the pad of his thumb. "Let's fix that."

"I don't need—"

"C'moooon."

They rewrite Denny's bio and extend his radius to include Chicago.

"Hey, so," Ryan says, handing back the phone, "I was gonna ask—Anabel's planning to visit. Next month. If that's all right with your dad. And you."

"Oh," Denny says, "for sure."

"Don't sound too excited."

"I just thought, maybe you guys broke up? Since you moved."

"Oh. Nah. She won't leave Gao's and we've always been long distance. I just wanted to, I dunno, do something on my own. Learn something new." Which is a little silly, Denny doesn't say, because just as his job with Gao was only possible through Anabel, this gig was only possible through him.

"Ever think of starting your own club?" Ryan asks.

"Uh, why?"

Ryan leans back and props his arms expansively behind his head. "Maybe we could do one, if your old man will let me in on the secret."

"What about that place in New York?"

"Didn't know what they were doing."

From what his father said, it was Ryan who didn't know what to do. Partying, getting too friendly with the owners, even (most scandalously to Senior) "chasing the spotlight" in that documentary, for which Denny happily interviewed. He has no desire for anything like that, nor a club of his own. But a desire to feel how Ryan looks when he says Anabel's name keeps him swiping, through monosyllabic replies and baffling biographies. Next time they get sushi, Ryan photographs Denny with the sake glass at his lips. He vets Denny's messages. A week later, they secure a date.

•

You must, Dennis knows, expect changes in your child. Most parents err in expecting to see forever, through accumulating mannerisms and flesh, the kid they first drove to kindergarten. Dennis Senior hears the echoing sorrow of such mistakes when parents pick up their children and cannot fathom reports that they have not tried hard in practice or belittled other children; or, conversely, that they are at the top of their age group, hardy and willing to suffer.

Ironically, Dennis has seen only sameness in his son. Junior has always been mulish—persevering, set in a dumb straight line. He has always been kind, too, which requires selective ignorance. In his father's quibbles with Ryan, Junior initially adopts a stooge-ish neutrality, tiptoeing past the room where Dennis Senior delivers his reproach; or, if he must be present, as during the expletive incident, staring at the wall with static behind his eyes. He's done similarly when Dennis needed to dress down umpires for bad calls or other parents for unsportsmanlike conduct.

Sometime after the first month, though, Junior's words and movement acquire an unnatural velocity. He plods across the room then nearly hops the threshold. *Forsure*, he blurs, instead of *Ohkaaay* or *Alll right*. He crumples the kitchen towels, fingers flexing violently. An edge absorbed from Ryan's game, though off the court Ryan still moves, mostly, with the deliberation of the good-looking and desired, apparent at any speed. (When Dennis catches him in the other moments—slurping from a takeout trough at the crack of dawn, eyes pink and ratty mustache hairs dangling crumbs of dry skin; swilling beers on the couch and burping explosively when Junior is gone and he thinks Dennis can't hear from upstairs; balancing on his "bad leg" in the entryway after removing his shoes, arms outflung like a kid playing airplane, mouth agape with idiot hope that it will feel good as new; crying to someone over the phone, or in the bathroom with the faucet on, probably mourning his descent in the world, though within hours he is imperturbable once more—he cannot help but savor it.)

Then there's the dating. At any and every hour on Junior's days off, he drives to meet girls from the internet. The first time, at 1:00 P.M. on a Saturday, Junior simply catches Dennis's eye as he's lacing his shoes and says, "Oh, I'm going on a date." They're meeting forty minutes away to play mini golf. Dennis Senior can only say, "All right." In return for Junior's transparency, he maintains a mild temper, an assumption of best intentions. The two times it has backfired—Junior stranded at the Havana airport because a college friend angered the visa officer; Junior violently ill after doing drugs out of a whipped cream canister—his son begged forgiveness with a self-aware remorse most parents only dream of.

Junior returns from the first date unscathed, if glum and unforthcoming. He describes the woman as "nice, kinda air-headed," before thumping up the stairs to Ryan. It's unbecoming to pass judgment, Dennis thinks, and to ascend the stairs so fast the soles of your feet part from the earth.

Ryan's hooting laugh ricochets down the stairwell. To keep from eavesdropping, Dennis forces himself on a nighttime walk, though it requires stuffing his feet into two pairs of wool socks and his head into a balaclava. They walked all the time when Junior was sixteen, his year of yips. The looping figure eight of a planned suburb, the levitating orbs of porch lights and crunch of gravel beneath tires, drained the tension lap by lap from his broadening frame. Near the end of their ten laps, Dennis Senior always pressed a palm between his son's shoulder blades, like burping an infant, prepared but never called to endure the stiffening of rejection. Now the loop takes him past the lighted window of his den, where the boys have begun to watch basketball on the monitors and play music from the speakers which Dennis bought on clearance and sat unused until Ryan came.

The dates increase in frequency. If Dennis asks, his son still concedes details: a nurse, a librarian, a music therapist for children. The way he says it suggests putting pearls before swine.

Ryan adapts irreproachably to Dennis's coaching style. It feels taunting. He says aloud rules that Dennis expects students to follow by habit. When they lie down in the bleachers or track water down the aisles in their outdoor shoes, he tsks at them, snapping fingers and barking, "Hey! Don't." Discipline is not about the rules, but rather their invisible effect. To expose the scaffolding of his philosophy is to challenge it. It's like everyone seeing an x-ray of Dennis's bowels, like the skeleton jumpsuit Junior wore every Halloween until the crotch seam ripped and they upgraded him, for a single high school party, to Darth Vader. But Dennis cannot formulate an authoritative, ego-free way to deliver such feedback. "Don't say the rules"? "Don't be so clear"? Several times, he mentions the walls of nails behind tables in Chinese training centers: "The coaches never have to *tell* them to stay close to the table."

The students like Ryan, too, except for a surly twelve-year-old who has set himself against everything. Having never shown much deference before, the kid begins to gravitate toward Senior during downtimes. Watching Ryan and Junior exchange jubilant rallies during water break, he clenches a fist and scoffs, "Show-off."

"What do you mean?" Dennis must reply, in a sage tone.

The kid huffs, disappointed, and jabs a hand toward the offender. His fingers are locked and quivering.

"You'll do that, too, someday," Dennis replies, a lie that sends the boy skulking away. But for the rest of the session, he tries harder, despite his scowl.

A few days later, Ryan approaches this boy and says, with the ease of a seasoned coach: "Let the ball breathe. Make friends. Let it come to you." It's phrased more casually than Dennis would think to, more wishy-washy. It's perfect and Dennis hates it.

But the weekly nightmares have ceased, and Junior's game has improved. A month into Ryan's stay, the boys begin to talk of driving to big tournaments. In two months, Dennis will host their club's semiannual tournament. Ryan has only competed once since returning from Germany and in practice appears evenly matched with Junior, Junior steadier as always. After Denny beats him, Dennis finds himself thinking, the groundswell of unwanted changes will dissipate.

•

The front walk bites Denny's kneecaps. It seems too spiky. His dad repoured it just last spring.

Ryan's arms circle Denny's waist and hoist. "Wrecked, buddy," his friend says. "How much'd you have?"

"'Twas fun," Denny slurs as his feet bump over the threshold. Ryan peels off his beanie, coat, scarf, boots ("Yech, my man, you need foot spray"), and supports him up the stairs. His breath smells, too, herby gin to Denny's whiskey. Light shines beneath Senior's door. Ryan sees Denny looking and says, "Don't worry about him. But no more nurses, okay?" He shoves Denny onto his bed, tosses the duvet over him, and turns off the light.

It's Denny's eleventh first date in two months. They keep track in a shared document: occupation, key information, vibe; second date potential? Other information, stored only in jokes and the recesses of Denny's mind: The librarian said she didn't like to read. The anesthesiology resident fell asleep on the bar.

Denny is having fun. He's having the most fun outside table tennis in years, since he was a kid and simply existing was fun; maybe ever. He's ostensibly having more fun than Ryan, even, who never seems to go out, whose main outlet seems to have become table tennis. It was never like this before. At tournaments, Ryan tried to sneak drinks in Vegas casinos, escape onto the street outside the convention centers, run off to meet Anabel. Now he wants to play on their off days. And though Denny should relish becoming the fun one, he still suspects he's missed something—that if Ryan doesn't want to do something, it's not worth wanting, even if Ryan encourages him, even if it's the path to something like what Ryan so cherishes: his relationship.

Ryan usually calls Anabel outside, kicking sprays of ice from snowdrifts when they pile up along the curbs, but the few calls he takes in the house, Denny overhears:

"Yeah, no, if I just think about my wrist—don't worry, I *am* resting. Are *you* resting? Why? Oh, I see. Yeah, it's midlife crisis season. Could you take her to Florida? Yeah, fine. Santa Monica. Ibiza!

"Nah, you have enough money.

"No, we only charge forty.

"Fuck off. No"—laughing—"seriously, fuck off, Bel."

It would be nice to be with someone who played table tennis, or at least understood. Denny looks for former college athletes and sports-related photos. "I like caveman types," said the ex-lacrosse player, hugging Denny goodbye, "so see ya never." The woman who played ultimate frisbee was weirdly into Asian stuff. The Chinese American golfer was repulsed by table tennis because it was *too* Asian. He's supposed to be himself, Denny knows. Ryan graciously disclaims: "Not that I know what I'm really talking about, man, I've really only dated one chick." But Denny sometimes slips and tells a date something he thinks Ryan would say, knowing that he said it because of that. Even more disturbing, as it surfaces through the rising dark tide of sleep, is the idea that it may not be what Ryan would say; that Denny's understanding outdates itself day by day; that he will never catch up.

Three days after the nurse date, Anabel arrives. Right away, she's sharper with Denny than when he saw her in New York last fall. "Hello, Denny, nope, I'll carry my own suitcase." At dinner, the four of them around a table of classic Chinese entrées prepared by Ryan (who only allowed Denny to rinse pans), she says: "You guys should come train for the summer."

"Sounds nice," Denny says.

She turns to Ryan. "Do you think so, too?"

"We'll have to sort our schedule," Dennis Senior says.

"When was the last time you went out of state, Denny?" Anabel asks.

"Last weekend," Denny says. "Chicago. Date. Online date."

"Oh," she says, and Denny is disproportionately, possibly meanly, happy to have caught her off guard.

"We made him a Tinder," Ryan says.

"It'll be better in the tristate area."

"He doesn't *have* to go anywhere."

"It's just an invitation. You guys could be roommates . . ."

"When was the last time *you* left Jersey?"

Turning squarely toward Denny, Anabel asks, "Has he mentioned any plans to you, Denny? Anything besides hanging out here?"

"Bel," Ryan says. "Leave him out of it."

"We'll sort our schedule," Senior says, "and, you know, it should"—he glances at Denny—"permit a week or two away."

Anabel and Ryan stay in a hotel ten minutes away and attend every practice. All week, Ryan seems happier. Even when he slumps into a chair in the crappy office, plants his face in his hands, and groans, "Dude, it is not going well," he seems happier: more talkative with students, faster at the table, quietly on fire. The students listen attentively to Anabel, though with a wider range of attitudes than toward Ryan, for whom they developed an immediate fondness, or his father, whose self-seriousness demands an amused but ultimately effective obedience. Arrayed before this reedy-voiced new coach, who makes no particular demands as to how they stand or talk, and herself stands awkwardly straight-armed with hands flattened atop her thighs, they either fall into slack-jawed hypnosis or seethe with confusion about the authority she exudes. There's an analogous incongruity in her playing, which Denny can only later trace to the fissured nature of that moment in their lives, beyond the court yet obscured by the court's predominance: her form (like his, Denny must admit) has fossilized with time and a lack of training she brusquely bemoans, the strokes' characteristic punch a rush, the bold simple set-ups a monotony. This unexpected, unflattering mirroring of himself saddens Denny; in the spirit of his father's teaching he tries to convert his sorrow into motivation, taking over from Anabel and practicing with Ryan as long as they can stand.

Most jarringly, though, something betrays that Anabel no longer feels the same toward table tennis as Denny or Ryan. Neither her coaching nor playing lacks discipline, and when she makes unforced errors she hisses through her teeth, sharp gears of desire turning in her eyes, just like before. Maybe it is off the court—a dismissive slant to her shoulders as she surveys the club, an indifference as she steps across the threshold into the rhythmless, objectiveless sunlight.

At the club, in the last moments of training on her last day in town, Anabel catches Denny alone. As Ryan corrects the serve of a student across the hall, she comes up behind him, presses a chilly fingertip to his tricep, and says, "I'm sorry, Denny, this is going to put you in an awkward spot—or maybe there's a way for it not to, but I don't know how to ask that way—and I have to ask: Has he seen anyone else?"

"No," Denny says.

"Like. Romantically, I mean."

"No." The finger retracts.

"And you would tell me if he did."

"But why would he?"

"He cheated on me in the fall," Anabel says. Two clicks and an exhilarated laugh mark the student's first successful Tomahawk; the walls echo Ryan's high-five. "And no, I don't want to talk about it. Thanks."

On the walk out to their cars in the dark, Ryan and Anabel talk normally ahead of him. What Denny thought was normally. Maybe she used to talk more, but he attributed her reticence to tiredness, new responsibilities. The parking lot lights honey the rumpled arm of Ryan's coat over her shoulders, the part in her hair that goes dark beneath his kiss.

•

Ultimately, the girl is a distraction, even if Dennis Senior respects her game and considers her coach one of the best. Distraction to Ryan could be welcome, given the imminent tournament.

He also cannot help but think that Ryan would have fared better close to Anabel, as she so desperately wants, at least until he vanquishes whatever folly brought him home. It wouldn't be so bad if Junior found someone to depend on. His promise to let the boys leave over the summer is the first concession he's made in a while; for extracting that, he must admire Anabel.

Alone in his bedroom, he scrolls to the familiar timestamp in the documentary. "I was never out," Ryan said, smirking into the camera. Foolish boy! Then Anabel's hand descended onto his shoulder, nails colorlessly glossed, the shadows of tendons snaking up her forearm as she squeezed with a loving force Dennis suddenly wishes someone could apply to him.

●

Two days after Anabel leaves, Denny opens Ryan's bedroom door without knocking, a habit from living without secrets. Ryan, late to meet them at the car, sits cross-legged in bed, tissues piled in his lap. "Oh, fuck." He swallows, gurgling, and swipes a hand across his face. "Sorry, dude."

"Oh, no no. It's all good." Denny hesitates. "You coming?"

His friend clears his throat. A web of red splotches the upper half of his face. Salted white trails trisect his upper lip. "Yeah. Just need like. Twenty seconds."

"Do you wanna, um, talk . . . ?"

"No. I mean, maybe later, but, just." He taps his forehead. "My brain's eating itself." Denny touches his own head. "Not like, cancer. Ha. Sorry to scare you." Ryan shunts the tissues into the wire trash can under his nightstand. Dennis would have hated that he put it there, dirty emissions so close to his vulnerable sleeping lungs. "I went off my meds this week. I wanted to see Bel without them, you know, see how I 'really' felt. Which is so fucking dumb. I'm still me, blah blah blah." Ryan swings his feet to the ground. "Let's go before your dad loses it."

"Need anything?"

"Maybe an extra Gatorade . . ."

The pantry has been emptied of Gatorade. Senior, suspicious of artificial coloring, never restocks it. Denny hears Ryan's uneven staccato steps on the stairs and must brace himself against the counter before meeting him at the door.

"I'm so sorry," he says, stomach heavy and cold, "but we're out . . ."

"Oh. No worries, dude." Besides pinkness around his eyes, Ryan looks recovered. Denny releases an unconsciously held breath.

At the club, the Yaos need help regluing their rubber. Senior's with them, his craned neck telling Denny that he's nearly out of patience. To Denny and Ryan, he says, "We shouldn't do anything until Mrs. Yao is satisfied," meaning, *Practice starts in ten minutes and God help me if I'm gluing rubber then.*

Ryan volunteers. "Thank you," Mrs. Yao says, a space between the words suggesting she has not missed Senior's evasion. As he straightens the barrier and rolls the caddies into position, Denny watches Ryan squat on a bleacher, Mrs. Yao's blade laid on the row above, and chat with the couple as he swabs a tiny sponge across fresh rubber, fans it with the paper packaging until it's dried, and rolls rubber onto wood with his forearm. Mr. Yao remarks how strong he is. Mrs. Yao raises the paddle and marvels at the evenness. Ryan dusts off his hands. Mr. Yao gives him trembling thumbs-up, a smile laxening his gentle, liver-spotted face. It's more gratitude than Denny has seen the Yaos show his dad, though they comment that Denny is a "nice boy" whenever he drives them home. Denny knows it's a balm to help others when you feel hopeless, that that is one of the few times you can do good without ego. Ryan needs their gratitude more than him. And yet, he cannot dispel his stomachful of sour, sludgy resentment, which stems from jealousy, which stems from insecurity, which, according to his dad, stems from lies you tell yourself. Such lies as Ryan has apparently told, but Denny has not.

During the break, he sidles up to Mrs. Yao to ask about her vegetable garden, and then, so that she will hand it to him: "Ryan did a nice job on your racket."

"He's a very nice boy," Mrs. Yao says. Denny spots a single, irrelevant air bubble near the base. Denny's father glued his rackets until Denny left for college, at which point he played with bumpy rubber and crudely snipped edges until he learned better.

Denny tells himself: Ryan had no Ryan Senior to glue his rackets. Ryan is sad, far from home, disgraced in several ways. And miraculously, or boringly, that does the trick. He returns the racket to Mrs. Yao's expectant hands and she grips it tightly like she suspected ill will. Ryan approaches to beg a few rallies of Denny before training resumes. It's good he's here. Everything between the two of them has been settled. Denny's loss at the cadet team trials, which Ryan won off an edge but celebrated anyway. Denny's twenty-first birthday in Vegas, where he didn't stop other boys from feeding Denny an Irish car bomb. The moment Denny realized Ryan had left for Germany without texting any of them goodbye.

No matter his feelings, Denny cannot lay claim on anything else.

•

The morning of the tournament, their printer runs out of ink. The last round-robin draws bleed to gray, then nothing.

It was Junior's job to check their inventory: tournament-grade balls, pencils, clipboards, cotton-lined pill bottles. (Over the years, angry players have thrown an astounding number of clipboards, shattering pencil lead and dislodging the velcroed bottles.) Junior claimed to have done it, staying with Ryan after practice, but Dennis heard them come home late and rowdy. The garage door was left open.

Junior tells Dennis not to worry, they can handwrite brackets until Ryan gets cartridges, but it's the weekend and the office supply store doesn't open until eleven. The tournament starts at nine. Junior yawns and rubs his eyes with the heel of his palm, which Dennis taught him not to do because it destroys the corneas. He's playing the Under-25 round-robin at noon, the last match of which will be against Ryan; they are the two best players by a large margin.

Dennis snaps, "Do it, then," violating his parenting principles, and leaves his son with the printer, which coughs up hot, rancid paper crisscrossed by the names of people they've been hosting for a decade. The home tournaments always force Dennis to confront that he is not, at heart, a service-oriented man. When he cannot claim credit for the new maturity of a child, the new meaning in an elder's life, or at least money in his pocket to raise Junior, he seethes at petty responsibilities.

Still, he does everything he can.

They unlock the club at six thirty. Junior and Ryan set up the courts last night. Before arranging the tables and bulletin boards of his battle station, Dennis straightens every barrier, most of which conform to ninety-degree angles, and slams the few infracting ones for emphasis. The boys, conferring in the corner, Ryan sipping a can of an intestinally damaging energy drink, too-long hair sticking in all directions, are probably mocking his fastidiousness.

At eight fifteen, the Yaos call. They're playing Over-70, which starts at three, but their daughter can no longer drive them. It would mean so much, says Mrs. Yao, they've been looking forward to the tournament all month, and in the background Mr. Yao emits a wild despairing groan. Any time he can pick them up, Mrs. Yao says, they're ready to go, they don't mind waiting at the tournament. Their daughter bought them folding chairs for their balcony; they've yet to use them, but today's the perfect occasion. Dennis hears plastic thud against flimsy wood, Mrs. Yao hoisting the chair for emphasis.

He says he'll be there after the tournament starts. "I need to give opening statements," he says. Again, the speaking of the preferably unspoken. His need for recognition.

As the hours pass, Mrs. Yao texts him, a skill she has not previously exhibited. She sends their address, though he's driven there countless times, and the name of the nurse who will check them out. She is worried Dennis won't show up or will show up too late. In a haze of what he's loath to recognize as warranted anxiety—it's been a while since anything went haywire; of course Ryan is here to see it; or is it happening because of him somehow?—Dennis finishes assembling the tournament director station, plugs in his laptop, prepares the software to print new draws, clusters all the bulletin board tacks in the upper lefthand corner, greets the concession stand worker and umpire, swipes a finger along the farthest table to ensure Junior and Ryan wiped it down. At nine, he delivers the welcome address—four sentences, plus one to acknowledge Ryan's contribution to the club, whose members constitute a plurality of the tournament attendees—and distributes the first batch of clipboards. At ten-thirty, he distributes the second batch. People flag down Ryan for questions if he happens to be closer; he points them to Dennis. Dennis knows the resentment he feels toward these rerouted people, some of whom he's known for a decade, comes from an ignoble place—possibly, as Denny and Ryan's match approaches, from the long-festering wound of Denny's losses. 2004, a dozen of Ryan's Tomahawk serves looped into the net. 2007, Ryan's round-the-side forehand too quick for Denny's backhand to defend. 2009, two lucky edges to push Denny out of the national team. 2011, the year of yips, Ryan looking bored as he alternated backhand and forehand loops until Denny missed the predictable down-the-line finisher. 2012, a drop shot that winded Junior, who reached his highest weight that year. And just over three years ago, the last time they played, at the French tournament where a Bundesliga scout approached Ryan: an absurd switch-handed chop when Ryan was out of position, which Denny, surprised, let pop off his racket. It wouldn't have been Junior instead—Dennis couldn't spare Junior anyway, he told people—but it needn't have been Junior he beat, Junior's humbled head his final springboard to glory.

Around eleven, the onslaught of recollected defeats becomes unbearable, and Dennis goes to fetch the Yaos. Junior is in the bathroom, so Dennis can only wave Ryan over and ask him to keep the tournament afloat.

"Sure thing, Coach," Ryan says, and then, quite seriously: "Keep your ringer on."

He returns, an hour later, to the ambience of a smoothly proceeding tournament, punctuated by only shouts from Court One. It takes a moment to understand, through the suffocating mental grille of tournament logistics, that it is his son and Ryan, playing their match early. The scoreboard reads one set to zero, 6–4, Ryan ahead. Dennis thinks the score could be worse; silently snarls at the fact that was his first, kowtowing reaction.

"Oh . . . h-how thrilling," says Mr. Yao, still holding Dennis's arm. Now that Dennis has shown himself willing to help under extraordinary circumstances, the old man is more willing to display vulnerability. This should move Dennis, who will lean on his son's shoulder soon enough. He should be sitting in Junior's corner. Instead, there is a woman with a rhinestone butterfly clip in her hair, hands buried elbow-deep in the leather purse on her lap. She's texting, even as Junior barrels a foot from the barriers. The Yaos putter off to spectate. Dennis hides in the director's station and watches from between two monitors. Junior claws back the second set. In the third set, he forgets to avoid Ryan's mid-court backhand; Ryan flicks again and again down the line. He's beaten Junior this way at least a dozen times, and after every flubbed forehand Junior glances toward the girl. She looks up, but at Ryan, who's clicked into the level of performance that reasserts his dominance. He's waiting for the ball before its trajectory appears readable.

"Cho!" the boys begin to shout, "c'mon!" Junior misses and mimes smacking his forehand. Ryan misses and inspects his backhand rubber. *Please God*, Dennis finds himself thinking, *let him trip, let him fall. I'll do anything.* He stops looking at the scoreboard. He only knows Ryan has won when the boy falls to his knees in slow motion and joins his elbows to make the face from *The Scream*. Junior runs over and slaps the backs of Ryan's hands. Ryan grabs Junior's waist and bulldozes him back across the court.

They fall, laughing, below Butterfly Clip. She wobbles up onto narrow wedge heels and stumbles delicately to the barrier. Junior stands and performs intent listening, knitting his brows, nodding so deeply it bunches the skin beneath his jaw. Butterfly Clip talks at Junior, but her chest and gesturing hands point toward Ryan, seated and leaning into leg stretches. Denny does not notice; has eyes only for the deceiver they have welcomed into their home, who even now extends the deception by sticking out his tongue in a charade of camaraderie.

Dennis lets Junior approach at his own pace, which is leisurely: the boys chat with the umpire, who abandons professionalism and stands with thumbs looped in his belt, hip cocked to expose two inches of lemon-printed yellow sock. Junior smiles, even reenacts a few of Ryan's best shots. He scrubs his towel over his head, too hard, a dog shaking itself of rain. Leaving the court, he trips on a barrier, catches himself charmingly—or alarmingly, depending; the girl's posture doesn't say—on Butterfly Clip's forearm. She lets it stay there—humoring him, Dennis thinks. They migrate to the concession stand, where Junior buys her a hot dog to eat beside him in the bleachers, his knees nearly bumping his chest.

Ryan comes to Dennis first, holding their match clipboard and trailing the umpire. 11–9, 10–12, 15–13, 11–6. Junior gave up in the last set.

"D's improved," Ryan says. His face shines, but no sweat has broken through. His eyes flare huge and dark like a raccoon's. "A lot of oomph on that backhand serve."

The umpire claps Ryan's shoulder. "Didn't tell me this guy was gonna be here, Dennis."

Behind them, Junior and the woman are still talking. She dabs something off the hem of his white shorts. "Been here a few months," Dennis says.

It's good to see Ryan back on the circuit, the umpire says; is he playing the new Chicago tournament? There's big prize money.

"Couldn't keep me away," Ryan says. "Can I get that weekend off, Boss? I'll bring Denny with me. Quick boys' trip, you can hold down the fort. He's got a good fort, doesn't he, Kagin?"

His every rushed syllable pings painfully in Dennis's chest.

"One hundred percent," the ump says. "A good fort."

"Congratulations, son." Mrs. Yao hobbles up to the director's station and braces herself against the rickety table. "Dennis—could you fold up those chairs? We're blocking an aisle."

Dennis folds and moves the chairs. He scribbles names in brackets, fingers smushed around a Ticonderoga stub, and watches as Butterfly Clip flutters a silver-pedicured goodbye, as Denny hesitates then lunges for a single-armed hug. Halfway to the door, she flutters at Ryan, too, both hands. Dennis replugs the wheezing computer and decides that Ryan played underhandedly, soft shots, cowardly, nothing like how they've been practicing. Like a girl. No better than Anabel. It shouldn't count, even; except Dennis is the one who's reminded Junior, for twenty years, that every stroke you make, not to mention every point at a tournament, counts. "No," he tells an impatient player, "we pushed it back so the previous event can finish," and swallows thrice in quick succession, anger clotting his tonsils.

Ten minutes later, feeling himself sliding toward inefficacy, he goes outside to take a break. The weather has half-heartedly warmed, so that his gloved hands itch but his nose still runs. He stands in the back lot they never use. Instead of smoking, as he did briefly as a young man and has craved ever since, he swings his arms and bounces on the balls of his feet, humming. *The mystery of your presence, Lord, no mortal tongue can tell, whom all the world cannot contain comes in our hearts to dwell.*

He's about to go back when he sees the boy sidle around the building. He must have left through the side door. Still in his competition shoes—not to be worn outside, grippy rubber sensitive to dirt—he jogs to a sedan at the far end of the lot. His back blocks Dennis's view of the driver, but he can hear their laughter, and thinks he catches a metallic shimmer as a hand extends above the tinted window and returns Ryan's phone to him.

Printing brackets, distributing clipboards, answering questions, he doesn't get to speak with Junior until the tournament has ended and the players have left. Sitting in the station, watching the boys fold up bleachers, straighten barriers, and wipe down tables, he has to admit: he can barely wait. Once, Junior asked why they needed to clean the tournament tables at night and again in the morning, but then, as always, Dennis only needed to give him a second to contemplate, to see its lode-bearing place in the gruelingly assembled structure of their lives.

In the main lot, golden hour sunlight flooding the asphalt, Dennis can finally squint up at Junior and say, "Good match you boys had."

"Yes," Junior says. "It was fun."

"It was magic, man," Ryan says. He's squinting, too, and shielding his face. "Can't remember the last time I had fun at a tournament."

"Don't mock him," Dennis asks. The clot of anger thickens.

"Mock . . . ? No, man, I'm serious. I'm so fucking grateful—"

"Language!" Dennis barks.

"—so grateful to be here with you guys. I'm not mocking anything." Now there's sweat, an enragingly even lattice across the bridge of his nose.

"Oh, so, *so* grateful. I'm sure you're grateful to humiliate my son again."

"Dad, come on." Junior steps forward. "We were just having fun. It's not Nationals. We can play for fun. I mean, what else is there to do here?"

"Go on dates," Dennis says, "right?"

"I like it here," Ryan says.

"It's a hard adjustment," Junior presses on. "We live in bumfuck—sorry, the middle of nowhere, and he's had to deal with the crappy pharmacy to change his meds, and—"

"Was it the meds," Dennis says (and now he feels the full and awful force of his protective duty, the weight of an angel's adamantine blade swung high above his head), "that made you get that girl's number?"

Denny begins, "I invited her—"

"I'm talking to Ryan. He had separate business with the young woman. In the parking lot, after your match. Care to explain, Assistant Coach Lo?"

Ryan stares at the tops of his sneakers, which, since moving into their house, he's polished every weekend. Several times as Dennis passed him in the kitchen, he saw the soiled soles held a mere inch from the freshly wiped counter. He held in his reprimands. He had to trust the boy, he told himself. He was obviously trying. Now it's obvious he risks meeting the fate he most fears: becoming a sentimental old fool.

"Can we just go home and talk?" Denny says. He still believes in the power of calm conversation. He was raised well.

Prayers, works, joys, and sufferings. Dreams are dreams. Dennis's life is still his to dictate. He will recommend the boy to another club. But—he finds himself shamefully relieved to have an excuse to conclude—he can't stay.

●

It *was* a fun match. Ryan proposed they start early, since their opponents defaulted. It didn't matter who won, Denny reminded himself in the bathroom as he shat a habitual nervous shit. It didn't matter what happened. It didn't matter when they played—he could do it now, or in an hour, or in two days, because he was not nervous. Not even with his date there, no. It was never acceptable to let nerves hamper you. The more nervous he appeared, the more his dad prodded at, if not exactly bullied, him. He summoned Senior's voice: "Are you defusing a bomb? Doing brain surgery? So what's the problem?"

More than that, it was Ryan's vacant stare, exposed to the hall when it should have been private, that led Denny to start with a trick serve. Ryan pushed it into the net. "Hell yeah," Denny said, and pumped his fist. "*Cho*, fucker."

Ryan laughed. "I'll get you," he said, and jumped in place, exaggeratedly high.

He had never seen his friend so unexcited before a match; just like, until a month ago, he had never seen him cry. It was a new era. Ryan needed his help.

They relaxed into a loose, if not quite silly, match, chop blocks and lobs, stuck-out tongues and feints, and while Denny could not have said with full honesty (the only kind of honesty, Senior says) that he threw the match, he did feel, for the first time, that the outcome did not matter, that he would recover within days or even hours, that he might not even add it to their lifelong match record and, if he did, only in the interest of integrity. He didn't even notice his father had returned until the Yaos, on the sideline, began clapping for them both.

Ryan had suggested Denny invite his date to the tournament. Denny had driven all the way to Chicago to see Shedd Aquarium with her. The shouts of children and murmured discontents of adults reminded him of the table tennis club. The date asked whether everything reminded him of the club, which seemed to impress Ryan. "Show her," he said.

Before the tournament ended and she drove back to the city, Denny savored, like the late low sunlight across his face, its bold Easter yellow the first hint of spring, how she had not looked at Ryan admiringly, not even while he was beating Denny for the twenty-fourth time.

Ryan locks himself into the bathroom without asking Denny if he needs it. As Denny waits, seated in the hallway, forearms propped across tented knees, the euphoria of his untroubled conversation with his date, his hateless match against Ryan, his passionate defense to his dad, loses its heat. The moisture-warped cracks around the door release hiccupping echoes. Drips of paint hang calcified from the last time his dad repainted. Despite the proximity of the last months, even before he unlocks Ryan's phone with the code he's seen him type a thousand times and finds his date's phone number in the contact list, Denny knows he will never feel as close to his friend again.

"Ryan?" he says. Downstairs, his dad is whistling. This means he is feeling beatific, and safe.

2017

MARCY

The summer after college, at Alvin's bidding, she worked in the fitness room at the Chinese Community Center. That was how it went: Alvin lobbied for Marcy to staff the new fitness room; Marcy showed up when she was told. Alvin proposed three days before graduation; Marcy said yes. Alvin secured a tech job just outside their hometown and the condo his parents rented out for passive income; Marcy did not protest the implication of staying forever.

"Cuuuute," her sorority sisters chorused as they admired her ring. Only her House Mom dared ask whether it was not just feminist enough, but *good* enough for her. Because Marcy had been raised by women, House Mom saw her as a saintly ingenue.

She had more fantastical ideas of where life could go, but most days, they seemed safest unacted-upon. When yearning was fulfilled, its magic vanished. An idea from an English seminar. All those years in musty classrooms out east, reduced now to an autumnal daydream.

After its renovation, the center was almost new to her, as Alvin had seemed almost unknown, unknowable, down on one knee with the diamond whose wink still startled her beneath faucets. As a teenager she had volunteered there, taking out trash, packing up mahjong sets, and directing Mandarin-speaking senior citizens to the service desk to fill out Social Security and Medicaid forms. Now the buckling linoleum in the lobby was granite, the folding tables wooden slabs screwed to the floor. And what had been a daycare was transformed, by a squat rack, dumbbells, cable machine, and wall mirrors, into a gym whose legality Marcy didn't question. Nothing Alvin did without permission—applying to Rutgers after he found out she had, pranking their rival school with a weather balloon on their football field, ripping up the carpet in his parents' condo—had yet required him to ask forgiveness.

Just in case, Marcy was stationed at a desk facing the glass half wall, back discreetly turned, the partition a wan mirror in which to spot trouble. Her own watery reflection was inhumanly stretched, her plain features hideous without their appearance of well-adjustment, and she tried to avoid it. Until Ryan showed up during the last week of May, her only clients were grandpas who'd putter in, tug at the cables, and putter back out without signing the guest clipboard.

At first, she thought he had come to the wrong room. "It's around the corner," she said, "in Lucy Liu."

"Sorry," he said, "what is *where*?"

"Tae kwon do? Is in the Lucy Liu Room?" She eyed his upper arms, clefted lengthwise even in repose.

"That's funny. Martial arts, in the—"

"Yup," she said, "martial arts, Lucy Liu, ha ha."

"I'm just here to work out." He swung his fists as if shuffling ski poles. She slid over the sign-in sheet, blank but for a doodle of her sorority house in the upper right-hand corner. His fingers choked the ballpoint, which Marcy thought she heard creak. The paper ripped. *RYAN LO.* "Damn," he said, running an index down the unmarked page, as Marcy often did for the feel of the ink ridges, "people in our community are *not* prioritizing gains." He tapped the house. "What's that?"

"My sorority."

"Nice ivy," he said. She had, in fact, lavished hours on the ivy detailing, dabbing and curlicuing stem and leaf between each unique brick, draping bangs of it over House Mom's window on the second floor. Behind that window frame, she had even rendered House Mom's perennially visible menorah.

Ryan used the machines with a more reasonable force, reracking safely like Alvin had demonstrated during her training, for which he (though technically the center) paid her twelve bucks an hour to deploy. When, a few days later, new plaques went up in the entry hall, she recognized Ryan. US Champion of Table Tennis, the metal nameplate declared. In the picture he lunged toward a ball, hair vertical, cartilage rippling his knee. Despite his contorted expression, Marcy remembered that she had met him once at a homecoming. He hung between his father, a nationally acclaimed neurosurgeon and major donor, and a girl three years older than Marcy who'd been elected to the Milpitas city council.

The second time Ryan came, Marcy tried to pick out the telling traits of a table tennis star. He was fit, comfortable in a gym, but no more so than Alvin, whom he had met playing as kids.

He caught her eyes in the mirror, held contact to let her know he'd seen, then looked away.

That night, she told Alvin: "You know Ryan Lo's been coming to the fitness room?"

"Ha!"

"What?"

Alvin swigged half his can of seltzer and burped. "That's impossible. He's playing pro ball in Germany."

"Maybe he's visiting."

He drummed his fingers on the table. "Hm. If you see him again, tell him to holler?"

Marcy didn't. For two more weeks, she watched Ryan yank at cables and bare his teeth at the bottom of rep after rep, and her suspicions solidified: unlike Alvin, but maybe like her, Ryan was not where he was supposed to be.

When Marcy left the Bay after high school, she had imagined herself writing for an advertising firm, marketing for a movie studio, or even illustrating for some faceless but benevolent multinational company. Superheroes, anthropomorphic tampons, cartoon bears dancing around toilet paper towers; she could have drawn any of it. Alvin hadn't featured in that dream, but it did not preclude him, especially since they went to the same college. She adored his goofiness and sureness, which were complementary, jokes reinforcing something secure and irreproachable within him. *Maybe I'll work for SpaceX*, he'd say, pretending to launch a rocket from his crotch; but it was not impossible, he had finished his computer science major by sophomore year. Marcy was the one who vacillated between communications, accounting, marketing, graphic design. She rushed Greek life because Alvin did. When she balked at recruiting and job postings, her desultory offer from a medical equipment retailer in Wisconsin, Alvin reassured her: he'd make enough money for them both. Especially given his parental rent reduction. Come back with him and it'd be easy to set her up.

She had helped design the flyers for the fitness room; that was a start. And once Alvin was established at his new company, he would connect her. Don't worry, don't worry. She repeated his promise to her mother until it acquired the sheen of virtue. Who else had a fiancé who provided for them at the ripe young age of twenty-two? They didn't even have to pay for dinner most days, since he could load takeout boxes in his work cafeteria. Until her first days in the fitness room, Marcy felt mostly convinced, mostly virtuous. Mostly cared for. The rest was decorative aspiration, fluttering prettily on its dead stalk.

The fifth week Ryan came in, she finally said, as he was leaving: "Aren't you supposed to be in Europe or something?"

He laughed and shook his head. "The aunties gossiping?"

"Alvin. My fiancé."

"Holy shit. *Marcy.* You guys are back? I thought Al'd be living in the city."

"Nope, we're in his parents' second place. He says to give him a holler."

"Ah."

"I get why you wouldn't, though," she said. Insecurity and a craving for privacy, the same reasons she had stopped replying to her sorority's alumni group chat.

He rapped the clipboard. "Nah, I'll definitely holler. See you Monday."

Down the hall, Intermediate Adult Dance's boom box shrilled "Mo Li Hua." Two rooms over, the martial artists shouted *ha!* Marcy sat back and turned up Paramore in her earbuds, humming happily and shading a sketch of Ryan's face until another grandpa wandered in. She convinced him to try the pull-down bar and write his name. By Monday, she'd get to turn the full page.

•

On Monday, Ryan asked, "So who's in charge of the classes?"

"Mo Li Hua" and *ha! ha!* shook the glass partition.

"Rina. In the Jet Li Room."

He signed in. He'd started testing different scripts: lowercase cursive yesterday, a gothic *R* and *L* today. Tongue between his incisors, diagonally shading the base of the L, he asked, "D'you think people would want to learn table tennis?"

Marcy triumphantly flipped to a fresh sheet. "From you, definitely."

"Wanna come ask with me?"

"Why?"

"Give me a little extra authority."

"I don't have any."

"Then just moral support. If you want."

She led him down the hall. Rina greeted them with an admirable shamelessness as she set down her phone, empty desktop amplifying the abortive tinkles of Candy Crush.

"We've got an idea for another program," Marcy said. "Ryan, Ryan *Lo*, wanted to teach table tennis."

"Of course," Rina cried, "it's our most popular activity! Here's the form, honey, and no need to describe experience. Duh. You arranged this, Marcy?"

"Yup," Ryan said, voice deepened and slowed, "we knew each other in school."

"I love organizing volunteers," Marcy said. In college, she was assistant treasurer for the sorority's Giving Tuesday. She had mailed three hundred handwritten thank-you cards. "I'd love to help."

"I'll onboard you to scheduling," Rina said. "Give you something to do, while you're sitting over there . . ."

The next day, Marcy's profile appeared on the center's website under *Staff*. Assistant volunteer liaison. That was a start.

●

They invited Ryan for dinner on Thursday. Alvin wanted to thank him for helping Marcy. He returned early from work with a plastic elephant plant and cut-glass whiskey tumblers beneath his arms, cloth placemats and a chicken in a reusable shopping bag.

"What is this?" Marcy laughed. The placemats said NOM NOM NOM in pale brown cursive.

"Everything I could carry on the train." Alvin squatted to set down the plant and nearly tipped over. Marcy relieved him of the tumbler box.

"I could've done this . . ."

"You had work." She had told him she was on the job hunt, which meant she guiltily slammed her laptop shut every time a senior citizen wandered by, freezing her tabs of dance competitions, how-to videos, days-in-the-life. "Also, Ryan's my buddy and this was my idea."

She unpacked and rinsed everything as he chopped vegetables. Their wok was new and they'd never roasted a whole chicken. They didn't have time to marinate properly; Alvin slapped the carcass's trussed flanks, saying that stimulated flavor.

"I'll stimulate *your* flavor," said Marcy, and aimed a kick at his ass. She hadn't seen him so worked up since job recruiting, and it helped her calm what she wouldn't let herself consider nerves.

Ryan arrived balancing a platter of beef Rouladen, potatoes and braised red cabbage, a Black Forest cake, and a bottle of Korn. The beef rolls, tender pink, would have passed inspection in a restaurant. The cabbage tingled pleasantly on the palate. Anabel loved braised cabbage, he said, and Alvin nodded so knowingly Marcy held back her clarifying question (Anabel?). Ryan's dishes made theirs look amateur.

Alvin raised a tumbler of Korn toward the plastic chandelier they had been meaning to replace since they moved in. "So what *are* you up to now?"

Ryan drained his liquor and said he was planning to finish his bachelor's. The university had agreed to reenroll him after two years. He was taking the summer to catch up on coursework.

"Must be a drag," Alvin said.

"Yeah," Ryan said, "it makes me feel like a dumbass."

"I get that," said Marcy. "I look at job postings and it's like, 'What *is* that? But didn't I *just* learn it?'"

"You always got good grades," Alvin said.

"That's not the same as being good at stuff." She nearly failed to graduate on time because she forgot to enroll in her last requirement, Introduction to American Literature. Alvin had come the closest ever to being mad at her, then wrote it off as putting too much pressure on herself. Self-sabotage. Unknown to him, she had also slept through a job interview and neglected to submit her résumé to several recruiters.

"Man," Alvin said, "I remember getting walloped by you. Bring that energy, and you're good."

"Thanks, homie. You still play?"

"Nah, I'm a simple gym rat."

"You ever go to the fitness room?"

It wouldn't have been good enough for Alvin. He had brought Marcy to work once, and the gym there was five times as big and overlooked a vast quad with lollipop trees and grass that looked digitally colored. "The hours don't work out," he said.

"It could use some heavier dumbbells," Ryan said, "but otherwise, pretty nice."

"Yeah, they just can't have people hurting themselves. Marcy couldn't move a hundred pounds."

"I could figure it out," Marcy said.

"No," both boys said.

Alvin poured Ryan more Korn. "Can you believe we're back, man? It's kinda fucked up."

"You're doing great, though," Marcy said. "Your life is great."

"Cheers to that," Ryan said. They smashed glasses.

•

"You're bored, too, right?"

It was four days after dinner. Ryan had come in later than usual. All day, Marcy had languished with the blank clipboard on her knee, drawing Asian grandpas in yoga poses and watching videos about how to start an Etsy shop. Last night, Alvin said he'd met a director in the marketing department. Their teams were collaborating, and if it went well, he'd forward Marcy's résumé.

"I'm trying to move forward in life," Marcy told Ryan curtly, "just like you."

"I get it," he said. His workout had been erratic and short. It occurred to Marcy that dinner had pricked his ego, too, but he had not thought to empathize with her at the time, to refrain from chumming it up with Alvin at her expense.

"I'm sure you do," she sniffed.

"Listen, wanna go do something fun?"

"Right now?"

"Whenever this shit's done."

"'This shit' is my job," she said.

"I know. Sorry. I'll just . . ."

He dropped himself at one of the lobby tables. Over her laptop, Marcy watched him scroll his phone for an hour. She had planned to spray and wipe all the surfaces extra slow, but by what seemed the hundredth short video he watched, each punch line jerking his shoulders but leaving his eyes unamused behind its moving reflection, could not bring herself to. He stood when she did and followed her around as she cleaned up and returned the clipboard to Rina. "I'll DD," he declared, rattling his keys. "Let's go dancing!"

"I need to change," Marcy said. She was wearing her volunteer polo, the gray of sun-faded asphalt, and baggy joggers severely pilled at the inner thigh.

"C'mon, we don't have anyone to impress . . . Marcy. Come on. You look fine."

The honesty of "fine" persuaded her. She lay in the reclined passenger seat of his otherwise immaculate red SUV—"My bad," he said, "my friend Denny's fat ass broke it"—and tried to assimilate the sights of the new route he took downtown, the back porches of houses that always presented her their facades, little creeks and ponds shielded from her preferred roads by thickets of trees. From his rearview swung a jade Guanyin charm, a translucent bead bracelet in shades of violet, and a thumb-sized vanilla scent bottle, their light spots spraying the dash as Ryan drummed the wheel to Tame Impala.

At the third stop light, he raised a hand to flick the scent bottle. Anabel had given it to him, he said. She had made the bracelet, too, an activity she introduced for the little kids at her coach's summer bootcamp. They were going to eat at Anabel's favorite restaurant.

"Anabel's your girlfriend, right?"

"Kind of." Ryan twisted the bottle on its leather string; released as the light turned green and floored it to a clacking disco whirl of color. "I'm not sure if we're still dating. Anyway. There's my old barber." They were passing strip malls Marcy had overlooked every day of her life. "There's me and Coach's victory shawarma. There's the fro-yo place where I almost beat up your boyfriend—fiancé—after homecoming."

Marcy did not remember that. By pointing out his landmarks and memories, Ryan was laying stakes on their shared territory. It would have been cheap and unoriginal to reply in kind, so to reestablish herself Marcy asked, over their miso in an unremarkable sushi shop, "So what was it like, playing in Europe?"

He swirled his soup and peered into the sandy vortex. "The facilities were great. The money was good, comparatively. They take it seriously."

"But you came back."

"*I* wasn't great. I played fine, but there was too much baggage." He hooked his soup spoon on the rim of his bowl and snapped off a disposable chopstick to spin on the base of his finger.

"Too much pressure?"

"Baggage. Also, I lived in a crappy dorm and my teammate was sixteen and it was like—am I gonna be stuck here forever?"

"You outgrew it."

"You hungry enough to splurge on a Dragon Boat?"

He ate most of the Dragon Boat. Marcy observed, with the heightened but detached awareness House Mom trained them to adopt in sketchy situations, that she was nervous about taking out her phone and texting Alvin. It would disappoint Ryan that she wasn't playing along. The fiery but harmless upset of a kid. The way he plunked sashimi into his brimming sauce dish suggested childishness, as did the anime T-shirt. He should have been FaceTiming his kind-of girlfriend instead.

When he got up to use the bathroom, Marcy considered calling a car home.

But she followed him around the mall, rubbing the hems of T-shirts on front tables and rooting through candy dispensers. Then they drove to a bar to kill more time. Her cheap pants soaked through with sweat and dried back to what felt like cleanness. Alvin was right, she should have invested in nicer work clothes. It was only seven; he was still on the train from work. One more hour until the club opened. She texted him that a middle school friend had asked to get drinks last minute, would he mind? Of course not.

"What're your favorite things about Al?" Ryan asked. He leaned his elbow on the bar, his head on his fist. He talked slightly too loud.

"That's silly," Marcy said, "you know him."

"No. People are secrets."

"Guess."

"Hmm. Responsible. Hands-off, except the whole married thing—no, *now that* he has the married thing. Never gets mad."

"That's just a generic nice guy," Marcy protested.

"Then what?" He raised his head, freeing his fingers to glide forward and rest around Marcy's ring. Against the webbing between her fingers, they were hot, unexpectedly soft. He wiggled the gold loop. Alvin had sized it well. He was as exacting about daily things as Ryan must have been about table tennis.

She withdrew her hand. "So what's the deal with Anabel?"

"Oh, Anabel! Ha. Her deal is: she's got it all figured out. She was great at school and great at table tennis. Her coach loves her and she loves her coach. She's gonna work at the club where she grew up until she dies. Jersey to Jersey, dust to dust."

"Sounds . . . fun."

"You know, she is, actually. But mostly with me. And I like that."

"Why are you only 'kind of' dating? 'Cause you don't have it all figured out?"

"Bingo," Ryan said. "When you say it like that, it's amazing I even get 'kind of.'"

"Well. Sorry. You're also, you know, an impressive person."

He signaled for the check. He drove to the club five below the speed limit and circled the block twice before parking. If they had not been the first people in line, Marcy might have gone home, but—feeling, also, that her pointed question about Anabel extended her sentence for the night—she showed her ID and accepted a stamp on her hand. They descended to an empty, dark dance floor. A hit from their early teens hummed in her feet.

Ryan turned his back to the DJ booth and presented Marcy three white pills, stuck in a perfect triangle to his palm. "Pick-me-up?"

"No, thank you." *If you can't name it, don't take it*, said House Mom's voice, though Marcy had seen her toss back mystery pills on several occasions, with some of the same seductive resignation as Ryan now took his, tongue cushioning the end of the pill's short flight and curling it into a self-deprecating grin.

"More for me," he said. Then he began to air-guitar, stomp, and lip-sync, every vowel crinkling his nose. Not as if no one were watching, but as if he needed to be seen looking ridiculous. Marcy looked toward the head-bobbing DJ in the corner, all motion of neon-glossed hair part, headphones, stick-and-poked hands; thought of the tae kwon do students' endless, shameless shouts. All these small, modestly witnessed exertions. She could do that for him. She raised her arms, twirled her wrists, thrashed her head; her hair tie shook loose and her flailing earrings stung her neck. Lyrics rattled from her throat.

Maybe moving back could be worth this, autonomy and joy washing out so much childhood drear, so much monotony that being with

Alvin had given shape to but never pierced. Her mother's anxiety about her future, her grandmother's loneliness after she moved here to help raise her, the hollow light of Sunday afternoons, which she had feared so much then one day felt a total frightening indifference toward, because it seemed no bleaker than how *she* was inside, the blank plaster wall of her mind—all of that shaken to the surface and then off her sweating skin; flecking the dance floor, then trampled.

Ten songs later, thirst ended their spell. When she looked up, dazed from screaming *I! feel! so untouched right now!* a cluster of kids was imitating them, arms unevenly windmilling. They looked barely teenaged. More came down the steps, and in the hungry glaze of their eyes Marcy saw their own inconsequentiality.

Ryan stood breathing hard. "Should we be here?" Marcy half shouted, half laughed. He pointed toward the men's restroom. "Okay! Want me to get you a drink?"

"Come!"

"I don't need to pee."

He looped two fingers around her wrist. "We're friends, right?"

She let him guide her into the empty bathroom. He pulled a plastic baggie from his pocket.

"Oh," she said, "I don't do that, either."

"It's okay," he said. "Don't stress. We're just hanging out." He dabbed a finger in powder and ran it around the insides of his lips, then followed it with another pill. "Just stay with me for a minute."

She had seen Alvin dabble in college. It made him rambunctious and domineering, sometimes calculatedly charming, but she had never felt that it reached anything deep and meaningful within him.

Could it reach something deep and meaningful within her? What was down there?

All she could imagine was something out of a campy children's cartoon, ink strokes whipping a Medusa whirl from atop her cloven heart.

"It's nice to do this with somebody," Ryan said, as if forgetting she had declined; or to release the action coiled in her private question, to make her extend her hand and take the baggie. She tapped the powder along the opening and brought her finger pad to the triangle above her front teeth. Her gums tingled and numbed. In the mirror, she could see only Ryan's dim profile. She felt his eyes inches from her cheek, wanting to meet hers, and some small part of her—the cruel and mighty part, inert for so long—compelled her to deny him.

●

Four months later, at her wedding, more distinctly than her made-up face in the dressing room mirror or her mother's shaking hands, the fragrance of petals or Alvin's mouth syrupy hot during the kiss, Marcy remembered—because her presence was unexpected—Anabel, pale arm hooked over the back of Ryan's chair, its plastic ear pressing up a beauty mark on the creamy skin behind her armpit, speaking wry observations into Ryan's ear, tapping his shoulder as he leaned into her on each laugh.

Did she know what he had been up to? She must not have known.

After their night at the club, Ryan never returned to the fitness room. Alvin attended his packed coaching sessions. Sometime during those sessions, he decided to host their after-party at the center, in the Annie and Justin Lo Auditorium. He asked Ryan, who said they could use it for free. They set the wedding for November. For a small ceremony, as Alvin said, why wait longer?

By mid-August, Marcy was selling stickers on Etsy, cartoon watercolors of Asian elders stir-frying, tossing Chinese yo-yos, playing table tennis. Alvin loaned her most of the seed money . . . and sorority sisters contributed the rest. She sold her first sticker after a month and pumped her fists in the empty fitness room. Refilling her water bottle in the lobby, she overheard two aunties say Ryan had postponed school. Competing again, one of them said. He just couldn't hack it at either, the other countered.

By the end of September, she had quit the fitness room. She was selling enough stickers to justify staying home, singing Mariah Carey as the printer whirred sweet plastic fumes. Two weeks ago, her sorority had put in a huge order, her biggest yet. If they liked the first batch, they'd recommend her to other chapters.

Only after Anabel and Ryan left for their hotel, after Alvin and Marcy drove through a shower of rice back to the condo, where they made pancakes and decided they were happy just kissing ("Once-in-a-lifetime emotions get me soft," Alvin said, one arm over Marcy's shoulders and the other digging between misshapen couch cushions for the remote), as white morning knifed along the dark horizon, did she remember that she had forgotten to ship the box. Five hundred stickers: two hundred tai chi, two hundred kickboxing, one hundred stir-frying. She'd meant to do it the day before her wedding. Self-sabotage if she had ever seen it. But she wouldn't have to admit it to the sleeping Alvin. She tapped into his phone and texted herself Ryan's number.

Anabel could take it for her, Ryan said. They'd pay for the carry-on. He'd come now.

She barely registered his face in the blue dawn as she tucked the box into the back of his SUV, bedazzled address label irradiated by earliest gray sun. The last she saw of him was in disappearing profile, wreathed by exhaust in the morning's unseasonal cold, wisps hanging long after the car had barreled away down the steep curved road.

After he left their place, he visited a Starbucks and drove four hours east. (By this point, Anabel had called Alvin, who called Ryan but went to voicemail.) He stopped at a gas station and a Vietnamese restaurant. He filled his tank and bought a chicken banh mi. (His location had been turned off.) Then he kept driving along I-80 until, an hour west of Elko, he swerved, crashed into a sedan in the next lane, and rolled them both off the shoulder into a ditch. The autopsy found alcohol, cocaine, and tricyclic antidepressants in his bloodstream. The death was ruled accidental. All this they learned two days later from Mr. Lo who came to break the news. Despite his ringed eyes, he looked younger and spryer than on his plaque. All the bright, boyish parts of Ryan were recognizably his. "You must have been close," he said. "I wanted you to hear it from me."

Also, they had found Marcy's box in the trunk, one corner crumpled, rhinestones strewn among the shards of windshield glass.

The night of the club, Ryan had sped them to a house in a loop of toothlike duplexes. The living room windows were lit and curtained. It was his coach's house, he said, and they stood at the end of the driveway, and as they stood, the quality of the light in the window seemed to change. When Marcy moved out of the sorority, she had asked Alvin to drive by once more, and the sight of a makeup bag on the stoop and iridescent confetti glittering in the lawn was like trying to drink from an inexplicably emptied cup, a feeling that now seeped from the coach's window toward her memories of home, the empty soccer field where she and Alvin had fallen in love, the old community center, Alvin, even of dancing just an hour before, the memory of every time she had danced to any of those songs. Soon, she had felt, everything would be corrupted. Soon she too would be lost to whatever haunted him. But then he turned away and took her home.

She told them the basic details of all that. What else was there to tell? That at the wedding reception, in his parents' auditorium, Ryan had made a fool of himself, climbing up to the catwalks and flipping Alvin the bird while their childhood friends, all table tennis players, jeered; and that she found this heartening rather than disturbing? That Alvin had said, while Ryan was up there, "I'm glad I didn't turn out like that"? That it had suddenly seemed too late to worry about *turning out*, and when Marcy's tears began to flow at the end of the night, it was for this lateness? This premature but somehow relieving lateness.

DEUCE

2004

KRISTIAN

If he wins the tournament, I can come home.

I think it between sets during Ryan's semifinal, despite neither wanting nor believing it; despite Düsseldorf no longer being home; despite having given up bargaining ten years ago, when I left. As if hearing me, Ryan says, "I can still beat him!," bobbing his head twice for emphasis, shaking sweat from pink cheeks onto scarlet floor. He's an open child, unembarrassed by affection, vulnerability, need. If there weren't a court barrier between us, and if I were a different kind of coach, he might have rocked sideways and bumped me reassuringly, as I've seen him do at practice with the other boys, even the young assistant coaches, who cannot help but smile as his cheek brushes their armpits.

He *can* still win. We made it this far without dropping a set. His opponent is a nobody, a farm boy contemplating how many sauerkrauts to later snarf. His coach, whom I've inspected as closely as I can from across the court, trying to place his caterpillar brows and boxer's nose, too caveman to be my old teammate Eckert, even allowing for ten years' wear and tear, is a nobody, too, one of the countless nobodies who have not recognized me, which surely someone will, in this tournament hall where I used to play. If not Eckert, whom I'd be glad to see, someone. Sure, there is new carpeting in the lobby, fresh scarlet paint on the railings, padding on the VIP seats, a utilities giant advertised on the fresh polyester floor, and from all that, a scratchy chemical scent atop the brine of sweat and racket glue; another row of tables, twenty altogether now; two more cooks in the cafeteria and a smaller training hall across the plaza where they've parked jingling sauerkraut stands. Sure, new faces smile and shout from the banners circling the cinder block walls, though the cinder block is the same gray, the purple gray of a nightmare you want to remember for the thrill of your subconsciousness freed, dark horse raging in a dark field. Sure, a cattail-fringed lake ripples where we used to kick footballs behind the main hall, beneath the green hills that witnessed and enforced our sequestration from normal life. But surely, still, someone will know me.

Will they kick me out? Will they know why I left? My Bundesliga coach gloated that he'd "saved my life" by keeping it "behind closed doors," but rumors seep beneath doors. Maybe I would have been safer dealing in facts—the boy's massage, the mother's complaint, the dismissal. Too late to relitigate now. Eckert recommended me to the club in California, where he knew the head coach, and I've been there ever since. Ten years. When they recognize me here, I'll tell the facts: that I brought Ryan to this children's tournament in Düsseldorf to play some real table tennis, that was all; that thoughts of return or redemption, or whatever else they suspect, did not occur when I called to register him and heard German at last, the language like dry pavement after ten years of icy gravel.

"Coach," Ryan says, "should I try the serve?" He can tell I've drifted. It happens to the best of us: sometimes you know, before the ball leaves the racket, who will win. Ryan's only trailing because of his right leg, tight from a quarterfinal dive—the ball focusing every line of his body but that leg, beautiful and strong, the poor leg that spent itself to launch him from the ground. He was up ten to five but dove anyway, because I teach them (core lesson one) to play every point like it's zero–zero. I should be proud. I *am* proud. Ryan is the best I've ever coached. A blessing that his parents found me, after months wasted on tennis, as if anyone, watching the boy's eyes follow rallies, fingers tapping their iambs onto his thigh, could think that sport would use his gift to the fullest. Now, for example, I tell him: "Run him. Left, left, right. Left, right, middle. Catch him off," and he'll magic the ball around till the farm boy keels, though he's taken no more than four steps in any single direction. Where else can you experience such concentrated power? What better sport, I always ask my students, than this one of millimeter margins and symmetry, jewel-toned surfaces and sound, speed and brute perseverance?

"And yes," I conclude, "try the serve. Mixed with short underspin. Keep him guessing."

Ryan nods. "Special serve," he whispers, and fist bumps himself. "Special serve. Special serve."

As he shakes out his limbs and bounces on the balls of his feet, working back into the rhythm of the game, I hand him an orange sports drink, the flavor of tight scraps and comebacks. Lemon-lime is for holding leads, breezy confidence; we've been drinking it for two days straight. Ryan gulps too fast, remembers himself and lowers the bottle. Excess fluid slows you. At practice, I issue standard 750 mL bottles. The students may drink one every two hours. *If I give everything*, I bargained ten years ago, when I arrived in California, *let me start over, let this go right*. My last deliberate bargain, and it worked. So I give everything. I teach them everything. I come early and leave late. I reduce my fees and give rides, sometimes crisscrossing the Bay for hours. I take in strays and delinquents, kids who'd otherwise be setting squirrels afire behind their middle schools. In return, they hear my lessons. They ration water. They run penalty miles. From Ryan down to the meanest, most hateful boy, they are my new grace.

Before the umpire calls time, Ryan whispers one last thing, too quiet for me to hear. Something clicks into place behind his eyes, contracting the pupils, snuffing the watery pinpricks of doubt. He prowls back to the table without spinning his racket, rubbing his eyes, or any of the tics that plagued the first set. The farm boy starts hopping side to side, face jiggling. He knows he's about to be killed.

"Zero–zero," the umpire says, flipping the score board to what I've taught the kids to call the golden goose eggs. "Service: Lo."

Ryan catches the ball, dribbles it on his end of the table, and crouches for Eckert's old Tomahawk serve. There's enough time, as the ball flies up and the old pressure squeezes its way up from my shoulder sockets, to consider other bargains. Less selfish, less audacious. If he wins the tournament, I will take another gifted student to be his companion. If he wins the tournament I will invite his parents to spectate again. If he wins . . .

I know, simultaneously, that the serve is an ace, and that I could not honor those things.

I stopped bargaining because of the injured boy. If his parents came on time, I thought that night ten years ago, the last night I would ever coach in Germany, I'll let them deal with it. If they're late (and they were, often), I'll take care of it myself, because how quietly ruinous, for a child, on the evening he first experiences real pain, to feel neglected.

To that, my Bundesliga coach said, "We bargain for what we know we want, no?" By the time we had that conversation, after the boy's mother reported me and the club suspended me, it was too late to explain it all, or really any of it—how, as the boy himself testified, I'd only been easing his groin strain; how many hours I had devoted in libraries, memorizing the human body, and before that, watching my childhood coach point out every muscle down another boy's leg, *to steady, to pivot, to lift, to stop*; how I never bargained during matches, so it was not for petty outcomes or easy desires; how when I first started playing at eleven, when life was a suit of nails tight on my skin, I thought: *If I am good today, let it be easier; if I win this match, let me sleep tonight* . . . I could have joined the military, or killed myself; instead, I played table tennis. But there are too many such sob stories in sports. To people who'd understand, it's not worth telling. As with the bargains, the only true audience is the inchoate thing in the night, dark horse in a dark field.

The ball spins to a stop behind the farm boy, expending itself against the flap of the barrier. He groans and glares at his racket. "One–zero," says the ump.

I've given Ryan Jean-Philippe Gatien's footwork, Kalinikos Kreanga's backhand, my old teammate Eckert's Tomahawk. He'll win, because it's his destiny, which crystallized when he won Under 11 at last month's US Open. I saw it and knew we had to come here. This tournament, the big California Opens, the US Open, US Nationals, Pan American Games, Junior Olympics, the ITTF circuit and world ranking points, going pro in Europe by twenty-one: if he wins here, I think, as he pumps his fist in triumph, we'll go all the way, we'll chase it all. He steps around and zings a forehand into farm boy's elbow. This match is over; the first set was a fluke. When did I come into the idea of destiny? Maybe by the time I was Ryan's age, ten, entering that period when you learn how to live. How deeply it cuts, how you're treated when you feel your ugliest and least lovable. I brought him here, to Europe's largest Juniors tournament, to show him: here is victory, abundance, your future.

Eleven to seven, eleven to six, eleven to three. By the third set, farm boy stops trying to step around, letting shots to the middle burrow into his sour black shirt.

"Match, Lo," says the umpire. The stands applaud. People are piled all the way up the high walls, wielding inflatable clapping sticks and pulling knees to breathless chests. In the US, you'd never get so many spectators, especially not for Juniors. I stand and jab my fists into the air. One terse punch, a strike to both cheeks. Ryan laughs and jabs back before shaking his opponent's hand, the umpire's hand, the other coach's hand, vising hard and pumping twice like I teach them. I let the other coach come to me, his own handshake limp as unglued rubber.

Ryan sprints at the barriers, as if to vault them; skids to a halt on his toes. He caught a second wind that didn't spend itself, and now he's just a hyperactive kid again.

"Oh my god," he says, "that was like Choji's Chunin fight." It's a cartoon he likes—ninjas, friendship, the power of perseverance. Not the worst thing he could watch, though I don't know when: the only time we don't train is Sunday nights, habit from my childhood Sundays of church and closed grocery stores. He does half his homework in the backseat of my car, driving to or from practice, pen ripping paper when the fickle California traffic, the sun-crazed teenagers in open Jeeps, force me to brake. "Oh yeah, Choji's a fat ninja who eats a lot. He gets stuck in the wall when he tries to attack, so Dosu gets him. Except, I'm not really Dosu."

"What's a Dosu?" I ask.

"It's not important. He died."

As we all must, Eckert might have replied, with extraordinary cheer. "So who are you?" I ask.

"Hm. Shikamaru? No, Shika's too lazy."

"You're not that."

"Noooope." He pops the *p*. "Oh! I'm Rock Lee. He can't do jutsu, but he trains so hard it doesn't matter."

Wrong, I want to say: *there's nothing you can't do*. I notice my fingers tapping my thumbs in rapid succession, then tapping the caps of the remaining sport drinks. They want to trace the triangular pockets above Ryan's collarbones, to squeeze out my expectations. To pick him up like a groom his bride or set him atop my shoulders, my hands tight around the bases of his legs. To—

No. *I* don't want to do that. I don't *want* to do that. Core lesson two: speak reality into existence. I haven't felt the old pressure in years, and the boy that brought it on quit table tennis soon after to focus on school. Like we should have, Eckert and I always said, not meaning it.

"That makes you Guy Sensei," Ryan says. "You kinda have his haircut." He giggles, canines missing, one dusky new tip poking from the gum. He traces a line across his eyebrows. In the barbershop last week, I had them leave it longer; I must have been hoping to exude a careless, Californian aura. It feels wrong sticking to my forehead and the nape of my neck.

"Eight gates," Ryan says, lowering his voice and striking a sumo stance, "open!"

"Open indeed." I hold up his jacket behind him. He stabs his arms through the sleeves, puffing little ninja nothings beneath his breath; zips to his chin; smooths the tag perfectly along the track. A few feet away, kids thump up and down the aisles, hands swinging loosely, feet kicking inefficiently outward, knees rubbery and spry. We sit, and I watch Ryan watch the other semifinal. A boy in head-to-toe neon green screams in triumph. He loops the next point past his opponent and turns to the stands, arms outstretched like he's grabbed the horns of a tiny bull. A gesture doubtless drilled by a coach or father, which belies his age: in imitating Schwarzenegger or Vin Diesel, he looks no older than seven.

"He's pretty good," Ryan says.

He's fast, but not as strong as Ryan, whom I've trained with weights for months, his growing power pinning shots to the end line. In the last set against the farm boy, he strung together a flawless point: long serve to the pocket, counterloop to backhand corner, loop to forehand corner, arcing drop shot. The ball kissed the table and fell to the floor. The farm boy, annihilated, finally smiled.

The skin beneath my fingernails buzzes.

"He's weak in the backhand and pocket," I say. "You just need to play your game."

"That's against everyone, though."

"Exactly. How's the leg?"

"All good."

"Really?"

"Really!" He kicks it up, taps his toe, grins again.

I want to give him a massage. Instead—though if I do feel a thrill when my fingers work through a neglected muscle, a round of fat untouched by sun, a thrill I cannot compare to what others feel because, how can you? what are you supposed to ask or compare? why should it not come from the usefulness of that touch, the care, the good it does a child?—I offer him a bottle of water from my duffel, the same electric-blue one I carried as a kid traveling around Europe and a professional competing in the Bundesliga.

"Can I have a lemon-lime?" he asks, tentative, smile faltering. According to my rules, we only drink water between matches. His face falls further as a group of boys flows past us, stopping and dispersing and doubling back on themselves like swallows.

I suddenly pity him, separate from the other kids. Just like I used to be, though he for more admirable reasons. For a purpose.

The pressure ripples down to my toenails.

I dig in my bag. We're out of lemon-limes.

The final starts in an hour. If I leave, I bargain, if I go and get the drinks and deal with myself, let him win the whole thing.

"I'll be back in ten," I tell Ryan. I urge him to stretch, to avoid getting stiff. He stands and raises a knee to his chest, still watching the boys, perhaps not knowing, or simply not accepting yet, that he is the hawk to their birds.

If I deal with myself, let him win.

At the kiosk six blocks away, there's an unfamiliar woman behind the counter, dopily young behind her thick glasses, with no immediate resemblance to the old couple who used to sell me and

Eckert cigarettes, condoms, lighters, flotsam we'd bury behind the training hall before tournaments. Superstition, tomfoolery. Like back then, the fridge stares blankly from the back wall. To its left, a rusted door hangs open, revealing the hallway to the single-person bathroom I sometimes used on my way back from long runs around the neighborhood. The new woman doesn't look up from her book.

As I traverse the kiosk aisle, the shelves of plastic bright dry goods, the darkness of the ammoniac hallway, I summon memories of the Swedish boy at my first international tournament serving a reverse pendulum, Eckert backhand-flicking a serve from the forehand corner, because maybe it started with the Swedish boy or Eckert, but the question of origin is pointless; who hasn't wanted to inhabit the body of a superior person? I do this every time the pressure descends. Sometimes I watch reels of Waldner, Samsonov, Joo Sae-hyuk. Sometimes I run until my arches ache, do a hundred push-ups, then another hundred. Sometimes it dissipates for a while, but in the end, I still have to deal with it.

The bathroom reeks of urine, bleach, and chamomile soap. They've installed a new doorknob, with a proper lock. I twist it and hook the old chain, too. Between the toilet and wall, a new mop sits in the old bucket, its wood handle resting against the sill of the frosted-glass window. The sink is chipped in the same Rorschach blobs along the white wall tiles. I don't pause before the misty, purpled mirror before I straddle the familiar toilet basin, facing the tank. I count from one to sixty-nine in intervals of four, up and down, an exercise the students do before tournaments, and let the pressure diffuse and run its course. Core lesson three: you must know what can be changed and what must be accommodated. Whether your disposition is nervous or calm, whether you face a match with trepidation or bloodlust.

I finish on the fifth round. Seventeen, thirteen, nine, five, one. All you can do is acknowledge and channel your nature. I smear off residual drops with the base of my thumb, flush the toilet, and wash my hands. The mop, leant and leering like a man with a knife in an alley, urges me to wipe the floors, too, but I know nothing got down there. It's just that the mop was my only witness.

Back in the kiosk, two kids are blocking the fridge, one nearly inside, arm and leg two fleshy ellipses against the fogged door. The other, taller, has a hand curled protectively around the handle. His shorts are table tennis–branded, and as I watch, he slides a bottle of soda into their left pocket.

"Hello," I say. The shorter one startles and drops a drink. It explodes against the floor. The taller angles himself between us, glaring, and it clicks: brothers, with the same square cheekbones and wavy black hair, long, an impractical style I've seen Ryan admiring on the Korean assistant coach. Little brother, dressed like a green highlighter, is Ryan's opponent in the final.

"We'll pay for it," big brother says. Defensive but cool. He'd find a way to get them out of it, even if I wanted to raise trouble— he looks responsible, straitlaced. The most dangerous kind of kid. My pulse slows. They don't know anything, couldn't know anything. The mop was my only witness.

"You don't have to tell me," I say, and shrug. I doubt the cashier heard through the glass, or whatever sounds from her book fill her mind. Backfiring cars, rustling leaves, lusty moans. I ask if they have the drink Ryan needs. Little brother's smearing the edge of the puddle with his toe, eyes widening as it thins and seemingly evaporates, then sticks his shoe to the linoleum.

"Leave it, Kay," says big brother. "Yeah. How many you want?"

He passes them to me, one at a time. He wants me to leave before them.

"You have enough money?" I ask.

"Of course," he says.

If I let them go, Ryan will win.

"Don't forget," I can't help but say as I go, "the one in your pocket." At my club, they'd run penalty miles for this—six, maybe eight.

The cashier thumbs her book as she scans my bottles. Plastic bag looped around my wrist, I lap the block and wait three doors down, beneath a bakery awning, to watch the boys leave. Little brother's holding the orange soda, doesn't bother looking around before cracking the top and chugging, just like Ryan. He'll be impatient at the table, susceptible to long, spinny rallies and surprise serves. He'll feel bloated and slow.

I give them a few blocks' head start. The farther I imagine them going, the more at ease I feel, magnanimous, the unpeopled street a fresh start. *If Ryan wins*, I let myself think again, as I pass the phone booth on the next corner, *I can come home*, the thought's facetiousness emphasized by the booth: I don't know if my parents would pick up if I called them in Koblenz. I have no guess as to what they're doing. They don't know why I'm here or why I really left. *Go, then*, my father said, *go, of course; nothing here was ever good enough for you*, and it was a flash of healing sunlight, the fact that I had finally become someone others might say that about. In California, I lost touch with everyone. My childhood coach died in the fourth year. My father always hated him. *What the fuck is this*, he asked, the first time he saw the tables where we trained, in a renovated bunker, the irregularly dyed surfaces (gray-pocked forest green, dusty violet) and their peeling edge tape. What kind of man approached kids on the street to play table tennis in his basement? I couldn't have said to him then, though I say it now to my students' parents, who want to understand my *philosophy*, my *life story*, that I already felt, at eleven, that I wouldn't amount to anything, though I knew I should want to, and even the smallest amount of that wanting, the little bit I was able to scrape for myself from the news or the presence of a glittering boy at school, pained me, because nothing around me suggested it could be fulfilled. I was eleven, mediocre at books and football and life, an only child, and everything hurt. *If I am good at this, let it be easier* . . .

The American parents love to hear I only started when I was eleven, that I quit young and dedicated myself to coaching. I was meant to play table tennis, meant to teach, meant to bring wisdom from a foreign land. They are blindly confident in me, especially Ryan's parents, two surgeons who are too busy to travel and, understanding the cost of excellence, too circumspect to question my decisions. I pared them away so Ryan could experience the sport purely, with me, undisturbed.

The bank clock says it's been twenty minutes. I've never left Ryan alone for that long. At other tournaments, we fill spare time with exercises and drills, and we always fill it together. I walk faster. By the time I hit the fifth block, I'm jogging, and by the time I run through the lobby doors, it's like I never left: my arms are buzzing, my face, my ears.

As I turn into the hall, Ryan is sprinting toward me, the little brother ahead, all four of their arms extended backward, counterbalancing as they plunge forward, so fast they miss me by millimeters as they swerve, little brother's sweat flecking my arm. Ryan is panting; his jacket zipper has shaken down.

"What is this?" I demand in German.

"We . . ." Little brother, chest heaving, cradles his forearms and looks to the bleachers, where big brother, arms crossed and right foot propped on a VIP seat, stands speaking with an older man. I know the man.

"Was this your idea?" I can see how it happened: the scampering return to the hall, the adrenaline from his near-miss with me, the instant boredom as his brother left to consult their father, the uninhibited approach of Ryan, who was alone in the bleachers, bored as well. The lack of recognition, even from this small child, of who I am, that Ryan is my student.

"It's the Naruto run," Ryan says, over little brother's head. "It was—it was my idea."

The lie—he would never approach a strange child first—surprises me more than the horseplay. Naruto, I recall, is an orphan boy, rebellious out of neglect. Ryan is no orphan—he has me, who only made the mistake of leaving him. I'll never make it again.

"Han!" little brother screams, perhaps emboldened by my hesitation. Big brother and my former teammate, Jun Qiu, turn. They descend the bleachers. I consider pretending I don't know the man, but that would violate core lesson three, because neither our acquaintance nor this reckoning can be changed.

"Jun," I say, "it's Kristian."

Jun still holds his arms away from his body. The anger that used to explode from him on the court, his expression placid until he was slapping at his racket mid-set, has carved harsh furrows between his brows. "Kristian . . . ?"

"Borussia. Ninety-four to -five."

Behind Jun, big brother's eyes widen.

"Kristian. Ah." Jun clasps his hands behind his back. "My apologies. You've . . ."

"Darkened? Aged?"

"Maybe that's what it is," Jun says. He talks more slowly, the muscles of his face at ease, with less of the old implication that he expects you to say something stupid. Kids force you to let go. "You've been in Düsseldorf?"

"Just for the tournament. I coach in California."

"Long way."

"Good tournament." If Ryan wins, he'll earn two thousand euros. "Is this"—I raise my hand to indicate little brother, but he's darted behind the big one; I raise my eyebrows instead—"your son?"

"Kay," Jun says, "and Han. Han plays for Borussia now."

"Congratulations," I say. "At such a young age."

"Well. Eighteen."

"Not so impressive," Han says, "since I've played my whole life." He half smiles at me, as if to say: *You see what I deal with? Wouldn't you rather be on my side?* As if knowing that I will suddenly remember him as a five-year-old, some team gathering at the

Qius', Eckert and I laughing in the corner, Han penned behind a barricade of plastic panels, pulling in circles a wheeled wooden tiger, his face stormy and determined.

Eighteen-year-old Han squats before Ryan and asks, in English: "What's your name? I'm Han."

Ryan looks to me.

"Shake," I tell him.

So he says his name and extends a hand. It barely fits around Han's, the webbing going white, but he squeezes firmly.

"*Freut mich*, Ryan," says Han.

"*Freut mich*," he ventures, the *r* clear and piping.

"Very nice," Jun says. "A very exciting final. Go warm up."

"There's still soooo much time," Kay protests. He slumps onto Han's back. How quickly he's dismissed the threat I posed. He gets away with it because he's more talented than his brother, I'd guess, or less damaged by expectations.

Han clamps Kay's arms around his neck and staggers up, pretending to dump his brother, who squeals and kicks his feet.

"Fatty," Han groans. "Less bread!"

"I'm not! Fat! Ha ha ha!"

Ryan stands stiff and seemingly indifferent, hands tightly clasped, but his eyes, wide and shiny and rapt, give him away; Jun says, "Take Ryan, too."

"I do his warm-ups," I say.

"Just ten minutes," Jun says. "Our apology for the mischief."

It's promising that he has offered, I tell myself. Jun and I were never close; my first year on the team was his last, with three years between our retirements. By the time I joined, he was the cranky veteran. Maybe he doesn't know.

Ryan follows Han onto a court, beneath a banner of the older boy mid-serve, and chews his zipper tag—nervous, starstruck.

Jun asks where we are staying. I name the hotel across the river, in Oberkassel, not far, I recall, from where they used to live. "I remember Han," I say, "when he was this tall." I pat the air by my hip. It was all so long ago Jun may not remember me, may not know; it is reasonable for him to ask, even if he doesn't know: "And just the two of you?"

"He was the only one worth bringing," I say.

"The only one?"

Out of my forty juniors, I clarify. I run a large club outside San Francisco, I explain. A hundred students; forty kids; seven days of league nights, group sessions, and private lessons.

"Impressive," Jun says.

"Do you coach Juniors?"

"No."

"Only yours," I guess.

"His parents couldn't make it?"

"They're surgeons."

"How impressive."

"Busy, I mean. Operating on brains."

"Not good-for-nothings like us, eh?"

"You're surely proud of Han," I venture. "Bundesliga at eighteen."

"He was Dieter's last hire," Jun says. Our Bundesliga coach. "He died last year."

Eckert loved Dieter. Eckert, whose hands looked inordinately, impudently massive around the Qius' tea mug, and looked that way anytime they weren't choking a racket. Returning from the kiosk, he carried everything in one fist.

"I'm sorry," I say. "About Dieter. But the club seems well."

"All his work."

"Of course."

"And you're still coaching. Many students."

"I have assistants."

"I didn't recognize you," Jun says. "I've been watching him, but . . . I wouldn't expect you here."

"I wouldn't, either," I concede. I give him the spiel: how table tennis in America staggers along on the backs of immigrants and foreigners, ails in a system disorganized and laughably ill-funded; how I wanted to show Ryan the life he could have abroad. "He's very good," I say. "The best student I've had, anywhere."

Maybe the "anywhere" triggers the memory, or the decision to act on it. Jun shifts his weight forward, nearly arching onto his toes, and pompously scans the tournament hall. Around the edges, they're folding up the tables, baring more and more of the red floor.

"It's inspiring to play here," I continue. "To see people like Han, to compete against the other children. We were looking into summer training camps, I don't know if you're familiar with any . . ."

"Of course," Jun says. Han is blocking Ryan's loops, carving ruler-straight lines across the court, arm and torso ticking machine-like. Outside, he was a rebellious teenager; here, he is a role model. *More spin*, he tells Ryan. "But I cannot recommend you to them."

"He's as good as any boy here." The indignation, natural and true, cuts me off from pretending or even considering pretension.

"He is. I've watched him."

"So—"

"I cannot recommend *you*. Because of the . . . your departure."

"I'm back."

Jun shakes his head and stares behind me. "I'm leading the search for Dieter's replacement. I have a responsibility to the club. And you, Dieter said . . . are not allowed."

"Because . . . ?" I ask. But I already see, in the rootedness of his feet, his imposition between me and the hall (the protective stance Han took in the kiosk; learned, despite whatever disdain he holds for his father), an unyielding opponent.

"Because," he reassures himself, "you are not allowed."

"Well, then," I say, "congratulations are in order. To Kay."

"Ha," Jun scoffs, "still petty. Your boy can play his match."

"So gracious."

"It's nothing against him. I wish the best, for him."

That's me, I want to say. *I am the best for him.*

"I'll tell them to finish up," Jun says.

He walks away. I stand alone in the aisle, for the time it takes to cross twenty yards to Han's court, for Han to escort Ryan back over. Less than a minute, but long enough to register the pressure has settled somewhere deeper than the nerves. Like a layer of mercury; like the fat my childhood coach described pressed between our muscles, a glistening white net.

"Good luck," Han says, already impersonal as he turns to rejoin his family, as he says to me: "Tell him I look forward to seeing him play here."

Ryan is flushed, hair spiky and shirt askew. I tug it straight. His eyes follow Han down the aisle, into Kay's court, where they will play in half an hour.

"Earlier," I ask, "why were you running like that?"

He bites the insides of his cheeks. A tiny muscle flutters beneath his eye. I mimic the run, mouth gaping and hands flopping. I run past him once, twice. "You looked like a loser," I say. "Like someone who's not serious." I run again, lolling my tongue and stuttering my steps.

"Okay," he says. "I won't do it anymore."

I straighten and shake out my wrists. "What should you have done instead?"

"Think about my match," he says.

"What else?"

"Meditate."

"What else?"

"The counting exercise."

"What else?"

"Um . . . stretch."

"What else?"

"I . . ." The tears well up. He balls his fists.

"What else can we do, that is not running like someone who's not serious about winning?"

"I . . . wall sits."

"Good. What else?"

"Suicides. Zigzag. Calf raises. Hot foot. Burpees. Supermans—"

"Good," I say. "Let's do those now."

Uncomplaining, as behooves my best student, he shucks off the jacket, pads to the barrier, and swings his leg into the court. It's never too early or late to do the right thing. We do grapevines and suicides and sit-ups. We shuffle round one side of the table, slapping damp handprints behind the net posts. We hold a plank for two minutes. I feel people watching, Jun and Han and Kay surely among them.

When I permit us—him—to flop to the ground, Ryan says quietly, the polyester against his face: "Coach. My leg . . ."

He rolls over, plants hands and feet, tries to jump up. The right leg buckles; he hops and steadies himself on the table.

"Sit down," I say. He does, legs akimbo, one extended naturally and the other tipped sideways, crooked at the knee. I sit and pull the bad leg across my lap.

"Where does it hurt?" I ask. He taps behind his knee.

"From one to ten," I say, "tell me how sore." My hand circles the muscle. You must be methodical, moving up inch by inch, squeezing as hard as you can, so hard it overwhelms the old pressure, the buzzing fingers.

"Three," Ryan says. "Three. Four. Four. Ah! Seven."

My fingers close again, slower. "Seven?"

"Um. No. Five."

I go higher. He flinches. "Six."

High hamstring. For extending and hinging. I get the painkillers and a lemon-lime from the duffel, drop the pills and tip the liquid into his mouth.

"In ten minutes," I promise, "you'll be all good." The other boy was, ten years ago. He walked out to his tardy parents without limp or qualm.

I palpate the soreness until the leg goes limp, and the other leg also, all resistance eased away. Soon, the painkillers will kick in. I have him lie back so I can bend the leg at each necessary angle (hip extension, knee bend, full flexion), foot pointing toward the ground, then straight forward, then back behind Ryan's head. When a groan escapes his clenched teeth, I instruct: "Yes, breathe it out."

Ryan huffs.

"Out of ten?" I prompt.

"Five."

". . . Now?"

"Four."

"Now?"

"Three."

"Let's stand," I say.

The bad leg holds, but he's tense and immobile, anticipating pain.

"You're better than that boy," I say. I extend my right leg backward. Ryan follows, eyes narrowing, lips pressing down a complaint.

"I'm better than him," he says.

"You are." I sit down, right leg crooked, and flex the heel into the ground.

"I am." He follows me down, crooking his leg and flexing his heel.

I stand and bend at the waist, letting my torso hang, and slowly bounce at the hips. "You'll beat him," I say.

I hear my posture mirrored in the muffled waver of his voice as he says, "I'll beat him."

I straighten. "You can play."

He faces me. His face has cooled to a calm tan, each tiny plane shining with an understanding of what we are about to do. "I can play."

Twenty minutes to go. He starts to repeat the stretches, and I begin: "One. Five. Nine."

"Thirteen," he says. "Seventeen. Twenty-one."

"Twenty-five. Twenty-nine. Thirty-three."

"Thirty-seven. Forty-one. Forty-five."

Up and down we go, faster and faster, so many times I lose track. By five minutes before the match, Ryan is bouncing in place again, eyes closed and face tipped sightlessly toward the cold lights. The umpire circles the court, official clipboard beneath her arm. Kay is still rallying with his brother, grunting on each hit. He's warmed up too much, going for one last winner as one ump checks the net and another flips the scoreboard to the golden goose eggs.

I know he is going to win. I don't need to be there, really, beside the court as Ryan smashes Kay's serves into the corners, as he spins Tomahawks deep into Kay's elbow, as he blocks and loops, even lobs, as if the ball were iron and his racket the world's strongest magnet, screaming and pumping his fist every time. I don't need to tell him to keep the pressure on, or to hear Kay sniffling on the podium below us, the carnations in his runner's-up bouquet quivering against my elbow as he stills himself for the photo. I don't need Jun to confirm that he is too cowardly to reject the hand I extend from on high, my arm around Ryan's victorious shoulders, the squared shoulders of a boy proud and unoppressed, who walked stoically through the resurging pain, which we will overcome. I didn't need to say goodbye to my childhood coach, or to Eckert. I don't even need the coach from a club in Berlin to approach afterward, with two hammy thumbs-ups and a series of questions that will end with an invitation to train with them, his face full of surprise when I say we're from America.

"The yellow of the egg," he says. The best of the best. My childhood coach used to call us that, in turn, to keep us going until the next fiercely scrapped win, until the next time the ball felt more blessing than curse against our rackets. A new chicken every month, we joked. Out of us all, I made it farthest, and still: a disgrace in the end. My childhood coach was too soft.

The work has already been done; that is core lesson four. You can't regret a match: it was decided in practice months ago. You can't seek the past; it has turned its back on you, and you cannot choose, if it ever does turn again, which face it presents to you.

If we do well enough, I bet—as the tram carries us over the Oberkasseler Bridge, through a sky still white with sun, above the waxy white Rhine and the white blots spreading north along its meadowed bank, which make Ryan rock up onto his good leg, press his hands to the window, and shout "Sheep!"; as I remember how I enjoy California's Pacific dusks and domineering highways, its cavernous shops and loud nosy people; as I consider, for the briefest moment, perhaps half the rotation of a ball, the river cliffs of Koblenz, the thud of my mother's chopping knife, some maudlin idea of an idyllic Rhineland; as the mercury hardens beneath my skin and we travel home, home, home—we will never have to defend ourselves again.

2018

JOAN

Gao was selling her club. Joan didn't want to care, wished she didn't know, but her husband brought her the news like a Labrador, thinking her as eager as him to remuddle their recently simplified lives. A few months ago, Barry retired from work and competition. In six months, their son was going to college. They had finally saved enough to pay three-quarters of his tuition.

Gao has cancer, Joan said. See what a club does to you?

She's selling it for peanuts, he said. And it's only stage two.

At another point in their lives, he would have spoken of death's advancing shadow reverentially. He used to be quite poetic, but losing a lot, or winning among known losers, cut down a man's capacity for seriousness. For anything beyond the raucous, pint-sized circus in his head. Joan retired a decade ago, and though she still believed she could run a marathon tomorrow, though the twin flames of envy and admiration had still flickered when she watched Barry compete, such delusions were relatively contained.

Even for peanuts, she says, I don't want cancer.

She was standing by the sink while Barry sat behind her at the dining table, spinning his phone; the kitchen window reflected a sprite of light whirling round its black face. She'd filled the sink with scalding water to soak dishes. Finding ways to elongate all required action, to savor the new excess in a day. Maybe not much longer. Also in the window, on the other side of the glass, the car Barry jacked up on their lawn last week to change its oil and de-rust its fender. When she chose that sedan at the dealership, he'd gently mocked its pragmatism. For their whole life, he'd been waiting for her stern "facade" to shatter. A dog's bark shivered the glass, then a neighbor's passing car. Lately, these January nights had the quality of damp tracing paper.

Kristian will lend us the money, Barry said.

He'd gone to Kristian without asking. She should have known: earlier, she heard his laugh from down the block, and he always called Kristian while he was walking, sometimes even running. They met not long after they immigrated, chummed it up at tournaments, for ten years sat together on the board that ran table tennis across the United States. In Kristian Barry saw one of his only equals here, though he was more successful than Barry could have aspired to; no matter that he did not play as Barry and Joan persisted in playing, taking big scraps off this country's miserly competition table. Several times over the years, Barry suggested that they could have run a club as lucrative as Kristian's, given the chance, but never moved to produce such a chance, happy to subsist off Gao's labor. Until now, too late.

I'm not taking his money, Joan said.

Sure, Barry said, and got up to plant a kiss on her earlobe and plunge a hapless hand into the suds. She wouldn't play nurse if he cut himself, Joan swore, even as she imagined the delicate width of his gleaming, bleeding finger between her dull and responsible ones.

●

Her knee was fucked up. Both knees were fucked up, but the left one more debilitatingly so. Their son Adam, who followed up Barry's retirement announcements with a declaration that he planned to *devote his life to personal training, or maybe physical therapy*, advised her to strengthen her glutes and roll out her hamstrings.

Yes, doc, she said. They were in the car the next day, bringing cake to Barry's retirement party. Gao was hosting at her club, where, after the festivities, they would sit down to talk about the prospective sale. Joan had been made to play at work again, a new hire, an Ivy League business major herded up to the table by her giggling colleagues, Joan summoned from beside the microwave where her lunch, packed by Barry, rotated four seconds from freedom. She had not given them the full crouch, barely moved her feet in their kitten heels, but she went for one last smash just to show the kid and the habitual stomp of her foot jammed pain beneath her kneecap. *Woo-hoo, Joan!* the colleagues squealed. *I'm an Olympian*, she had to say, over and over, when yet another coworker was told she *played a mean game of Ping-Pong*. One advantage of running a table tennis club: people grasped the respect due.

I'm going to do it, she thought as she splashed her face in the bathroom and stretched her quad high behind her, not caring that a coworker might see her ass up her skirt. She was sick of them, sick of this. She too wanted to feel like Kristian, authoritative and proud.

Gao had folded all the training tables and pushed them against the walls. GOODBYE BARRY! said a string of shiny letters over the door, both *B*s accordioned like they'd been sat on or got drunk. Walking beneath, Adam jumped and slapped his father's name against the cinderblock, nearly dropping the white cake box. Folding picnic tables in horseshoe formations occupied Courts One and Two, flowery plastic tablecloth jellyfishing in the A/C. Five courts, six rolling caddies, five to seven hundred balls (kids stomped them at a devilish rate), six scooper nets, one bathroom, one drinking fountain, fifteen folding chairs, six folding tables: Joan could not help counting what was once for pure enjoyment.

Hello, hello, have a seat, Gao said, as if they were late to someone else's celebration. She was in a gray silk blouse too tight beneath the armpits, her ancient track pants from Henan Provincial Team (where Joan and Barry had also played; one of the reasons they immigrated to this corner of New Jersey, of all places), and a pair of wedge-heeled flip-flops. Her hair was down for once, a curtain of normal-seeming thickness. Her face, still round and malleable like a girl's, looked lively and unusually glossy, glitter in the outer creases of her eyes. Probably applied by her sister, who beamed by her elbow, the only sign of something amiss. According to Barry, those two fought and made up like star-crossed lovers. Barry was hustled to his seat at the head of Court One. The younger students craned their necks for cake. Joan remembered Gao beside them in the '08 Olympic Village, harrumphing in the food line as she watched a Portuguese pole vaulter take the last chocolate muffin. That had been it for all three of them, despite valiant efforts; Barry lost in the group stage of the 2012 trials. This was one of the accomplishments Gao listed, standing astride a barrier between the courts, among many half-truths about Barry's career. Olympian (only after someone else dropped out). Board member (half-hearted). USA Table Tennis Hall of Famer (true). The youngsters chewed their bottom lips. Gao's sister led a round of applause, and Adam delicately peeled back the paperboard panels of the box, flattening each to the tablecloth as if it were an injured bird's wing. Gao led the room in belting "Happy Birthday!", after which Barry hooked out a fingerful of vanilla icing and smeared it across their son's cheek.

They could be happy here, Joan thought. They had been.

Congrats again, said Anabel, seated at the end of the horseshoe beside Gao's empty chair. She was in a white shirt and navy cardigan, fresh as the napkins Gao was scattering into kids' laps from their torn package. Begrudging her effortlessness, Joan noted the product caking her hair, forming harsh, icy strands as they streaked into a high ponytail. Six years ago, Anabel knocked Joan out of her penultimate tournament, ran her to death in the Women's Singles quarterfinal. Gao made a point of excusing herself before the match. Joan wouldn't say the girl ended her career, she'd known she was on her way out, but the knee problems worsened expeditiously after that match.

Not for much, Barry said, twirling his hand in a jester's bow. Congrats on your board seat.

Joan thought of the twelve faces she saw on Barry's monitor every month, faces she knew from tournaments, galas, induction ceremonies, and airports, talking—too passionately and in fuzzy-edged slow motion—about such matters as the algorithm for amateur ratings and the barrier budget at the US Open. What twenty-four-year-old joined a sports governing body?

Heard you're taking over here, Joan, Anabel said, congratulations.

Oh, Joan said, we're still working it out.

Well, I hope you do. I think the club could use—

Anabel! Gao waved icing-streaked forearms. More forks! They're smashing them!

We might have more in the closet . . .

The girl speedwalked away, legs perfectly fluid in form-fitting gray jeans. At least Barry didn't watch; he was more interested in the spheres of honey melon and cantaloupe trapped in his buttercream.

If you guys don't want it, Gao said, she'll take loans and buy. But what does she know about that kind of responsibility? Better not let her.

By the time extra silverware was procured, cake finished, and kids dispersed, the floor mats were strewn with debris and Barry had turned talk to the sale. Gao laid out three rows of crisp balance sheets and recited their contents. Anabel chimed in with the occasional figure, but otherwise stood over her elders, arms crossed, wearing a look of disproportionate concentration.

To buy the club outright, they needed fifty thousand dollars—hardly "peanuts"; hypothetically all their liquid savings and ten thousand out of Adam's college fund. Kristian had offered thirty thousand, Barry said. It was profitable, but at the cost of seven-day weeks, eleven-hour days. On the way home, Barry said to think of Adam: they could cover the remainder of his tuition, sending him into the world debt-free.

You should do it for yourselves, Adam said. It'd be so cool.

No offense, sweetie, Joan said, but your input doesn't count.

He's an adult now, said Barry.

Nope, Joan said.

I defer to Mom, her son said.

What did they know about the responsibility, either? Most of the time they spent in Gao's club these last twenty years was to train, paying peanuts for off-hours table time. Joan occasionally volunteered—Friday nights, weekends Adam went away for school trips. Barry coached more, and took Gao's money, but his efforts amounted to a fraction of Anabel's—Anabel, who had postponed medical school indefinitely to maintain the glorified warehouse. But all night, Joan's sleeping mind decorated its walls with figures, zeroes and threes flickering hopefully like white paper lanterns. At work the next morning, her conscious mind was running numbers on the toilet—something disagreeable in the cake; she should have done better than a premade—when an email came from Anabel.

Hi Ms. Chen, are you free for coffee this week? I can come to you anywhere, anytime.

Hi Annabel, Joan replied, leaving the autocorrect typo. *12–1 P.M. lunch breaks. Café in my office park?*

Perfect, Anabel replied. *Would today work?*

Someone got in the stall behind Joan, groaning and yanking at her pants in a rustling flurry.

Fine, Joan replied, and pushed herself upright, squeezing the muscle above her traitorous knee. She needed to make another PT appointment. It felt like she'd just finished with her PT, a lugubrious twenty-six-year-old who laughed exclusively at the custodian's jokes about killing herself. At least Barry was cheerful, unlike all of these youngsters.

The café line extended ten feet down the sidewalk, polyester-blend butts soaking heat from idling SUVs. Joan was five minutes early, and so was the gray sedan she knew, even before she messaged *here*, belonged to Anabel. She jumped as Joan rapped the passenger window, phone sliding across her fingertips, but caught it nimbly over the underseat chasm.

Too crowded, Joan said. Let's drive somewhere. She suddenly felt chagrined about her venom toward Anabel, who looked more tired today, her slightly more formal attire—black chinos, a white buttondown beneath her gray puffer—rendering her stiffer, less certain. They could go to the park across the street. Joan's secret, hidden by a slope of dense cedars, breezy, benches ringing a sun-soaked glade and cherub-topped birdbath.

I'd prefer to talk in here, Anabel said, if you don't mind.

We're still considering about the club, Joan said, lowering herself into the passenger seat. The heat was off and the frozen leather down her back reprimanded her for lying. Gao said you might be interested as well, and—

I'm going to report Kristian for sexual misconduct, Anabel said.

What?

Anabel stared through the windshield. The cold pimpling her pale neck tightened Joan's throat, too. My friend Ryan, Ryan Lo, you knew—? He told me, not long before he died . . .

Ah. The boy. He had knocked Barry out of the 2012 Olympic trials. A shock, the randomness of the death. Gao closed her club the week of the funeral.

He said it only happened once, Anabel went on, but I don't believe that.

It was here, Joan felt, for a ringingly clear second: the monster binding the core of the earth, the brutality of the sport which devoured their younger days—or, no: the days when they had just begun to realize what youth was, when they were still young but just old enough to intuit the existential repetition that seeped poisonous from the fifteen dull fluorescent minutes at the end of lunch, the vacuum's path around yet another mess left to you, the distracted missing of sunset, moon quarter-full then suddenly quarter-full again and the bird's nests always emptied and torn—and seemed, over time, to fade into legend, a power the simplicity of whose rule they craved. It was both to avenge himself on and revive this force that Barry kept playing for so long.

Then she returned to the surface of her life, its topographies of doubt and normalcy.

Why are you telling me? she said.

I was wondering if you knew anything. That might . . . confirm things. Evidence.

The question flattened everything she knew about Kristian, anvil stamping the landscape of memory. And if Joan thought she knew something like that, wouldn't she have acted already?

You know we're family friends, right? she said.

That's why I'm asking.

Have you talked to Barry?

I figured he'd be . . . less receptive. And maybe you could ask him, if he knows anything . . .

Joan tried not to feel smug about her assignation. I understand, she said, but I can't promise anything. What do you have so far?

Just Ryan's word, Anabel said, so far.

No text messages, DNA—anything?

He's dead.

No notes, Barry had said, no clues as to why. The most straightforward explanation was addiction and stupidity.

But I want to report it now, Anabel went on. We implemented a new SafeSport law, after the gymnastics stuff. They have to investigate.

Barry must have mentioned a new reporting law after his meeting last month. Right? Surely even he minded about something so serious. They had another meeting in two days. She thought back to the metal table in her sports academy's "medical ward," in a former factory, muggy white sky in barred casements. When the girls turned sixteen, their wizened doctor began gynecological exams. *Lie back*, the girls would imitate in their bunks, *make your legs like a frog's*. They joked about farting in her face. The doctor could no more have deviated from her mocked script than a table could from its stoic, four-legged posture.

When did it happen? Joan asked.

Three years ago? Maybe longer.

So you'll bring a four-year-old accusation against the best coach in the United States, with no evidence. For someone who is no longer with us.

Doesn't the fact he died mean something? What if it happens again? What if it's been happening? In the windshield, the café line inched forward, the woman attached to a pair of bubblegum-pink haunches squinting triple-chinned at her phone. Maybe if we say something, Anabel said, someone else will come forward.

I still don't know if I'm the right person to ask, Joan said.

When you buy the club, Anabel said, you'll be my boss. I'd hoped I could at least talk to you.

God damn Gao. God damn Barry.

After work, Joan drove to Gao's. She hasn't told me, Gao said. Beneath the fluorescent strips in her office, she did look sick. It did not help that she slumped on the broken couch while Joan sat on her desk, legs sternly extended. They had traveled to London together in 2012, putting the ghosts to rest, and skipped the Round of 16 to visit Stonehenge. The stones moved them unexpectedly: Joan remembered standing transfixed at the vantage point shown on so many postcards, listening to Gao speak at length about the poignancy of the cavemen's faith and wisdom.

If she'd told me, Gao said, I would have done something.

What?

Spoken to Kristian. Spoken to people at his club.

Could we still do that?

If there's any evidence, sure . . . the assistant coaches, or the kids, they'd be the ones who might know . . . Gao closed her eyes, and with two fingers tapped the golden stomach of the Buddha on the windowsill. Among the cleared shelves and desk, the shriveled black potted plant, he was the sole survivor of her former life.

Is there a chance?

There's always a chance. Who knows.

Even if she's wrong, that club shuts down, Joan said.

A long, strange motion wrung Gao's throat from sternum to chin. Clubs shut down, she said, it's not the end of the world. Let's sleep on it. You should tell Barry.

He wants to buy the club with Kristian's money . . .

I'd still sell to you, Gao said.

That's not my main worry.

I'm just letting you know that, even if it is, it's all okay. It's still yours. Just talk to Barry.

But Gao, how are you doing, with—

Not tonight, Gao said.

Back at home, the sedan sat untouched on the lawn. The men were doing burpees in the living room, their shadows intermingled on the wall. Barry was winded, Adam breathing deliberately through pursed lips. Tighten your core, Dad, he said, tuck your elbows. He saw her and stopped first. Barry did one more burpee, wobbly-cored and dripping, and fell onto his back.

Everything took place as if behind a heavy curtain. On the other side stood another table, another set of stakes, the shadows of table legs and human feet extending graspingly through the gap. Immaterial, silent, undeniably present.

Order takeout, Joan said. I'm exhausted.

Your knee still hurting? You could try—

I've tried everything, Joan said, it's just age.

She should tell him now. But for what? The last time they saw him, in Beijing, her father-in-law told Joan: Stay strong. You are the man. Joan had insisted on bringing Adam, then six; she'd known it would be the last time he saw all four grandparents alive. Barry had denied this. Barry said it would distract them but let himself get eliminated in the first round.

Kristian video called as she was applying her nighttime creams—pure ceremony now, as stress had long since claimed its pits and runnels. Still, she rubbed in the excess before picking up. A roving frame of sunbeams and treetops flickered around Kristian. Behind him sounded the *pock* of a struck baseball. I owe you an apology, Joan, he said. Barry and I should not have discussed the money without you.

That's all right, she said. Was this it, the face of a child molester? In their living room, five years ago, deferentially unblinking as it listened to Adam's lecture about the greatest hockey goalies of all time? Taking in, intently, the movements of Barry's hand as it demonstrated his favorite soup recipe? Smiling wanly at the neighbors on a run with Joan and Barry, spring air passing through its sensitively flaring nostrils the same as theirs, the vista atop a local hill edging its features with the same clement, vernal joy?

I don't think we can take the money, she said. I know Barry said yes already, but—

A pale palm, serene and diplomatic. Of course, Kristian said. I wired it to your account, but it can be returned anytime. All's fair in friendship and business.

Barry was slumped on the couch, watching European soccer; did not turn his head as Joan asked, Did the board pass a sexual misconduct law?

Yeah, he said, we went around about it for *two* months—Kagin drafted it because he runs Ethics and everybody had to approve every word before it even went to a lawyer—and what do *we* know? Oh, fuck!—he half stood—no, it's offsides.

He turned up the volume, shouts and whistles shaking their elephant plant as a Spanish striker threw himself writhing to the grass.

Late into the night, Barry sound asleep, she sat at the dining table with the numbers. Adam came out of his room for water and told her, Don't do what you don't wanna, Ma, you're tired. He raised a hand as if to squeeze her shoulder, then considered better and thumped to the kettle in his flannel pajamas. Surely he thought the scales were beginning to tip, while she, having been him, knew it would be many more years, likely many frustrating ones, before he stopped bringing the same pajamas home for her to wash and properly, indulgently, iron once a season.

●

The next morning, the day of the monthly board meeting, Barry hoisted himself beneath the jacked-up car. (Custom jacks, twice as expensive as the generic ones.) He freed a hand to wave as Joan left for work, wobbled, kicked his feet to rebalance.

So we can drive to our club, he called. *Our* club!

At the office, she printed summaries of their finances. Did it make sense? Despite the years of retirement, she'd barely had a chance to miss it. Attending Barry's tournaments and listening to Barry's gripes about the board. Listening to Barry talk to Kristian.

She emailed Anabel to meet her in the park. Light collected on the cherub's shoulders and belly.

Have you talked to Kristian? Joan asked.

No, Anabel said. The sunlight whitened; the cologne of cold sap intensified. If he's innocent, there won't be a problem.

If he's innocent, shouldn't you let him make his case first?

Whose side are you on?

I need more time to think.

Do you know something or not? Anabel said.

Just give me a day.

She was just a kid, unattached, dogmatic. So little life to burn down, if that's what she decided to do. She had no real idea, Joan reasoned as she limped across the parking lot, accelerated breath piquing the first flush of indignance, what she was demanding of Joan in such brusque black-and-white.

At home, the forms to buy the club lay on the dining table, all grinning white signatory lines. Anabel had shown her the online reporting form she would fill, toggle-down menus and the narrow visor slits of word entry, encouraging succinctness. One could be a Claimant, Victim, Advisor to the Claimant, Witness—Gao had agreed to be an Advisor, but there was no natural role for Joan. Come on, honey, Barry said, you want to. Can't let that girl snatch it.

Joan's knee twinged. Her palms sweated. She did want it. She'd driven by on her way back. She admired the cinderblock face, the resolution of its craggy, scoured whiteness. Like Anabel's face in her car, and this afternoon. Everything it took—she missed the monstrous demand.

Right after dinner, as Barry sat down at their computer to join the board meeting, she told him about Anabel's accusation, her request for support.

I wouldn't tell you, she said, if I didn't think there was—

Kristian? Barry said. Our Kristian?

It's . . . it's never someone expected, right? You could never *really* suspect it. It shouldn't matter who it is.

Do you hear yourself?

I'm just telling you—

Whatever it is she wants, you have nothing to do with it. Or too much. It's *our* friend. It's Kristian! She's never liked him anyway, the situation with the boy—

Gao's backing her.

Sure, she'd do anything for her. It's selfish to involve Gao, really, the state she's in.

He couldn't tell her what to do. That was never how he asserted his influence; they both remembered as he kneeled between her knees, supplicant, outspread hands collaring the base of her neck. Joanie, he moaned, Joanie, Joanie. Today, as every day, he wore athletic gear from when he was young, vintage teals and yellows, hair gel in tropical flavors. He hadn't told her to support his continued competition, no matter her reservations: she loved watching him play. The real power wasn't haranguing or bullying.

She thought of Kristian's soft-spokenness, his glowing watchfulness.

She hasn't done anything yet, she said.

It doesn't matter, Barry said. I bet she'll tell everyone at the meeting. That's the point in these cases, isn't it—airing it out, venting, making a villain. Her boyfriend dies and *now* she wants to bring up something, from years ago?

Barry.

I need to join, he said. He shuffled back on his knees and settled into the desk chair, let Joan sit on the edge of the bed, out of sight, and played the meeting on speaker. They knew, on some level, what would happen: right after the president's welcome, Anabel announced her intention to report sexual assault. In the name of transparency, she said, and the new bylaws. She did not name anyone, but her eyes seemed to seek Kristian's across the screen.

It's . . . thank you for this, the president said. We'll be looking into it, per our new protocols. Which there is now, ah, *renewed* urgency to finish!

One of the longest-tenured members raised a digital hand. We'll save discussion for official channels, the president said.

The man unmuted. Those of us with personal involvement, he said, should be given the opportunity to recuse ourselves.

I agree, Barry said, and also, let me just say—

Joan went downstairs to stand before the kitchen window. The sink was clear. Adam was doing his homework at the dining table, beneath a framed watercolor of the London skyline that Kristian gave them, congratulations to Joan for her Olympics run.

Adam set down his pencil. Wanna come to the gym with me, Ma? Maintaining bone density is important, for women your age.

And what age is that?

Middle-aged?

Kristian holding Adam as a baby, back when they were all young. No, that had never happened. Just beneath Adam's skin, the shape of another person he would become, who was just a suggestion of the shape of the next. She felt a rush of mournfulness for their imminent meeting, for her love whose form would always lag behind his.

•

The next day, an assessor came to the club. Gao would start chemo in a week. As they put on their coats to leave, Anabel's head popped out from the dark office.

Can I talk to you, Joan?

Honey, Barry said, looking to Gao, maybe—

Hit with me, Barry, Gao said. They're just talking.

They sat as Joan and Gao had two nights ago, Joan on the couch this time. In the interior window, Gao lobbed and Barry wafted soft hits back. Gao's feet barely moved. Her knees looked stiff.

Kristian had called Anabel. He offered his condolences and said it was a massive misunderstanding, but he and Haesun would do whatever needed. He said he understood the depth of her pain. That in the face of the void, one had to do something.

If you're going to do it, Joan said, just do it. You should have before you told everyone.

Do you have any evidence to add? Anabel said.

No.

The next day, they signed the club papers. The family celebrated over dinner; Barry drank four glasses of wine and Joan fell asleep on the living room couch. When she woke, to windows full of a strangely bright, paralyzing dusk, Barry was on the phone. Thank you again, he said. I don't know how we'll pay you back. Well, with money, yes, but—yes, anytime. We'd love to see you.

•

At first, with Gao still leading, it was energizing to coach a few nights a week, slipping out of her kitten heels into a new pair of the flat-soled sneakers she'd worn to Beijing, to Vegas, to so many places that shaped her down to the marrow. To learn the quirks of the two other assistant coaches and feel dozens of table tennis balls kissing the edges of her feet as she stood in a corner and watched the kids drill. In the mornings, Barry dropped off her and Adam, then headed straight to Gao's old office. Adam took the bus home, and his parents returned together. There was harmony. There was compromise and laughter, and even a brief, tentative liaison on the broken couch. (It doesn't *look* that poky, Barry concluded sagely.) It was harder without Anabel, who had resigned, but if they hired another part-timer, Barry insisted, it could be done.

On her last day, Anabel had not even said goodbye. Her resignation came as an email, cc'ing Gao, and the last a distracted Joan saw of her was her torso bent over the drinking fountain, hand clawing the rim of its shuddering metal belly, circle of sweat between her shoulders like a bullet wound.

Within a few weeks, talk of Kristian visiting tapered. What with the case, you know, Barry said. After.

Two months in, Gao left, eyebrows feathery. At her retirement party, held in a restaurant, kids cried. Parents cried. Joan watched Gao spit out a piece of braised pork. Too piggy, she said in the restroom later, apologetic and flushed. Without her, nights at the club went hard and timeless, the sounds of students' demands, snapping net posts, and rattling caddies deadened hammer blows on something never to be finished, its loose panels never to feel secured. Barry, manning the club from ten to ten, lost fifteen pounds. They divided Gao's coaching between them, and within two weeks Joan could not jog or bend on her knee.

The most steadying presence became the pressure of her old brace. Like the black sleeve of oncoming sleep, it comforted her. Kristian did not reach out. He's probably not allowed to talk to anyone, Barry said. But they'll get to the bottom of it.

Four months in, shortly after Adam's final exams, a parent asked after Anabel. He'd read something about her and a sexual harassment case.

It's about her ex-boyfriend, Joan said. He's dead.

The next day, Adam emailed her a link to a news story and a thread from a popular table tennis forum: *It's disgusting how young people make accusations for attention. If their club needed new students esp. after the ownership change—how's that for timing?!—they could hire new coaches or host better events, or better yet, this girl could run it herself and show everyone how it's done. To attack such a longstanding member of the community like Coach K is laughable. US Table Tennis would not exist on the world stage without him.*

First of all, the next comment began, but Joan could not bear to read it.

Five months in, the toilet overflowed. They shut down the club for a week to replace the plumbing. Then a section of the roof began to leak. They lost four thousand dollars that month.

Joan visited Gao, intending—she realized only as she lost her will to do it—to accuse Gao of not warning them sufficiently. But she had. She had shown the numbers, and her life. She left her head bare, and they smoked a cigarette on the balcony of her apartment while, from the other side of the glass, the tennis match her sister was watching flashed tinny blue light and cheers across the railings.

Are you mad at me, Gao finally said. Ah, why am I asking. I'd do it again. Sorry.

The parent who asked about Anabel stopped sending their child to lessons, citing Gao's retirement. Two more parents followed. Joan and Barry had not planned for students leaving with her. In a mania that saw him out of the house from 6:00 A.M. to 11:00 P.M., Barry campaigned in Asian language schools and senior living homes across the county. The new influx of students worked them all to the bone, and one of the assistant coaches demanded a raise of five dollars per hour. At thirty-five hours a week, it was not possible. He moved to a different club. For a week, the remaining four of them managed; then Joan's knee started burning when she walked. They were forced to cut back lessons. Adam joked that he could learn to toss balls out of the caddy.

Without consulting Joan, Barry talked to Anabel. I told her she'd always have a job here if she wants it, he said, but maybe she should just apply to medical school.

Adam graduated. On his high school football field, he and his friends posed kneeling, one arm outstretched and the other cocked "in Archer's Pose," he explained, half impatient and half elated, as he urged her to point the phone camera lower, "out of the sun!" Barry ran forward to re-drape Adam's fallen cords around his neck, and the flash of sun on egg-white and marigold silk was like the convention center light on the uniforms of Kristian's students, at the US Open it must have been, fifteen years ago now, all of them running in a line around the arena, sprinting the long sides and jogging the short, Kristian at a halfway point behind the head umpire's station, tapping each boy's shoulder as he passed, more of a slap for the laggers, "Good, good, faster, all right, faster, not good enough, good," and Joan remembered how his hand sometimes rose to meet the back of a boy's neck (all their hair was kept short), his lifetime's experience inflicted, through callused hands, upon the soft, fuzz-whorled embrasures that would soon harden into muscled ridges; and it was nothing against the hours Kristian had sat with her husband and talked, sat in their very living room; her own coaches had probably touched her like that and she forgot because it meant nothing, Adam's gym teachers had probably touched him like that; but it felt solid and sure as the perpetual longing for her son that had already mineralized in her aching gut.

She mailed two checks to Kristian. An indignity, her inability to pull the money from a single account, but one she felt she deserved. A week later, when the checks were delivered and Kristian called, followed by Barry, she sent both to voicemail. What Gao had given everything to preserve, they recklessly lost; the terminality that could sweep any time across a table, in two swings of an opponent's racket, had gotten its lead curtain around their lives. She walked slowly to the park after work and sat at a bench at the base of the hill. She could not see the ever-delayed sunset from there, but she could, she thought, smell the wind off the peaty birdbath water, the furred darkness creeping again up the cherubim's base.

●

A few days before Adam left for college, Gao forwarded an email from the board's new ethics committee. The initial investigation found insufficient evidence to escalate the case.

Adam found her in a lawn chair on the driveway, facing the sedan. Somehow, summer was over. The expansive, mournful light of August carrying on forward, from and toward the hollow glare of February. Tomorrow, she would call someone to tow the car to the shop.

What's wrong? Adam said. Your leg.

Glute squeezes, hamstring stretches, leg raises. She let him walk her through the motions he'd learned from his friend. His hands kind and deferential, trustworthy. Of course, she'd been touched inappropriately in her life. Not by the doctor, but any number of people she'd forgotten, boyfriends and male teammates. Grabbing, teasing. She never thought it would make a difference.

2022

HANNAH

Haesun brought me with him to bail out Coach. They arrested Coach yesterday at his house, where Haesun lived till he moved out last month and tried to start going by Hank. At security, he still gave his Korean name.

"You should wait outside, Hannah," he said.

"Then why'd you let me come in?"

"Listen to your dad," said one of the guards. I could see to the end of the hallway; I could have sprinted through before the guard manning the conveyer belt blinked.

Haesun chucked his keys back through the metal detector and I went out to wait in the passenger seat, staring down the stacked bug eyes of the high rise's black windows. Thirty minutes later Coach came out of the turquoise glass doors and saw me right away, despite Haesun's disgusting smeared windshield. He arched a hand over his forehead, like I was brighter than the sun, which all week had shone greasy and dull. He was wearing a gray T-shirt, basketball shorts, and mismatched socks, like they caught him in bed eating chips out of his lap and shouting at a basketball game, the way they'd catch my dad if they busted our house. When I got out to give him shotgun, I took a deep breath. Jail smelled like nothing. He still rocked the car as he sat; still had weight and those two super long hairs on his ankle, just like before.

"Why did you bring her, Hank?" he asked.

"She wanted to see you," Haesun said.

When Ma broke the news—Ba should have done it, but no matter how mean he acted, he was no good at difficult things—I grabbed my head and said *No no no no no*. She didn't stop me from googling and reading *Charged with misdemeanor child molestation of fourteen-year-old student*. I was fifteen but everyone would think it was me, though we always had separate rooms. For ten years. Always. No, no, no.

Coach tilted his head owl-like. His eyes looked bigger and flatter. Maybe his face had shrunk. He looked hungry. In jail they didn't have his oatmeal, fish pills, Diet Sierra Mist. "Why?" he asked me.

"The Open's next weekend," I said, as if he'd forget, even in jail. Haesun's head drooped. In his lap his fingers went at each other. Whenever my lungs hurt during multiball, I focused by counting splinters of skin on his raw cuticles.

"Why did you *bring her here*?" Coach's leg shook twice. I imagined his wrists in cuffs, but really they were propped on his knees, apart, free. I knew where his hands lay just by the angles of his shoulders.

"I wanted to see you, too," said Haesun.

Tears welled. I sucked air through my teeth, as if that would draw them back into my head.

"Do you want to ask me if I did it, Hannah?" Coach asked.

The air stung my gums. I wanted to reach over the console and tap his knee, but really, it was too late. Besides his hands guiding my arms, and one hug, he had never touched me.

"You shouldn't see me again," Coach said. "Go have a nice life."

•

No one at school talked about it. Their feeds showed other news. No one would care, though sometimes it felt like everyone in the world had shouted after me, on days they needed an ego boost, *Ping-pong, ping-pong, ping-pong!* Not like the school where Ryan Lo went, which wrote kiss-ass student paper articles Coach stacked in his office. I was Coach's best student since him. He still watched us in poster form, half hidden behind the bleachers. Ryan Ryan Ryan. At fifteen, he had accomplished more than me, and the comparison kept me going.

Coach never made me feel less-than. As soon as I showed more potential than the boys, he prioritized me. He could send me to the Bundesliga, too. Less competition on the women's side. Easy.

Ma and Ba thought I'd drop out of the Open. When I got home and saw the flight cancellation page on our living room computer, I vaulted the sofa and slapped the mouse from Ma's fingers.

"I'm going," I said.

She pinched the back of my hand and twisted so hard my skin whorled like rice paper. "And who takes you?"

"Haesun," I said.

"Haesun! *Haesun*, ha! Ha!"

"Haesun *and* Dana," I said. The rule, since the gymnastics thing, was that you couldn't travel alone. Coach always followed it, bringing Haesun or Dana or both. The club helped cover costs for me to sleep by myself.

"I'm going to win," I told Ma.

"It won't change who he is," Ma said. "You have no idea. Do you know how we feel? Your Baba and I, we feel like idiots. We feel like the world's worst parents. What if it was you?" *But it wasn't*, I knew better than to say; that really would have set her off. Already she was uncrossing and recrossing her legs, pinching the hem of her skirt, and looking toward the drawer with the rock candy that kept them going after they quit smoking. Coach made them quit and they never forgave him. I could imagine them whispering to each other: *see, that's the kind of man he was, he hated cigarettes and he molested children.*

I x-ed out the page. The mouse felt cool, like Ma was a vampire. "It's for me," I said. If I didn't go, everyone would think I was the girl.

Ma click-clacked into the kitchen and smoked half a cigarette through the open window. I liked the smell, I must have since I was a kid, and now there was no one to save us from it. I bowed my head and imagined the ball bouncing from corner to corner of the white tiles, smooth and shiny as Haesun's cheekbones were pimply and dull. I never missed.

•

"I was going to quit," Haesun said. We were sitting in his parked car outside the club, four days later. He had picked me up from school, like Coach used to, and driven me over. The club was closed indefinitely but I wanted to practice. Haesun was one of five people—him, Dana, two custodians, Coach—with a key. It was still the best place to practice in the Bay Area.

"That's why you moved out?"

"Yes."

"But you didn't know about—"

"No! How could you ask me that?"

"Well, how could he do something like that?"

"Not the same."

"Uh-huh."

"You shouldn't do this," he said. "You think it'll make you feel better but—"

"I am under no such illusion," I said. Why did people think everything was about *feeling better*? I didn't *feel better* after a four-hour practice. I felt endorphins, sure, I felt loose in a biological way, but for every bit of looseness there were five bits of nauseating exhaustion. The more potential you had, the more time you spent feeling bad. Haesun should have known that, but he'd given up on his own potential. It was a shame. I'd always rooted for him. I'd always wished I played elegantly like him, but I was more like Ryan, guns blazing.

Inside, we set up in silence. Things hadn't collected dust yet. The flickering light Coach replaced just before his arrest came on perfectly, a little whiter than the others, but only if you were looking for it. The best ball caddy was in Coach's office, but we didn't go there. Haesun slid a screen in front of the black window. Maybe it had happened in there one night, after everyone went home, one of the times I drove with my parents or Haesun. Almost never Haesun; he probably declined driving students to avoid suspicion about this very scenario. He was here as a huge favor. I hadn't even considered until we were grapevining around Court Two, Haesun watching his feet: What would someone think if they found us in the shuttered club? It started making me nervous, so nervous that by backhand time I had to stop every ten balls and catch my breath.

"You don't look good," Haesun said. He stopped serving. "This is wrong, isn't it? This is wrong." I missed being in sync like that, our thoughts gulped from the same cloud of weird air. It hurt to realize. He dropped his racket and propped himself against the table, white edge cutting into his yellower palms. "Do you think there are cameras?"

"You're asking *me*?"

"Do your parents know you're here?"

He was supposed to be reassuring me. Useless. I held my next breath until I achieved a lightheadedness very similar to anger. "If you're that scared," I said, "whatever, just take me home."

The sad thing was, I'd been hitting really well.

•

I skipped the Open. Eleven days after we visited Coach, his lawyers called, asking if I would testify.

The next afternoon, Haesun met me outside the Starbucks where the other kids flocked after school. I'd never had time to go. Haesun had stopped gelling his chin-length hair and it wisped around his face like Einstein's. His radio was on, talking, even as we spoke through the frame of his passenger window.

"Are you gonna do it?" he asked. Inside the coffee shop one of my classmates, faking a doubled-over laugh, knocked the green sign swinging.

"Did they call you, too?"

"Yes."

"Well, will you?"

He looked away, out the driver's window. He started rambling. He'd drafted a few cover letters for IT jobs, he said, which was what he came to the States to study. For a long time it had seemed less dignified than being a coach, all the sitting down, headsets, and dead-inside clients. And he'd have a hard time finding as inspiring of a boss. No one made him believe in himself as much as Coach had, he said, and I understood that. But during the intervening days the self-belief that underlay my table tennis, that belonged to table tennis the way water belonged to its lake or swamp, had flowed elsewhere. I walked around school wearing the dry spiked halo of the fact that I wasn't the raped girl. I literally knew her, she could only have been one of a few people, but that fact didn't pierce the pure *not-me*. I didn't know what to do with that.

We repeated ourselves:

"Did you know?" I asked.

"Why would I?"

"So you *do* think he did it."

"I don't know."

Would I serve as a character witness? the lawyers had asked. Coach never did anything to me, right? He had treated me well. No, nothing had happened to me. Why had nothing happened to me? I had considered texting the other girls, but any time I unlocked my phone to do so, I googled Ryan. The links were all purple. Coach used to pin every medal and clipping of mine next to his, but stopped just before Ryan died. Like he knew it was about to happen. I remembered because it made me so sad, the empty wall space next to Ryan's US Nationals plaque.

I needed to see the club again. Haesun, probably relieved I dropped the topic of testifying, agreed to take me. The air from his car vents smelled like the seafood warehouse down the road, whose reek had somehow never infiltrated our practice hall. Whenever Coach drove me to tournaments, up and down California and twice in Texas, he kept a stack of Little Trees in the glove compartment, crisp black cutouts in individual baggies. Sometimes I'd take one and press its plastic to my nose, smelling only the car wipes Coach used to clean every surface, including the tree baggies and the tissue box, after every long trip. Then Coach would ask if I was training to be a K-9.

Haesun parked by the doors and waited against the car as I stuck my nose up to their glass. I thought I could make out half of Ryan's face glowing in the dark practice hall.

"Do you think it's why Ryan killed himself?" I asked. My voice washed back over my face, damp, acid, and whiny.

"We don't know that he killed himself."

"What do you *think*?" *Think! Think!* Coach always yelled at lesser kids, the ones who, unlike me and Ryan, had no intuition for the game.

"I think he had his own problems."

Would they have said that about me? That I had my own problems? No matter what, I wouldn't have quit the Bundesliga. They'd have had to send me back in a packaged coffin, slide me out from the side of a jet like an excised organ.

This thought felt so terrible, I turned and jogged back to Haesun. I raised my arms, as if to hug him, or maybe shake a decisive thought from between his ears, but I wobbled and he caught me around the ribs. I saw his purple-cratered cheeks and pink O lips. His hair was gelled again. The tips of our noses brushed. We kind of kissed. He was thirty-seven, I remembered; his birthday had just passed.

I pushed him away, stumbled, and fell on my ass. Haesun, wiping his mouth, didn't help me up.

"You smell like him," I said.

Haesun scrubbed a finger across his nostrils. "What?"

"Did you move back to Coach's?" Coach's address was public in the case file. I couldn't guess the direction of his house and didn't look it up, just like I didn't click the other stories about child molestation beneath Coach's, glued one to the next, a white worm rising out of cyberspace hell.

"Well, there's mold," he said, "in the new place, there was mold, so I had to . . ."

I imagined Haesun lying across a sofa that could be Coach's, watching a show on Coach's TV. Coach would never lie down on a sofa or watch whatever shows Haesun did. "It's *his* house!"

"He's there, too," Haesun whined. "I posted his bail, he's home."

Coach was home.

He got to see Coach. If I wanted to testify, the lawyers said, I could not see Coach.

"So you're not testifying," I said.

"I don't know."

"But you don't think he did it," I said.

"Hannah," he said, "I don't know."

And then I thought, looking at this helpless man who had known Coach and Ryan for so long without getting any closer to understanding or being like them: what serious business would Coach have had with lesser people like Haesun or the other girls? "Why did you bring *her*," he had asked, because who cared if Haesun saw him in a jail cell, who cared if Haesun thought he had some right to the house where they'd arrested him or to keep living with someone he did not fully believe innocent, but *I* didn't belong among those lies. I had always played with conviction. I always knew which way I wanted to go.

It was clear now.

Ignoring Haesun's shouts, I sprinted away, all three miles home. Through the living room window I saw my parents were staggering around, mouths open. A sugar cube arced across the orange lamplight. Ma screamed, laughing, as it bounced off her cheek. Then she threw a cube and Ba gulped it out of the air like a trout. They had started smoking openly on the porch, and Ba, especially, was more relaxed than ever. They were saving a lot of money on my quitting. If they felt bad they'd given so much money to a rapist, the nicotine buzzed over it.

On the lawn, I called Coach's lawyers.

•

At the 2018 Pan American Games trials, I got my period between two rounds of matches. I hadn't brought tampons. I didn't want to get periods and thought if I left behind the equipment, maybe they couldn't follow. Coach walked me into the women's bathroom and handed me paper towels to roll into a pad.

"*Hola*," I heard him greet someone. Her footsteps went on calm and slow into the adjacent stall, sneakers squelching down against the tiles as she sighed and braced. I flushed when I thought it would cover the splash of her poop. By the time I emerged she was handing Coach two tampons, bundled in four yellow-wrapped pads.

"Do you want these now?" Coach asked.

"I made a pad."

To the woman, looking between us, to throw her off, I said, "*Mi papa*."

"*Vale*," she replied.

Coach and I both hated that I'd said that. For the rest of the tournament we didn't get along, and I didn't qualify for the games. Coach kept holding out tampons and I kept rolling my own pads, until I had to face the foamy white hotel sheets. Then I said "Fine" and took all the stupid crinkly things. He hugged me, our first-ever hug, and told me not to worry about the bed. One of those tampons was still rolling around the bottom of my duffel.

•

The next night, I told my parents they'd have to drive me to the pretrial hearing. That was when Ba finally lost it, swinging at the air and kicking at the carpet. "One wrong word and your future is over," he said.

They tried to get me to see another lawyer, but they couldn't make me do anything anymore. I lay on my bed, mentally zinging every angle of winner past the World Champion, until Haesun's name blacked out my phone screen.

"I was just thinking," he said, "you're right, there's no reason you should throw away your career—"

Coach wouldn't have posted his own bail, if he'd thought he committed the crime. Haesun had failed that test.

"What's funny?" Haesun asked. "Hannah. Hannah. Seriously."

"You're not him," I said. I wasn't *her*. She didn't exist. I blocked Haesun.

•

Ma and Ba took a long way round to the courthouse. Like at tournaments they were more nervous than me, but maybe they were trying to undermine me somehow, too.

The long way passed my old elementary school, a park where the saddest kids smoked weed, the yellow house to which we ran before practice, whose grassy hill I was dragged down—Ba, to encourage me, gave too hard a push—the one time my family tried to fly a kite. It almost passed behind the club, but Ba swerved just in time, drawing honks. During the pandemic Coach and I had done burpees on the back lawn, sometimes joined by Haesun. I'd tell my parents I was out walking and run the three miles. Not for a second, because of how strong the burpees made me feel, did we doubt it'd all blow over.

"So you know who it was?" Ba said.

"Wouldn't you like to know," I said. But the spiked halo behind me shivered and warped. Soon, I'd have to find out which girl he had supposedly chosen. I'd have to look her in the face and communicate how much more my conviction meant than hers, just like at the table. I rubbed the insides of my knees together, hoping the nylons Ma had thrown at my head that morning could catch a small fire.

"You're the kind of parents whose kid it'd happen to," I said. "Yeah, you know, it might as well have been me."

Ba whirled round as the car barreled into the courthouse lot, and for a second I thought we'd all be sent from the world in flames and hatred. Not hatred of me: the self-hatred that lights up adults' eyes like the reflection of an oncoming train.

"Leave it," Ma said, "she's just scared." Like I said, she was the one who could say hard things.

This time I went through the metal detector. Ba was sent back for an e-cigarette in his pocket. Haesun wasn't there yet. When he arrived, I'd use all the power that made me good at table tennis not to hate him. I could only hate him if he had done something wrong, but all he'd done was be stupid.

Waiting on a bench outside the courtroom, I saw Coach first. He looked normal. I guess I'd expected his eyes to keep enlarging, to take over his head like a piranha's. His lawyer was a woman in a cherry-red pantsuit with colorless lips. As they passed me, his gaze swiveled to keep me pinned. *Why did you bring her, Hank?*

He wasn't apologizing. He was pissed I hadn't walked away. That I wasn't off living a nice life, as if I knew what that was supposed to be.

"Be brave, Hannah!" Ba shouted, demented and three seconds too late, as Coach stepped through the wooden doors, glossy and dark as the chocolate I'd once left to melt on his dashboard, which he wiped away wordlessly before we pulled back onto the highway, heading home, all the mountains and deserts and oceans but a backdrop for my dreams. Our dreams.

Ma smacked Ba's arm. *You're nobodies*, I wanted to tell them, and everyone filing by, their legal pads warped by coffee and hand sweat, their legs jelly stumps—no one but Coach's lawyer looked like they could even run a mile—*you're fleas*. And Haesun, framed in the security scanner at the end of the hall, who couldn't have stopped me if I tried to kiss him a thousand more times, until his asshole-shaped mouth chapped off. He couldn't bring himself to give Coach up, either, but we were not the same. I had until he arrived to figure out how to say it; to ask Coach, heavy with a winner's sorrow: Would it ever have been me?

EPILOGUE

RYAN

The kid arrived at the museum half an hour before closing. The guards who waved him in had no idea that he'd played his best-ever match of table tennis that afternoon, nor that he had slipped from his hotel in Le Marais while his coach met with a Bundesliga scout. They were mostly eager to go home, to emerge into the cool coppery air whisking off the Tuileries pools, to end the extra-long shifts that late Fridays entailed. A few, grinding their rubber soles against the red marble fronting a Babylonian stele or squeaky parquet beneath the tumult of a Biblical painting, admired the boy's verve as he jogged past down the corridors of the Denon Wing, silver-capped hoodie strings bouncing at his back, winking the reflected violets of dusk. They had not seen him, twenty minutes earlier, tip himself through his slim hotel window onto a slimmer balcony, sore shins scraping down the twisted balusters, to watch sunset stain the mansard roofs, pigeons on spiked eaves across the courtyard fluffing feathers over their hearts, green and pink like the molten core of the sky, and consider lowering himself along the limestone wall's ivy or drainpipe, their bristle scratching his perpetually tense palms, before realizing, with a melancholy pang, that he could simply walk out through the narrow bluing hallways. As warning chimes sounded, the guards set their feet along terminal routes, not knowing how, six hours before, the feet of three hundred spectators had crammed along the bleachers in the Porte de Versailles convention center, all toes—scuffed and polished, leather and rubber—pointed toward the arena of red polyester, in a corner of which the boy stretched his arms one then the other, eyes blackened by purpose, lips sugary moist, the alien light and energy of the city coursing through him, despite or because his coach declared it a perverse place, beautiful but perverse, defiant, and it filled him with a warmth toward these strange spectators, a warmth he knew to be unwarranted and fanciful but stoked all the hotter for it. The guards had not seen him stalk up to the table and call *heads* with an insolence that seemed to have decided the match, then fling the ball for the first serve of warm-up against a boy whose name no one would remember two years later. At that point in the afternoon, they had been contemplating Goya and Titian, Rodin and the workshops of time-conquered Greeks, the tops of their shoes framing square feet of bathroom tile, aches stringing arches to hamstrings to lumbars, worries souring lactic between their pinched shoulder blades: traffic, climate, dusty covers and rugs, empty refrigerators, persistent pains, unvisited parents, unanswered messages, trash staining the stone along the Seine's water line. They had not seen the boy's first, debilitating serve, then the second, softened only to draw out the opponent, the path of the opposing racket as legible as the rise of his own finger, time but a braided rope of milliseconds, coiled simultaneity, levering his limbs to where they were needed. The guards had never experienced this; or, if so, perhaps as they tripped in front of a masterpiece, toes crossing the worn tread of tape but outstretched hand diverting from the paint, whose crackled surface compelled them, as the force of a hundred thousand hours of practice compelled the boy, through familiarity. The guards (except for one, whose nephew played table tennis and had asked him to attend; but he did not see the boy now, sloppy strides accordioning his kangaroo pocket, feet thudding and arms jolting laxly as they could not afford to at the table) had not followed the tournament announcer's voice, low, amplified, ubiquitous like a bored archangel's, into the seats of the central court in the Porte de Versailles, tucking their bags and disgruntlements behind their calves for the last time that day, only to find themselves leaning on knee-propped elbows, breathing down necks below as the two boys worked themselves into an ideal frenzy of competition. They had not gone lightheaded as the match hurtled toward the fulfillment of a spectator's headiest desire: technical mastery, seesawing the match to its uppermost breaking point, which seemed impossible in this case because one boy—the boy now running frame to frame across the zoetrope of the arched windows, flying over graying garden grounds beyond—was so much better than his opponent; but the universe had conspired to grant the lesser player a string of genius, courage, strength, luck that only emphasized the greatness of his superior, and which, after raising its witnesses above the cloud line of ultimate enjoyment (deuce in the fifth) let them see the dreariness of everything below, ordinary life, and embedded pearlescent in that drear, like the upturned faces of the saved in an apocalypse scene, their own tiny ambitions, catching the last light motes as nimbuses shut once more against the aspirational sky. The guards did not have the canvas of that match, forty minutes on the convention center floor in the Fifteenth Arrondissement, against which to see one of those reveries that blow in like painted scarves, brushing the mind's eye before dissolving against the frieze of the present: a trumpet clarion, for the seventy-year-old man in his dead brother's wool jacket, who attended the tournament every year except '68, the sound a bronze needle floating before a desolate de Chirico horizon; for the Chinese tourist who had left her group, that afternoon visiting Auvers-sur-Oise, not only her anguish at the idea of Van Gogh's grave (a *stone* squashing the maimed head of genius!), but also a dream-memory of floating on the aurora-splashed North Sea, which for fear of destroying she would never travel north of France; and, shared by two cousins in the top row, though they would never know it shared, a bus stop from their youth where they thought they had seen their grandmother smash a bouquet of lilacs over a man's bare white head, half the petals whipping away as the other half filled the man's collar and the crisscrosses of their shoelaces, their grandmother's gray dress anointed by a single amethyst bud; as the boy himself, watching a match of unattainable skill, would have seen a little girl in New Jersey baring her teeth at the reflection in her bedroom mirror, wood frame heavy and densely carved as the fretwork on Versailles. The guards did not have the chance to be one of the few who, watching the match, having been born with the frightening ability to perceive the world unclouded by past and future, by form and preconception, saw nothing but the match—impossible to describe, streaming purely through sense, click stomp grunt. As the boy ran past, some of the guards wished his feet would land lighter; some envied his fleetness; some, too jaded or tired to interpret such encounters, felt a wan rueful twinge of portent. Had they known about the afternoon's success, a few might have called congratulations, even those who detested children and teenagers, perhaps a sardonic *allez!* softened by a glimpse of the boy's unfocused eagerness, his evident anticipation of some great fulfillment he had not been taught, among all his techniques, to envision. They would have been endeared by the way he tucked his hair behind his ears mid-stride, though if they had seen the match, they would have known that that gesture heralded an apologetic advance toward the final outcome, killing touches light, footwork silent; though not that, for a moment before the final stroke of the final and inevitably anticlimactic point, allowing himself to take in the full range and hunger of the spectators' faces (and more distinct than all of their visages, the unseeable presence of his coach behind him), the boy had felt a totalizing emptiness, all god's confused and purposeless matter contracted to a pinprick. If they had known, they might have crept (or sauntered, or stepped; they felt different entitlements to patrons' reactions) around the corner to witness as the boy skidded to a halt before the Winged Victory of Samothrace on her volcanic dais, and—after the primal awe of her stature and brutal pleasure of her asymmetrically wounded wings, the strange recognition that this was what he had not known he was running to find—wondered that she was supposed to be something within or guiding him; that anyone had imagined the inchoate, tormented, glorious feelings of his most private life as a shape so bombastic and plain. They would have seen him spread his arms in challenge and laugh.

Acknowledgments

MRC, for taking a chance on me. I'm so honored to debut together. *Woo-hoo!!!*

Alexis Nowicki, Tiffany Gonzalez, and everyone at Astra House, for your work and care. Rodrigo Corral, for the thrilling cover. Julia Kardon, for all the advice and advocacy. Ella Wang, for your editorial eye and steady support.

Claire Messud, Laura van den Berg, Neel Mukherjee, Peter Ho Davies, Travis Holland, Gabe Habash, and Julie Buntin for your faith, encouragement, mentorship, and precious, precious time.

Max Delsohn, for talking me off the edge several times (and many more to come, surely).

Amanda Hayes, for tolerating my antisocial behavior. I'm sorry I never checked our mailbox.

The Helen Zell Writers' Program, for changing my life in unimaginable ways.

For the sport: everyone at STLTTC (especially Kam Chan, Dale Dressel, and Stan Sokol), Harvard TTC, NCTTA, Michigan TTC, Lily Yip TTC, WDCTT, TTC Champions Düsseldorf (especially Michael Eckert), and Borussia Düsseldorf (especially Andreas Preuß, Dang Qiu, Alexander Schilling, and Kay Stumper). Khaleel Asgarali. Alfredo Báez. Ryan Driskill. Sonjay and Sonya Henry.

Kagin Lee. Leslie Liu. Coach Sheri, Justen Yao, Alex Yao, and Jonathan Yao.

For otherwise shaping me, and making life worth thinking and writing about (and uninhibitedly living, once in a while): Devin Barricklow. Mark Bryk. Olivia Cheng. Coleman Dues. Sophie Geoghan. My HZWP fiction cohort—Zoë Carpenter, Seanie Civale, Marne Litfin, Kabelo Sandile Motsoeneng, Gwen Mugodi, Josh Olivier, Anna Widdowson—and all dear Ann Arbor friends. Hairol Ma. Ruby Epler. Sabriyya Pate. Michael Swerdlow. Katie Wood. Julius von Borcke. Clay Andreen, Nathaniel Bernstein, & the whole DC WashU crew. Dea Closson. Hal Sullivan. Alex Rodríguez. Schuyler Bailar. Angela Hui & Advo FicBo friends. Blessing Jee. Steph Johnson. Anant Pai. Celina Qi. Apoorva Rangan. Arthur Schott-Lopes. Jen Xu. Zayna Quader. Ms. Donovan. Mr. Nicholas. Mr. Salomon. Dr. Smith. Auntie Yanrong, Uncle Litong, and Ian. Vera Parkin. Nadine Hur. Will Crock. Aidan Ip. Jonah Lefkoe. Hejran Darya. Samuel Webber. James Barton.

Mom. Dad. Adam. Grandma.

If I omitted your name, I'm sorry! Pure forgetfulness. Call or text, I'd love to catch up.

About the Author

E. Y. Zhao is a writer from St. Louis. Her work has appeared in *The Georgia Review*, *Electric Lit*, and *Chicago Review of Books*, among others, and she edits fiction for *Joyland Magazine*. She holds an MFA in prose from the University of Michigan and a BA in history from Harvard College.

The team at Astra House would like to thank everyone who helped to publish *Underspin*.

PUBLISHER
Ben Schrank

EDITORIAL
Maya Raiford Cohen

CONTRACTS
Stella Iselin

PUBLICITY
Rachael Small
Alexis Nowicki

MARKETING
Tiffany Gonzalez

SALES
Jack W. Perry

DESIGN
Jacket: Rodrigo Corral Studio
Frances DiGiovanni
Interior: Alissa Theodor

PRODUCTION
Lisa Taylor

MANAGING EDITORIAL
Olivia Dontsov
Nancy Seitz
Jane Handa

COPYEDITING
Janine Barlow

PROOFREADER
Jane Becker

COMPOSITION
Westchester Publishing Services